PRAISE FOR MA

"*With* Thirteen Ways to Kill Lulabelle Rock, *it's like Maud Woolf has joined forces with Tarantino and Edgar Wright to rip apart the crime/thriller genre, then remould it into something bad-ass and new. A genre-smashing, satire-mashing, ideas-packed gem of a novel.*"
Adam Simcox, author of the *Dying Squad* trilogy

"*A doppeltastic delight that explores identity and skewers celebrity culture.*"
Ever Dundas, author of *Goblin* and *HellSans*

"*In* Thirteen Ways to Kill Lulabelle Rock, *Maud Woolf playfully and skilfully explores an intriguing premise - a protagonist created to kill her own clones.* Blade Runner *meets* Killing Eve *in this clever and funny speculative thriller.*"
Guy Morpuss, author of *Five Minds*

"Thirteen Ways *is iridescent, drawing you in with all its shiny colours and propelling you through the mystery and horror of Lulabelle Rock and Bubble City. It's complicated. And really quite brilliantly simple.*"
Joma West, author of *Face*

"*Original, funny and heartbreaking in equal measure,* Thirteen Ways to Kill Lulabelle Rock *is a brilliantly assured debut. Woolf's razor-sharp wit and prose delivers a unique, contemporary and existential thriller which had me hooked from the premise to the final page!*"
Adam Southward, author of *The Alex Madison* series

"Thirteen Ways to Kill Lulabelle Rock *is an addictively enthralling sci-fi thriller with razor sharp prose, cinematic scenes and a surprising tender exploration of experiencing the highs and lows of life and finding love.*"
Nils Shukla, *The Fantasy Hive*

"*Gentle and dark in equal parts, Woolf's debut highlights the importance of balance, rest, and asking just enough of oneself. A riveting read.*"

Shazzie, *Fantasy Book Critic*

"Thirteen Ways to Kill Lulabelle Rock *is a debut that is as riveting as it is emotionally charged. It is one that sunk its claws in early and kept moving right along with its imaginative storytelling and sardonic humor. Woolf is an author to keep an eye on.*"

FanFiAddict

"*An insightful look at the unrealities of fame, this book explores identity and independence in a near future setting. The Lulabelles are as memorable and heartbreaking as they are unique. Woolf leaves the reader feeling thoughtful and introspective with her debut novel.*"

Fiction Fans Podcast

"*This book altered my brain chemistry. I'll forever be fascinated by Lulabelle and her portraits.*"

Charli, @bookishcharli on Instagram

"Lulabelle Rock *is a must-read for fans of* Black Mirror, *Blake Crouch, and sci-fi that passes the Bechdel test. I don't often see books in this genre that can balance speculative elements with this much heart. Woolf is a debut author to watch.*"

Amber, @seekingdystopia on Instagram

"*Such a thought provoking and poignant read , makes you think, makes you feel, makes you just stop – fantasy at its best.*"

Steph, @bookslovereaders on Instagram & Tiktok

Maud Woolf

Thirteen Ways to Kill Lulabelle Rock

ANGRY ROBOT

ANGRY ROBOT
An imprint of Watkins Media Ltd

Unit 11, Shepperton House
89 Shepperton Road
London N1 3DF
UK

angryrobotbooks.com
twitter.com/angryrobotbooks
Bang, Bang, We Shot Us Down

An Angry Robot paperback original, 2024

Cover by Mark Ecob
Edited by Desola Coker, Simon Spanton and Robin Triggs
Set in Meridien

ISBN 978 1 91520 290 1
Ebook ISBN 978 1 91520 291 8

Printed and bound by CPI Group (UK) Ltd, Croydon CR0 4YY

9 8 7 6 5 4 3 2 1

This book is for Margaret. You read me so many books; I wish more than anything you could have read this one too.

CHAPTER ZERO

The Fool

The sun is shining as the fool sets out on his journey. Everything he owns in the world is slung over one shoulder and in one hand he clutches a white rose. A carefree vagabond, his eyes are fixed on the horizon, unaware that he is about to walk off the edge of a precipice...

Lulabelle Rock takes another swig from her Pepto-Bismol pink smoothie. A single pastel raindrop escapes onto the front of her white bathrobe, where it is immediately absorbed by the terry cloth. She doesn't notice or, if she does, she gives no indication.

Instead she smacks her lips, and levels a frank and serious gaze in my general direction.

"Can I tell you about my new movie? It's a total flop. A disaster."

I'm not sure if I should nod. I don't get the impression that she's actually asking for my permission. She doesn't go on, her head tipping slightly to one side as she waits.

We watch each other for a moment, and then I relent. "Please do."

Lulabelle preens, patting the white silk scarf around her head more firmly into place. A solitary blonde curl escapes and dangles perilously by the big wet strawberry of her mouth.

"Well," she starts, leaning across the table. "When I signed up, I thought it seemed a sure thing. Spencer, my agent Spencer, he called it a hit and run idea. Hit and run. Isn't that clever?"

I murmur in agreement.

"Well, it's an adaptation. Of some art house thing. Swedish or Polish or Italian or something. Black and white. Subtitles. The whole shebang. The director, and he's a good guy you understand, one of the best... Well, he's always loved it, ever since he was a starving film school student. Medea, it's called. It's about a mother."

"Your part?" I ask.

We're sitting outside on the balcony and between us is a large glass table. When the sun comes out from behind the clouds it becomes a blinding disk of light. In those brief moments I feel as though we could be talking to each other over the surface of the moon.

"Of course," she says, clearly a tad offended. "Anyway, this mother, she has children."

"Naturally."

"Two children. Two little boys. And a father, of course... Anyway, they all live in this big old house out in the countryside. It's very damp and misty. England probably – it's soggy."

"Are they happy?" I ask.

"Oh, I suppose so," Lulabelle says, slurping her drink. "They must be. But then a war starts. Or it's been going on for a long time... I don't think it's clear. Anyway, the father has to leave. He's a soldier you see. So, he leaves and then the mother is alone."

"With the children?"

"Obviously. And years pass in that spooky house and all the time they're hearing more and more news of the war through the radio, in those old-timey broadcasts, you know the ones... And this mother she's so frightened and paranoid and she's all alone in this big old house–"

"With the children," I remind her, and she waves her shiny lacquered nails impatiently.

"Yeah, yeah, obviously. But she's scared. She's jumping at shadows. She keeps thinking, what happens if there's an invasion? If the enemy finds us? What will they do? And then after years and years and years she hears a knock at the door."

She pauses and looks at me significantly.

After a moment I realise I'm expected to jump in.

"Is it the husband?" I venture.

"Well," she says and deflates a little. "Yes. But you aren't supposed to know that. It could be anyone. Anyway, she thinks it's the enemy, here to slaughter her and do unspeakable things to her babies. So, she kills them."

"Who?" I ask. "The enemy?"

"No... the children," she says, letting the horror drip from every syllable. "She murders her own children before the enemy can hurt them. And then, when they're both dead, she goes to open the door with a kitchen knife. But who's on the other side?"

She arches a single pale eyebrow over the hard rim of her dark glasses. For a moment we stare blankly at one another.

"The husband?" I say.

"The husband!" She claps her hands in delight. "And that's the end."

I think about it.

"Hmm," I say. "And this was black and white?"

"The original was," she says with a shrug. "But our version isn't. Our version has the most beautiful lighting. Red and blue and so on. Have you ever seen Suspiria?"

"No."

"Neither have I, but I'm told it's a dead-ringer. We weren't going to make one of those trashy big studio remakes you see, where everything is pastel and toned down and safe. We wanted – well the director wanted – to go all in on the blood. Raw. That was the word he used. Unflinching."

"The original wasn't bloody enough for him?" I ask. I'm starting to get a headache from the sun. I'm not used to headaches. I don't like them.

Lulabelle Rock has big dark sunglasses on. She can look at me all she wants, but I have to squint to make out the pink blot on her white swaddled body and the manicured gardens that stretch out behind her, the distant azure swimming pool and immaculate topiary hedges. It's nice out here in the countryside. It could be a film set or a painted background, it's so perfect. There must be fences at the perimeter to keep it so untouched but from here I can't see them.

"The original was..." She pauses, tapping an electric blue nail against her canine tooth. "It was mostly implied. The violence. Reaction shots, tasteful splashes of blood on a wall. A child's hand dropping a toy truck in slow motion. Yadda yadda. We didn't want to do that. We wanted to go all in. We wanted to create something so horrible that the audience would want to look away. But they couldn't. You see?"

"You showed the murders?"

"In excruciating detail. It was disgusting really. And inventive. It took twenty minutes for each child to die. Buckets of blood. Which of course was annoying because first of all, it stains and secondly, it was edible, so of course the kids kept licking it off their lips when they were supposed to be dead."

A dark shadow passes over her face.

"Never work with children," she advises me gravely. "They think it's all just make-believe. They take away all the dignity of acting."

"I won't," I promise her.

"But anyway," she says, with a sigh. "It was supposed to be a masterpiece. My shot at recognition. No more playing the wife or the timid secretary or the party girl. No more big budget motion capture green screen CGI bullshit or voiceover cameos as Snicklesnork the troll."

"I'm sure you were magnificent in that role."

"The critics were kind." She gives a gracious shrug and pulls out a packet of cigarettes from her pocket along with a cheap plastic lighter. The cigarette hovers in front of her mouth; her face is turned towards the sprawling grounds. For a moment she looks like Lulabelle Rock the movie star.

"Medea was supposed to be my redemption," she says with lip-quivering Shakespearean gravitas. "But it looks as though it will serve as an epitaph to my career. The pre-screenings have been a disaster. Catastrophic, that's what Spencer says."

"They found it offensive?"

"No," she says glumly. "Worse. They found it boring. Funny, at best. Spencer said they cackled when little Robbie got the axe."

"I'm sorry."

"I guess art is dead – but no use crying over spilled milk."

I smile sympathetically but I'm not really listening. I'm looking at the cigarette packet. It is placed almost exactly between us. LUCKY GIRL the packet reads in stark black letters. There's something authoritarian about the blockiness of the font.

Am I being told I'm a lucky girl? I wonder. Or are they exclusively for girls who are already lucky? Perhaps simply smoking them makes you luckier.

"It comes out in a week," Lulabelle says, suddenly business-like. "I need some press. Something to generate interest. Something to turn this from an embarrassment to a cult hit. I think it's alright to have made a bad film if it's a cult hit. That's what Spencer says anyway. Which is where you come in."

"Me?" I ask, surprised.

"Of course," Lulabelle says. "Aren't you wondering why you're here? Why I made you?"

I blink. Until this moment I hadn't thought about it. I feel a sudden, jarring sense of dislocation.

"How long have we been sitting here?" I ask.

Lulabelle Rock gives me a cool look over the rim of her sunglasses.

"Your whole life," she says. "Twenty minutes, if you want specifics. You know who you are, don't you?"

I blink again and look down at my electric blue nails. I wiggle them experimentally and they seem to blur and leave trails behind them in the air. My headache has reached a shrill, piercing climax.

"I'm Lulabelle," I say. "Lulabelle Rock."

Lulabelle smiles sympathetically and gives me a brisk pat on the hand.

"A Lulabelle Rock," she corrects. "I am the Lulabelle Rock. Have a cigarette. It helps."

"I don't smoke," I say. "It's bad for my complexion."

"No," Lulabelle says with a faint impatience. "I don't smoke. I have a career to worry about. And my health. And magazine covers. You can do what you want."

I pick up the cigarette packet and unseal the wrapper. With clumsy fingers I take out a pristine white stick and place it awkwardly in my mouth. I try three times to ignite the lighter and in the end Lulabelle sighs and takes it from me. She plucks the cigarette from my hands and takes another from the packet. Sticking them both in her mouth, she flicks the lighter with a practiced hand and for a moment twin flames appear in her dark glasses.

"Here," she says, passing me one. "Inhale. Look, you'll get the hang of this soon. They all do."

"Who's they?" I ask around the cigarette, which wobbles dangerously in the corner of my mouth.

"The other Portraits. I've made quite a few at this point. You'll be my thirteenth."

"Unlucky," I mumble, trying to understand. "I don't – I think – I–"

"Inhale," Lulabelle snaps.

I do as she says, and the smoke fills my mouth, the gaps between my teeth, forcing its way down my throat and catching at my tonsils. I feel it enter my lungs like a thick black smog, filling me up from the inside. I'm frightened. I cough and begin to retch, tears filling up my eyes.

"Oh, grow up," Lulabelle says, rolling her eyes. "A little smoke never hurt anybody. Inhale, hold and release."

I don't want to, but she's watching me, tapping her fingers on the tabletop, clack clack clack. By the third try I have the hang of it but still, my fingers shake.

"Do you remember now?" Lulabelle asks at last. She seems to have regained control of herself. She's even smiling at me now, gently, like I'm a child who's trying their best. When she takes a drag, it's smooth and easy.

"I think so," I say and try very hard to think about it.

My memories are two-layered. I remember very clearly the pink spot on Lulabelle's robe. I remember the glass table shining in the sun. I remember Medea. I remember being told never to work with children. I remember holding the cigarette when it was new and pristine. All these memories are in technicolour. I can smell them. They smell like fruits of the forest smoothie and cigarette smoke and the spice of Lulabelle's perfume.

Beneath these memories are others and these are sepia. Flat and scentless, like a photograph. These memories are far vaster; they span for thirty years. A lifetime's supply. I see two faces. I can put names to them. One of them is mum. The other is daddy. I feel nothing at all towards them. These memories are like a dream.

"I grew up," I say carefully, watching Lulabelle for confirmation, "In the countryside. That's why I bought this place. The estate."

"Yes," she says. "But you must try not to think like that. You'll only confuse yourself. I grew up in the countryside. You were fished out of a vat in my basement. What else?"

"I – You moved to the city."

"Yes," she says. "Good."

"You're an actress."

"Yes."

"You've done this before."

"Yes. Twelve times. You're the thirteenth. Why did I make the others?"

I think hard and across the table, Lulabelle smiles. It's not a very friendly smile. There are a lot of teeth, glistening like wet little pebbles.

"I don't know," I say.

"I made them because I'm a busy, busy girl and there are only so many hours in a day. I made them because I'm only one person and I can only do so much. I can only give the world so much."

"Yes," I say. The headache has subsided to a low buzz. The clouds part again, and I wince in the flash of sudden sunlight.

"Why did I make you?"

I pause. I know the answer but I'm not sure it can be true.

"You made me to kill them. The ones that came before."

"Dispose of," she corrects lightly, but then she nods and, without looking away, leans back in her chair and takes a final long slurp of her drink. I realise suddenly how dry my mouth is from the smoke. I look around in hopes that some helpful staff member will be hovering with a pitcher of cold, fresh-tasting water.

I think a lot of staff are employed here, at the villa. It's a big property. Hard to maintain, but worth it for the view and the solitude. I think, I think. It does one good to get away from the city sometimes. The fresh air is a tonic. Everyone knows that. Don't they? When I first bought this place all the staff stood outside to greet me in a long line. In my memory, the faces are all blank.

They must have been smiling at me. Everyone smiles at me. At her.

"Do you know why I want you to decommission them?" Lulabelle frowns. "Keep smoking. You're getting ash all over the table."

I take another half-hearted puff.

"I don't know," I admit. "It's strange. I remember doing

things, but I can't remember why I did them or how I felt about it at the time. How can I see it all so clearly now, but not understand what I was thinking? Why can't I remember?"

She shrugs, the corner of her red mouth twisting. "I don't know either. I don't really understand the technology. They tried to explain, but it was a very long and boring explanation. Think of it like magic. It's easier that way. Anyway, I'm getting rid of the others because I think a little death might make people interested in me again."

Lulabelle says this last part so off-handedly that for a moment I struggle to catch up.

"Will it be in the news?" I ask. "Even if it's just a Portrait who's dead and not a real person?"

"If it was just one Portrait then probably not. A Portrait is decommissioned every hour, especially in Bubble City. But all of my Portraits, destroyed in less than a week? That's a story! That's exciting. Especially if no one knows who's doing it. A serial killer with only one victim. Fun!"

"So a secret then. Will I have a disguise?" A more important question presents itself and I lower the cigarette. "Why me anyway? You must have someone better."

"Sweetheart," Lulabelle reaches over to pluck the stub from my hand. Her fingers are soft and very cold where they brush mine. "Don't be ridiculous. Of course I want you to do it. There's no one else in the world I trust more. And of course, only I'm allowed to kill me. "

"Of course," I murmur.

"That's not a line. It's a loophole. At least, according to my lawyers. Though Mitosis may still kick up a fuss..." She glances at my expression. "Never mind about that. It's not your problem."

I hold my breath as I watch her take a final deep drag. The cigarette flares up one last time and extinguishes itself, spent. As she lets out a long plume of smoke, dragon-like through her nostrils, her head dips. Her shoulders relax.

After that, we have very little to say to each other. We sit for a little bit and talk about the weather but Lulabelle must get bored at some point because she pulls out her phone. I look at the lawn and the small blots of colour in the rose garden.

It's another beautiful morning, just, I think, like all the ones that came before.

A chime goes off from Lulabelle's phone and, as if summoned, an employee materialises from within the house and hovers around Lulabelle's left shoulder. He isn't tall but he has the bearing of a tall man. He wears an expensive black suit but on him it looks almost anonymous. He has a haircut that would be unremarkable in most time periods and his shoes are very clean. The only thing that prevents him from looking like a completely nondescript human being is his beard, which is rusty and bristles against his mouth, reaching almost to the knot of his black tie.

A Viking in business clothes, I think, but not a particularly vicious or interesting or noble one. A Viking who would fade into the everyday bustle of a monastery raid. A Viking who would not rock the boat.

"Ready?" he asks.

Lulabelle clicks her tongue and pulls a sheet of paper from her bathrobe pocket. Narrowing her eyes, she scratches at the surface of the paper with the edge of her nail, making little skrttch skrttch sounds.

"I think that's everything," she says after a moment, tossing it onto the table. I try to read it upside down but I only have time to make out stray phrases (human life is sacred, trust the engineer) before Lulabelle is waving her hand. "Go on then. Take her."

I think this must refer to me, so I stand up quickly, tripping a little and grabbing onto the table for support. There is an uncomfortable breeze around my legs and looking down, I discover I'm wearing a white terry-cloth bathrobe. When I touch a hand to my head, I feel smooth silk instead of hair.

Instinctively, I check for a pink spot on my robe, but the cloth is a pure bone white. I look over and down at Lulabelle who offers me a wide dazzling smile. It's begun already, I realise. We are growing apart.

"Well," she says and then looks at a loss for words. "Good luck, I guess."

"Will I see you when it's done?" I ask.

She starts to shake her head, changes her mind and then nods.

"Maybe," she says decisively. "Definitely, maybe. Take the cigarettes."

I pick them up and turn to follow the dark-suited Viking. In the darkened doorway to the house I look back one last time.

She has discovered the pink stain on her robe and is blotting at it with her sleeve. There is a look of total devastation on her face. I think she's forgotten me but then she looks up.

"I did try to keep it simple," she says. "You understand, don't you?"

Before I can reply or even shake my head, the Viking takes me by the elbow and steers me into the house.

Between one moment and the next, Lulabelle is lost to me forever.

CHAPTER ONE

The Magician

The magician stands with one hand held aloft to the heavens and the other pointing down to the earth. A powerful conduit between worlds, everything he needs for his work is laid out before him. Something very important is about to begin. Around him strange flowers blossom into life.

I am taken to a small beige dressing room and here I see her again, this time in the mirror.

She stands about six feet tall. When I untie the silk scarf, her hair tumbles down over my shoulders, in a bouncy platinum waterfall. Each perfect curl is brittle to the touch. I untie the robe. Below it, Lulabelle's body is naked and perfectly neat. I turn and examine her from a variety of angles. There is something utterly competent about the bend of her knees, the small bones of her ankles and wrists. She looks as though she has been designed by an experienced and detail-orientated committee. I lift the inside of her wrist to my nose and sniff. The skin is completely odourless and slightly damp.

It is not completely her body. Some things are missing.

My palms are as smooth as a baby's. Smoother. Someone once told me – no, someone once told Lulabelle that it's important to remember that Portraits aren't human. For this reason, there are no lines. For everyone's peace of mind.

Remembering this, I lean close to the mirror and pinch the skin of my cheek hard between my thumb and finger. It hurts but there's no red mark.

I am just a photocopy of an original. Although the words may look handwritten from a distance, it's not hard to tell the difference on closer inspection.

The Viking waits patiently in the corner until I have completed my examination. He's looking away, at a small painting on the wall. I watch him in the mirror, wondering if he's giving me privacy or if he's just bored. Perhaps it's out of loyalty to Lulabelle. Uncomfortable to see your boss naked, I suppose. Maybe he's just seen it all too many times before. Twelve to be exact. With the dark bulk of his suit in the way I can't make out the painting. I imagine it is a windswept coast.

"What's next?" I ask at last, and he points silently to a folded pile of clothes on a chair.

"A polo shirt?" I ask critically as I look through them. "Khakis? Why am I wearing trainers?"

"They'll protect your feet," he says impassively. "If you have to run."

I scowl and pull them on. When I look in the mirror again, Lulabelle no longer looks like a movie star sex kitten. She looks like a person who wears sensible shoes.

"Here," the Viking says, holding out a hat and wraparound sunglasses. "Put these on. Tie up your hair."

"Is this a disguise?" I ask. The word I want to say is costume, and I have to remind myself that I'm not an actress anymore.

"Your eyes need time to adjust."

This makes sense. It must have been dark inside the vat.

When I look at the mirror a third time, I see a compact woman of above average height looking back at me with a blank expression. The only hint of Lulabelle left is her mouth. I'm struck by a sudden intense fear that the cigarette has already begun to yellow my expensively whitened teeth. Do I still need to worry about this? I step forward and grimace at the glass trying to see, and then the Viking is by my side.

"Enough of that now," he says sternly. "It's time to go."

As we leave I see that the painting is of a large and rather ugly blue eye.

With one rough gammon hand on my shoulder the Viking steers me through a series of rooms and corridors: up stairways, through arches, even briefly stepping over a little open walkway between buildings. Even with the sunglasses, I have to squint against the sunlight. I see flashes of tasteful mauve rooms, steel topped kitchen counters, glass walls that lead onto acid green squares of grass. Every space is brutally clean and devoid of any signs of life. As tidy as an airlock.

The Viking doesn't talk. I wonder if he is used to conducting these whistle-stop tours. I want to ask him what the others thought. If they too wanted to linger.

In the end I stay silent. I have an ingrained instinct not to chat with the help. Not because I am trying to be rude, but simply because it's so exhausting trying to make constant small talk in your own home, where you go to get away from others.

This thought is inherited, I realise, but like a hand-me-down jacket that doesn't make it any less comforting.

In a painfully bright elevator, we descend, shoulder to shoulder.

"Here," he says and when I turn my head, he is holding out a small plastic case.

When I take it, my arms buckle a little under an unexpected weight. I flick open the two latches. Inside, there is a gun nestled in black foam.

While I am still looking at the gun, there is a gentle chime and the elevator door slides open. It opens onto an underground parking lot that's just as oppressively well lit. This is our final destination, I can tell, but neither of us moves forward.

"There's a silencer in there," the Viking tells me softly. "And bullets. You know how to fire it."

"Yes," I hear myself say. I think I do. It's a wicked thing, this object. So beautifully crafted. The efficiency of its design makes me think of Lulabelle's body.

The Viking is looking at me, but I keep my eyes fixed forward.

"Portraits belong to their creator, the original. Think of it like copyright. Lulabelle has authorised you to dispose of the other Portraits. This is allowed. If you decommission a Portrait of someone else, that is illegal destruction of property. If you kill a person, that is murder. Don't try and do either of these things." His voice is soothing, almost like a lullaby. The words sound rhythmic. Familiar. I wonder if this is a rehearsed speech.

"I won't," I say.

"You can't," he corrects, and passes me a small silver button on a short chain.

"What's this?"

"Your key," he says. "Your car is in the third bay."

I fall in love the moment I see it. It's horrifically ugly. A soulless white monster of a car.

There is nothing distinctive or human about it at all. It looks dangerous, like a factory in full operation or a shark in open water. It looks fast. I come a little closer, wary but trying not to show it. Like an animal, I think it would sense my panic and lash out. I place a hand on its flank and think about pushing the accelerator down as far as it would go. I think about hearing the hiss of the wheels on the road beneath me. I think about shooting past stop lights, blaring my horn and I'm surprised by how much pleasure the thought gives me. I can't remember Lulabelle driving fast. I can't really remember her driving much at all.

"It's fully automated," the Viking tells me as he holds open the door.

I clamber in, throwing my sunglasses and gun onto the passenger seat, and take my first look at the comfortable leather interior. It smells like it's just rolled off the assembly line, and I feel an affectionate rush of kinship.

"How does it work?" I ask. There are no controls, and the dashboard is chestnut panelled and completely flat.

The Viking leans past me to touch the dashboard. A hidden seam splits open to reveal a glass screen. Green words emerge from the dark.

Welcome, it says. Where shall we go today?

"Does it have a manual setting?" I ask hopefully.

"For emergencies," the Viking says and presses a small hidden button below the dashboard.

Another panel slides away, and a steering wheel unfolds with a click. I duck my head and look at the footwell, where two pedals have popped up.

"I think I'll drive myself," I say and give him a smile that I hope is condescending.

"You can try," he says. "But the car probably won't let you. The manual setting really only exists to give passengers peace of mind."

"Hmmph." I'm suddenly impatient to leave. "Is that everything?"

"Almost," he says and for the first time, the bristles around his mouth move in a way that suggests a smile. I shoot him an alarmed glance. To my relief, his face stays settled in place. Maybe he was just clicking his jaw.

"What?" I snap. "What is it?"

"There's a binder in the glove compartment. It contains all the information you'll need to track down and dispose of the others. I've already set your first address but after that you'll need to enter the destinations yourself. If you need to contact us, do so through the messaging system in the dashboard. If you run low on energy then you find Fruel in the minifridge."

"Fuel? For the car?"

"Fruel. Fruel ™. It's what powers you."

"I eat it?"

"It's what powers you," he says again. It sounds like a slogan.

"Fine," I say. "Okay, whatever."

I close the door in his face, push my sunglasses back on my head, and jab my finger at the glowing screen on the dashboard. It tells me I can choose whatever music I like; that I can make a phone call if I want or maybe send an email. It recommends good restaurants in the area and gives me an inspirational quote of the day.

DON'T THINK, JUST DO.

"Okay," I tell it and keep scrolling.

I learn that the weather is sunny outside with highs of 27 degrees, that the traffic isn't too bad, that it is International Day Against Nuclear Testing and that on this date Ulysses S. Grant died, Ingrid Bergman was born, and the Beatles gave their last concert (although not in the same year). Once all of this information has been relayed to me, I am once again asked my destination.

I set my preferences to 'fast'. With a click, the engine comes to life. I sit back in my seat and wait.

And wait.

After a while, the Viking taps politely on the window. I press another button to scroll it down an inch.

"You have to put your seatbelt on," he tells me. "Or the car won't start."

I nod but as I start to scroll the window back up, he puts his hand on the edge of the glass to stop it. "There's a diner halfway to Bubble City. Aunt Julia's. They serve three types of ice cream."

"And?"

"I need to know which one is best."

I frown at him. "Does Lulabelle want this done?"

"No. I do." He reaches into his breast pocket and pulls out a few crisply folded bills.

I watch his face but it betrays nothing and after a moment, I pluck them out of his hand, buckling up at the same time. The moment the lock clicks into place, the car peels out. He holds up a hand but I just nod, my hand clenched tight around the money.

Outside the garage the sun is blinding, filling the car all at once with a frightening intensity of light and heat. The car's technology scrambles to counteract, the windows tinting to grey, the invisible fans whirring on but, for a moment, I am skewered by brightness. A long wide gravel avenue lined with tall hedges sprawls ahead and, at the end, tall metal gates drawing closer and larger as the car picks up speed.

I draw back, hissing, and look over my shoulder at the villa.

I don't want to leave! I want to call out. Lulabelle! Don't make me go!

Flecks of gravel fly up as the car accelerates, faster and faster. The gates are still shut tight. For a moment I think that some hidden mechanism has failed and my journey will end here, at the beginning, in a ball of twisted metal and fire but at the last moment they slide open and I am thrust without ceremony into the world.

I've left all the green behind me in the estate. When I look over my shoulder I can only see the hints of the topiary sticking over the top of the dusty concrete walls. The further away I drive the more it looks like a fortress, giant and impregnable.

The road is smooth tarmac and, while it's wide enough for three lanes, I have it to myself, a straight lonely line that I cannot see the end of. I spend the next hour hunched up in my seat with my face pressed into my kneecaps.

It's odd, learning this body which is both intimately familiar and entirely new. It makes sense to me to start with the basic mechanics so I practice breathing for a while and try to listen for my heartbeat. When this gets boring I begin to fiddle with the music channels. I unpack the gun and screw on the silencer. I would like to practice my aim but there isn't much room in the car, even though it's a five-seater.

I shake out the cigarettes onto the seat next to me and count them (eighteen). I pack them back into the packet very carefully so as not to tear the paper or crumple them. When this too stops being interesting, I finally look in the glove compartment.

The file is in fact a grey A4 ring-binder filled with twelve clear plastic sleeves. Some sleeves are thick and stiff with papers; others hold only a single sheaf.

I flick through. The targets are numbered but I don't know if it's in order of age. There are no dates listed and I have no idea who was created when. This bothers me for some reason but I put the thought aside for now. Perhaps a pattern will emerge as I proceed.

The information on my first target barely fills half a page.

Registration Code: PROCKL78912913
STANDARD TYPE. NO DEVIATIONS COSMETIC
OR OTHER
LOCATION: Bus stop just before the A21 turn off
on M73.
CHECK UPS: (NONE)

In emerald-green ink, Lulabelle has scribbled a brief note on the bottom left corner of the page.

Made her because I was depressed on Monday. Too tired to meet my friends for brunch. Meant to pick her up two days ago but forgot.

The car tells me I will arrive at my destination at 11.35 AM. That's still two hours away. I settle in to watch the view from my window.

There's still nothing to see but flat orange scrubland. It stretches off in every direction, until it flattens down to a thin line at the horizon. The sky presses down on it like a big blue hammer.

I try turning up the speed, but the car won't let me. I try to switch to manual but even though the steering wheel pops out, it spins uselessly in my hands. I feel like a child being given a toy phone to play with. Even so, I pretend for a while, going through the motions of driving with my useless disconnected controls. Accelerate, brake, switch lanes.

The car tolerates this for a while and then it retracts the pedals. The whir of machinery sounds faintly judgmental to my ears.

"Beep beep," I whisper into the void. My mouth is still dry. When I open the minifridge I see rows of plastic bottles printed with the word FRUEL under a cartoon white and yellow flower. When I unscrew the lid and take a hesitant sip, it's thick and tasteless and leaves the inside of my mouth feeling like it's coated in a faint residue.

There's no way to miss the diner when it appears.

It's the first sign of life I've seen since setting out, a lonely box of a building at the roadside. An old woman in a pink apron smiles benevolently from the billboard overhead, holding a spoon and a bowl with steam rising from the surface. Aunt Julia's Eatery, I read and then we're pulling into the parking lot.

As the car's engine clicks off, the display beeps at me reproachfully and tells me that staying longer than my allotted thirty minutes will affect my arrival time. I slam the car door with unnecessary force when I get out and my trainers crunch on the dry earth. The air is dusty on my tongue and tastes faintly of eucalyptus.

The diner is small and squat and grey but there are small purple flowers growing in boxes by the front door. I'm the only car parked outside and I wonder where Aunt Julia lives in order to get out here every day. A small neon sign in the window reads OPEN 24/7.

Inside, the place is almost completely deserted, save for one booth by the window where a scrawny goth kid is wolfing down a plate of apple pie and whipped cream. He doesn't look up as I pass him on my way to the bathroom, just hunkers his leather jacketed shoulders down over the plate.

I use the facilities and splash my face with cold water

from the sink. My skin feels faintly slick under my fingertips. Perhaps a lingering effect of the vat. I take a paper towel and scrub until my face stings. It feels satisfying, ridding myself of the last vestiges of that amniotic state.

When I come out of the bathroom, the only sign of the kid is a dirty plate and a crumpled-up napkin. I can hear voices floating through the hatch to the kitchen and I wonder if Aunt Julia herself is back there, stirring her big cauldron of soup. I ring the bell on the counter and after a moment a surly looking man emerges from a swinging door.

"Yes?"

Aunt Julia smiles at me from his shirt. There are yellow egg stains on her face.

"Ice cream," I say. "You have three flavours."

He grunts. "Blueberry, death by chocolate and sarsaparilla."

"I'll take a scoop of each."

While he's spooning it into a little paper cup, I flick through the postcard rack by the counter. There's a few desert scenes, tumbleweed, a ragged looking vulture but mostly it's just Bubble City, again and again. Glittering towers against blue skies. The statue of the saint on her high rock. The view from the valleyside at night. There's nothing here Lulabelle hasn't seen but the familiarity is strange. Like being homesick for a place you've only ever seen on the television.

I pick up one postcard with a stylized cartoon map and the words 'You Wish You Were Here' written below. I put it on the counter and it's rung up with my ice cream.

Outside the goth kid is sitting cross legged on the hood of my car, scrolling through the phone in his hand. When he hears the jingle of the door, he looks up, eyes hidden by a pair of perfectly circular sunglasses, and scrambles to stand.

"Is this your car?" he asks. His voice is high and reedy.

I look at him silently and take a thoughtful bite of blueberry. It's obviously my car. It's the only one in the parking lot.

"Are you going to Bubble City?" he asks. He's visibly sweating and I feel almost sorry for him. It can't be easy wearing all black in this heat.

"Why?" I ask him.

"Well, I wondered, I mean I was thinking maybe I could get a ride?"

The blueberry has a sweetly chemical aftertaste. I frown and poke at the sarsaparilla.

My would-be hitchhiker shifts and flushes. In the sunlight I can see that his hair has been inexpertly dyed; there are orange roots showing up beneath the black.

"The thing is," he says. "Money is a bit of an issue right now. But I could read your palm?"

I walk over to him, stick the little plastic spoon in my mouth and hold out my hand so he can see the smooth, anonymous skin. He has to bend down a little to look, the glasses nearly falling off his head before he pushes them back.

"Oh," he says, deflated. "You're a Portrait."

I nod, shifting the spoon from one side of my mouth to the other.

"You must be someone important then?"

I take off my wraparound sunglasses and give him a wink. He looks at me blankly.

"You don't recognise me?" I ask and then give him a hint. "You don't watch movies?"

He shrugs and scrubs a hand over the back of his head. "We didn't have a cinema where I was growing up and uh, my parents are pretty strict…"

I cock my head to one side. "How old are you?"

"Twenty-five," he says, too quickly. He must think I was born yesterday. He's one day off.

I surprise myself by letting out a short bark of laughter.

"I'll give you a lift," I say. "Hop in."

When he clambers into the car he has a wary expression on his face. I wonder how long he's been waiting for a lift. The red spots on his cheekbones haven't gone away and when he sees the interior his kohl smeared eyes get very wide. If he's impressed he's composed enough not to say anything but I notice he sits gingerly, as if afraid to touch the fabric.

As we hit the road and Aunt Julia begins to shrink in the in the rear-view mirror, I settle back in my seat, turning the little paper tub in my hands, watching the blue and brown and orange run into each other.

"So," I say. "Anywhere in particular?"

"Just Bubble City is fine. That's where my master lives."

I look at him from the corner of my eye and wonder if I've drawn the wrong conclusions from the silver chains and black leather. "Your master?"

"My teacher," he says, his expression almost painfully earnest. "I'm on my way to study under him in Bubble City. I've been his apprentice for five years now, but we've never met face to face before. It's very exciting."

"I see." I'm not really listening. I'm typing out a message to the Viking. Death by chocolate. What a pointless exercise. Chocolate is the only sweet thing that Lulabelle allows herself.

"So, what does he teach you?"

"So far, just the basics. Dream interpretation. Divination. Goal manifestation. A couple of incantations. Astrology."

"Magic?" I try not to sound too dubious. "And you said you've never met this man in the flesh? Did he teach you through astral projection? Or in your dreams or something?"

"No. Video chat. It was an online course. But when I get to the city our real work will begin."

"What's that?" I ask.

"Well, first I need to start reading the ancient texts. Then he'll see about getting me a fairy servant to do my bidding. With any luck, this time next year I'll be able to conjure up angels, transcend my material body and remember all of my past lives."

"You have a lot of those?" I say dubiously. Lulabelle has encountered precisely two people who claimed to be magicians in her lifetime. The first had been on a late-night talk show with her and had correctly guessed what was in her handbag. The other one had been at a birthday party for the child of a major politician. Neither of them had said anything about angels.

"Everyone does," he says enthusiastically. "My master says that souls are passed on endlessly from body to body. That's why some people seem very old, even when they're children. And others are new, and they've only had three or four lives. The best magicians have very old souls. But between you and me..." Here he lowers his voice and looks at me with big anxious eyes. "I think I must be new. Because a lot of the time I have no idea what's happening."

His voice isn't any less reedy, but I don't find it so annoying now.

"I know how that feels," I admit. I smile at him.

He smiles back shyly. "You know, I've never met a Portrait before."

"Neither have I."

"Are you the only one she made?"

"No," I say and then I hesitate, wondering how much I can tell him. I have a feeling I've already broken the rules just by letting him in the car. But he doesn't even know who Lulabelle is. "I'm the thirteenth."

His eyes light up.

"Thirteen!" he cries out. "An auspicious number!"

"Isn't it unlucky?" I ask and he shakes his head vigorously.

"Only for dinner parties."

I shoot him a glance and he clears his throat, looking excited.

"To have thirteen guests, I mean. Judas was the thirteenth to arrive at the last supper. And uh, Loki. In the Norse myths. He was the last one at the banquet. But thirteen is actually lucky."

"Are you sure about that?" I say, narrowing my eyes at the rear-view mirror. There's something creeping up behind us on the road. Too large to be another car.

"Well there are thirteen lunar months in the Mayan

calendar," the hitchhiker goes on, happily unaware of my distraction. "In Judaism you become a man at thirteen. There are thirteen star constellations in the zodiac. Thirteen treasures of Britain and King Arthur sleeps in Avalon with twelve knights by his side. And in all Germanic languages it's the first compound number–"

"Uh-huh," I say, craning my head round now to look back. I can see now that it's a van, white paint work glinting under the sun. It's kicking up a dust cloud behind it. I put the ice cream tub down.

"None of these things are lucky of course" the hitchhiker continues happily. "But mathematically it's lucky. It's a natural number in a set generated by a sieve."

"A sieve?" I'm already going as fast as the car will let me but I stab at the controls again, just in case.

"Like the sieve of Eratosthenes."

"Is he a magician too?" I say. I am distracted. The van is nearly on us. I can see a logo now, on the hood. A yellow and white flower. It means something important.

I've seen it before. Lulabelle's seen it before.

"Um," the hitchhiker says. "Your car is telling you something."

On the dashboard white text has bubbled out of the dark.

You are being asked to stop by an authority figure under traffic law GZ28999 DELTA. If you believe this stop is unnecessary/dangerous/unlawful please let us know once you have resumed your journey.

"What does…" the hitchhiker starts to say but I just shake my head, tight-lipped. The car is already slowing and pulling off to the side of the road.

"Are we in trouble?"

"You're fine," I say.

I know this for sure and what's more, I know where I've seen that flower. Even without it I can read the writing on the side of the van.

Mitosis.

For the second time today, I'm about to meet my maker.

The van pulls to a halt behind us and for a moment the dust swirls in the air between our two vehicles. Then, with a clunk, a sliding door opens and two people in suits step out. One of them is an older woman wearing pearls and heels that are very impractical for the terrain. She seems to realise this by the look on her face and she makes her way over gingerly, clutching at a computer bag slung over her shoulder. I can hear her cursing through the glass.

Her companion is a stout man with his sleeves rolled up. He's carrying a silver case and as he swings it, the light catches off the surface. The moment I see him I trust him completely.

"Who—" the hitchhiker asks.

"That's the engineer," I say and unbidden, my hand moves to lower the window. By the time they reach us, hot dusty air is already filling the car, drying out my mouth and nose.

"Lulabelle Rock, I presume." The engineer smiles down at me, and rests one hand on the roof.

I nod and he looks past me to the Hitchhiker before whistling through his teeth and straightening up. I hear a clunk on the roof and then the sound of metal clasps being clicked open.

"Lulabelle, Lulabelle..." the woman is muttering to herself, fishing a slim tablet out of her bag and flicking through it. "What model number? I can't see any new ones on the system."

"Hold on a minute," the engineer says, something clicking in his hands. From where I'm sitting he looks decapitated. All I can see is his tie, yellow with a pattern of little ducks.

"Um," the hitchhiker says. "Excuse me? What's going on?"

"Oh sorry," the woman says, ducking her head to look inside. "Nothing to worry about. If she's unverified we'll give you a lift. Were you the one that made the call?"

I look over at the hitchhiker but he just looks confused. "What call?"

"About her," the woman says and then frowns. "You know,

she doesn't look like a knock-off. My sister loves Lulabelle Rock. She must have made me watch that one with the bee farm a thousand times..."

"No offence Connie," the engineer says and then when he squats back down on his haunches, he's holding a silver instrument in his hand. "But that's my department not yours. Face me. Don't blink."

"Hey–" I hear the hitchhiker say but I trust the engineer, so I lean my face forward out of the window. He brings up the instrument and for a moment the long sharp point of it is suspended just three inches from my left eyeball. There is a faint click and I see a momentary burst of purple. Then the engineer is stepping away, back to his colleague.

"P-ROCK-L. Seven, eight, nine, six, one, three, one, three."

"Ell as in Echo, Lima, Lima?"

"L as in Lulabelle. C'mon Connie."

"It's the heat." She finishes typing into her tablet and squints at the screen in the glare.

I feel a hand on my arm. When I look over, the hitchhiker is frowning. "You okay?"

I nod slowly. Everything feels a little slower somehow. When I blink I see that same purple flash, blossoming behind my eyes.

"Ah-hah!" The woman is saying. "Found her. They must have just finished registering her."

"Cutting it close. She's already three hours old. Can you drop them a line and tell them to get their shit together next time? If we hadn't double checked..."

"I know, I know."

"The last thing I need is to get my head bitten off by Mike for putting the wrong Portrait back to factory settings."

"Fine but I don't want to get caught up in an email battle with some celebrity's shark legal team. Christ, Louis, as if I didn't have enough going on trying to keep up to date with all this crap–"

"Excuse me," the hitchhiker says.

"Well now that is actually your department so–"

"Excuse me!" the hitchhiker says again. This time they stop and turn.

"Oh yeah, you can go," the engineer says. "She's verified."

"What did you do? With that thing?"

"Relax, we just checked her code. It's stamped on the back of her eyeball. But like I said, she's verified."

The hitchhiker opens his mouth but the woman holds up her tablet with a stern expression. Her hair is escaping from its bun and strands of it are sticking to her damp forehead.

"Listen, young man. We appreciate your concern but we have three unverified footballers in the back of that van and a Ginger Rogers so badly forged that she's literally spoiling in the heat. If you're concerned about your friend here I advise you to consult the Morality and Ethics page on our website. And tell her original to fill out the paperwork next time."

"Hold on Connie. Pick a colour," the engineer tells me, holding up a screen of colour swatches. Dazed, I pick red at random.

He nods shortly at his coworker. "She's fine."

"Have a nice day," the woman says and then they turn to leave. At the door to the van, the engineer offers his arm but his colleague shakes him off. A moment later and the van is once again nothing but a dust cloud in the rear-view mirror.

As if nothing at all had happened, the car peels out. We sit in silence and slowly my mind begins to sharpen again. The oddly chemical sense of calm is fading leaving a kind of sick wrongness behind. The only fitting word that I can dredge up from Lulabelle's memories is hangover. I see that the ice cream has melted into a multicoloured soup in the coffee holder. The sight of it twists something in my chest.

I was enjoying the sarsaparilla.

"So they were…" the hitchhiker says at last.

"Mitosis. What were you saying before? About the number thirteen."

"Are you sure you're alright? I didn't call them. Really. I didn't even know you were a Portrait till you told me."

"I'm fine. They're gone now."

"What did they – did you hear them say factory settings?"

"The number thirteen," I say again, still looking down at the ice cream. I wish he would stop asking me these questions. I don't want to think about it but that's okay. I don't have to. It's not relevant right now. "What's special about the number thirteen?"

After a moment so long that I consider pulling over the car and making him get out, he says. "Well... it's Death."

"It's death?" I sit up in my seat. The ice cream doesn't seem important anymore.

"Death," he corrects. "The Death card, the thirteenth card of the major arcana. Look."

"Major arcana?"

"Of a tarot deck. You get the four houses: swords, cups, pentacles and wands. That's the minor arcana and then you have the major. Twenty-two of them. They're like, uh, how do I describe it? Characters almost. Symbols. The big guys. The trump cards."

He opens up his leather duster like a bat stretching out a wing. From one of many pockets he plucks out a set of dog-eared cards. They are held together by an elastic band. He shuffles through them until he produces one from the deck and holds it out. I take it gingerly, trying to avoid touching his hand, which is sticky with apple pie. It feels good to do something with my hands. It makes me forget the purple. It makes me forget the yellow flower.

"There," he says. "That's you. Death."

I look at the card for a long time. A skeleton in a suit of armour sits on a white horse, holding a scythe. The skull grins back from where it's half hidden in the folds of the rider's billowing cloak. I rub my finger over the blade of the scythe. I'm almost expecting a papercut but the card is soft and worn.

"Mind if I keep this?" I ask. "As payment for the ride. Just this card."

"Take them all," he says, happily and without hesitation. "You can't break up a set. You sure you want those ones though? I have others. This one is goddess themed. Or maybe you prefer birds? Or famous serial killers?"

I decide to keep the one I have. Something about the woodcut designs appeals to me, even if the cards are old and bent out of shape. I tuck them away in one of the many pockets of my khaki trousers.

"Do you want to know more about the history of tarot?" he asks me eagerly.

I think about it and then shake my head. "No, thanks. Let's listen to the radio."

I flick for a while through the music selection, but everything annoys me. Finally, I settle on a tinkling harpsichord concerto.

"What would have happened to you if you weren't registered?" he asks.

I turn up the volume.

"Do you like classical?" I have to raise my voice.

He makes a face. "Not really."

"Me neither," I say and smile. It's nice to find something in common with strangers. We listen to it all the way to Bubble City.

Maybe it's the landscape and heat playing tricks on me but there's something sudden and startling about the way it appears on the landscape. At first there's just the slow rise of the landscape as the road enters the valley. Ahead there's only a faint sparkle in the distance, like the light catching off a broken bottle. Then, blink-and-you-miss-it, there it is: Bubble City, an alien structure of metal and glass rising up from the dust.

"I thought it would be bigger," the hitchhiker murmurs beside me. "What a strange place for a city."

"It is," I say, knowing that this is something someone told Lulabelle once. "They can't spread out because of the landscape – see how high the valley walls go? It gets steeper further up."

I fish the postcard out of my pocket and pass it over. "It's... the whole thing is like a big thumbprint – a hollow with the city in the middle. And because they can't spread out it's..."

I can't actually think of how this ends. I think Lulabelle might have zoned out at this point in the explanation. The hitchhiker is looking at me expectantly.

"It's dense," I say confidently. "Very dense."

The hitchhiker frowns at the postcard. "This must be wrong," he says. "Are there really this many motorways? It's like a web. Where do they fit all the buildings in?"

"Oh they can build around the roads," I say. "Over and under and so on. There are a lot of – what do you call them? Sky roads, criss-crossing?"

I try and demonstrate with my hands, tangling my fingers up.

"Overpasses?"

"Yeah. Those. Well, you'll understand when you see it."

By the time we're inside the city limits and making our way down Park Street, the car has slowed to a crawl in the midday traffic and the hitchhiker is looking around him with something like horror on his face. I'm not unsympathetic to this reaction – I can only imagine that the name Park Street was a bleak joke on the part of the developer. The overpasses here are stacked on top of each other – we're sandwiched right in the middle. Aside from thin lances of sunlight coming down from the canopy of roads above us, it's a dim and twilight world of horns and snatches of music from car radios.

"Cheer up," I tell the hitchhiker. "It's always like this trying to get into the city."

"Is it better on the inside?"

"Yes," I say. "Absolutely. Probably."

I'm trying hard to seem confident. Lulabelle is used to seeing this from the backseat through tinted windows and she's usually looking at her phone instead.

There's what looks like a bus stop ahead, a steep set of stairs leading up to it from the streets below. If I squint, I can just make out a blonde woman sitting on the concrete bench amongst the crowd waiting there. It's hard to tell through the red haze of brake-lights.

"You better get out here," I tell the hitchhiker with a sigh as we crawl past a glowing green exit sign that hangs above a doorway. Through the gloom I can see a tunnel and what could be a flight of stairs. "I have work to do. Will you be alright?"

"Oh yeah," he says, peering out of the window and nodding. "This is great. Quite high up but–"

I have a feeling he doesn't really know what he's doing but I'm running late already. More importantly, it's not my problem. I force the car to stop, which it hates because we're still in the middle of the street and causing a mild traffic jam with the holdup. I have to raise my voice over the beeping to say goodbye.

"Thanks for the cards," I say. "Enjoy all those past lives."

"Thanks! Good luck with your mission!" he says, opening the door. Half in-half out of the car he contorts to look back at me over his shoulder. "Look, we probably won't see each other again in this life. But if you meet a winged tiger in your sleep, then it'll be me. That's the form I take when dreamwalking."

"Okay," I say absently, already distracted and wondering where I put my gun. "Winged tiger. Got it."

He waves cheerfully and closes the door. In a moment, his gaunt shape has disappeared down the passageway.

The car stops its irritated beeping and we set off again in smooth inches. I find the gun case under the passenger seat and open it. The silencer is still on. I wish I had practised back at the diner.

The bus stop is very close now. I cut into the bus lane and as I do, I see her properly for the first time. She's wearing a cute little sundress and a denim jacket. I don't need to see the labels to know that it's taken a lot of money to achieve that casual nonchalance. She's sitting on the bench and staring blankly forward. There's a white paper bag on her lap with a cartoon stencil of a smiling cup of coffee. She must have been here for days now. Her shoes are on the bench beside her. Her bare feet aren't bruised, of course, but they're very dirty.

I wonder why no one's sent a car for her, or why she doesn't have the money for a bus fare.

Maybe she doesn't know where to go. It's not really important.

She's not alone.

There's a queue of people lined up beside her. At first I think they're waiting for the bus too, until I see that they're holding scraps of paper, books, baseballs and hats. As I watch, a woman steps up and holds out her white shirt for the Portrait to sign. The next person takes a selfie and as the Portrait stretches her mouth into a toothy smile, I see the deep shadows under her glassy eyes.

I wonder how long it took for the crowd to organise itself like this. I wonder if they've worked out that she's not the real deal. It makes me feel better to see she's so obviously miserable. It makes me feel like what I will do next is in some way a favour. A merciful act.

I scooch over to the passenger seat, which now smells faintly of incense and cloves, and then I roll down the window, steadying the gun on the sill. When we draw level she looks up, and for a moment our two sets of identical eyes catch and hold. Her mouth opens in a red O of surprise.

I pull the trigger.

One shot is enough. I wind up the window. There are stale bagels rolling into the road. People are screaming. Soon they'll see she's a Portrait and then they'll stop.

There's a break in the traffic. My car glides on its way, its progress unhalted.

CHAPTER TWO

The High Priestess

The guardian of the temple threshold, the high priestess holds wisdom in her careful hands. Behind her is a shifting veil, a thin barrier between the conscious and unconscious mind, decorated with pomegranates ripe for the picking. The moon is at her feet, tangled in her blue and silver robes.

I'm feeling pretty pleased with myself when I see that the time is only 11.59. One Portrait down already and it's not even midday. I pull out the file to find the next address.

Registration Code: PROCKL78960913
MODIFIED TYPE (enhanced: 'luminescence')
LOCATION: Fashion District. See daily route marked out in map below.
CHECK UPS: DAILY (due to wear and tear, exposure to elements etc.)

According to the notes typed out below she spends most of her days walking up and down the stylish and expensive districts that lie in the heart of Bubble City.

Lulabelle created her, the notes tell me, as a contractual obligation to her various sponsors in the fashion industry. I will recognise her by her immaculate outfits and perfect poise.

Lulabelle's green pen has underlined this last part and next to it she has drawn an upside-down smile. Next to this, two words are scrawled. Polka dots.

I spend a while trying to work out what this could mean, but no matter how hard I try, I'm unable to crack the cypher. In the end I give up and head off.

Twenty minutes later, my ride safely deposited in a towering spiral parking lot, I am strolling through the deep canyons of the fashion district. Here in the centre the sun shines down unrestricted; already the overpass labyrinth feels like a distant nightmare. Lulabelle knows these places better than anywhere I've ever been before and I let her muscle memory take over as we walk, leaving my head free to swivel.

The pavements here are as wide as rivers and there are no trees here to get in the way of the view. Cars go past slowly, eminently respectful towards the pedestrians, who glitter and catch in the afternoon sun. Each one of them is an artwork in their own right. There's no need to look at the mannequins in the storefronts. The clothes are all out and walking around on tottering knife-edge heels.

A woman with blue butterflies stuck to her eyebrows glides majestically past in a haze of yellow silk. A deer-like creature trussed up in fetishistic black straps waits at a crossing light. A stunning androgynous couple in matching red-wine velvet bicker over whether to take a taxi.

The Portraits are fairly easy to pick out. It's not just that they're beautiful. There's an airbrushed quality to them, a strange stillness to them even as they walk and talk. They look as though their movements are composed from an endless string of photographs. As I pass a coffeeshop I see a fly land on the cheek of a woman sitting and laughing at a joke. She doesn't flinch; just raises a hand and gracefully brushes it away.

They all look as though they should be held behind glass. I am frightened to wander through them with nothing between us, in the same way I imagine someone might be frightened by an art gallery. I see snatches of Lulabelle everywhere I look – a tumble of white hair, an upturned nose, the flash of blue fingernails. On a second glance it's never her, just another gorgeous debutante out for a stroll. In this place, on this street, her beauty isn't remarkable but uniform.

When I finally see her, she's moving like a long shadow down the bright street. A severe grey skirt-suit is pulled tight across her body from below her knees to high on her neck. She's wearing long grey gloves and a wide, full brimmed black hat. She looks like a line of wispy pencil topped by an ink blot.

I follow her down three blocks, biding my time. After a while I realise I'm not alone. From a darkened alleyway, I watch her pass and across the street I see a small gaggle of men doing the same thing. Each of the men hold something in their hands, like a totem. When one of them raises it to his face, I recognise the flash of a camera.

Like catching sight of bugs twitching in long grass, now that I've seen the paparazzi, I realise they're everywhere. The street is crawling with them. Leaning from windows, slouched down in car seats, taking furtive glances from behind newspapers. One man sits astride an electric scooter, smoking a cigarette pensively and adjusting his telescopic zoom. His eyes have the brooding look of a gothic hero. He has adopted a curiously shaped beard and an elegantly droopy moustache. His black hair forms a strange triangle on his head. Even surrounded by the fake creatures of high fashion, his cable knit jumper stands out as a cool piece of clothing.

I tap him on the shoulder.

"Excuse me," I say. "But are you following Lulabelle Rock?"

"Yeah," he drawls, dark eyes fixed on her distant graphite silhouette. "Why do you care?"

"Well, you see that's me," I say and then take off my sunglasses rather grandly. "I am she."

He flicks a glance in my direction, and I see him take in my khakis.

"Hmm," he says, uninterested. "A Portrait."

"She's a Portrait too," I say, feeling wounded.

"I know that. But you aren't wearing designer."

I frown at him but he's already looking back across the street. I clear my throat unhappily and when this fails to make an impression, I do it again. Around the fourth throat-clearing, he gives me a sour look.

"Can I help you with something?" he asks.

"Yeah," I say. "What's her schedule? How long will she be out? I need to talk to her. Alone."

Ahead of us, Lulabelle is almost out of view. The paparazzo makes some final adjustment to his camera, spits out his cigarette and the scooter hums to life.

"Look," he tells me. "I know she left a dress at Wellsprings to be tailored. She'll probably be back there this afternoon."

"Thank you," I say but he's already gunned the motor. I am left in the fumes.

It's with some difficulty that I find Wellsprings, even though it's only a street or two away. In Lulabelle's foggy memories of the place, she's usually driven there by someone else.

In the end I have to ask directions twice – first from a man wearing yellow eye contacts and a Hawaiian shirt and then from a woman wearing a clear plastic three-piece suit over nothing at all. Both of them give me strange looks, as if they're trying to work out what the catch is. I don't think it's recognition but faint bafflement that someone would approach them.

The directions they give me lead me away from the large sparkling valleys and down the dirtier, darker edges and corners of the streets. Hurrying down a narrow gap squeezed in between two behemoth department stores, I look back and see someone framed in the mouth of the alleyway. Silhouetted against the sun, I can't make out her face, only the bright edges of her hair. Something about her stillness makes me reluctant to look away and because of this I trip on a gutter and reach out a hand to catch myself on a wall.

It's cold and smooth to the touch. A plaque.

Wellspring and Co. Est. 1822.

Careful Measures.

I've found it.

It's less than impressive. A cramped little building that at first I had taken for the wall of a parking garage. The plaque hasn't been polished in a long time and an unfortunate scratch has made the date on it almost unreadable. The windows are all shuttered and dark and there is a gate over the front door. When I pull at the bars they don't budge. They don't even rattle.

I notice a small stainless-steel buzzer to my left. It only has one button and I press it.

After a moment, there's a click and then a woman's voice comes through, softly crackling.

"Hello?"

I realise I don't have a story prepared.

"I'm here for a new outfit," I say and then, because it's true, "I hate what I'm wearing. I don't feel like myself in it. Can you help me?"

There's a pause that drags on for so long that I start to doubt there's anyone on the other end. I feel like I'm being watched but I can't see any cameras. At last, a small and almost imperceptible sound, like a hum at the back of the throat.

"I can help you," the voice says. The lock on the door buzzes. I step inside, casting one last glance back towards the street. The silhouette is gone.

As I step inside, I have a sudden and very brief sensation of entering into a large and echoing stone chamber, filled with shifting smoke and flickering lights. An altar behind gauze. The sound of dripping water.

Then I blink and I am looking at a perfectly ordinary corridor, with white windowless walls and wooden floors. No art on the walls, no rugs on the floors. I walk along it and come to another door which opens when I lay my hand on it to reveal a comfortable little sitting room.

I see a table with a pitcher of water and two glasses on it, a large sofa and in one corner, dominating the space, a three-panelled, full-length mirror. The room is impeccably tasteful and like the corridor, windowless.

The walls are all bare save for one huge painting on the wall facing the mirror: it's remarkably ugly. A large white dome set against a blue sky. I stand in front of it for a while, trying to work out if it's a temple or half of a boiled egg. There are a few straggly brown lines that could either be cracks or vines.

I'm looking at it when I feel a sudden lurch, a tug in my chest. It's not so much that the painting is drawing me closer, but that suddenly I feel as if it was a drop, a hole in the world that I am teetering on the edge of. I feel myself sway and then there's a hand at my shoulder.

"Sit down," a voice says. "Have some water."

The tone is soft and calm, yet so commanding that I obey without question. I set myself down heavily. A glass of water appears in front of me and picking it up I take a few long and greedy gulps.

When I can take a full breath and my heart stops racing, I look up. In the mirror, I see a tall well-dressed woman standing behind me looking down at me with infinite patience.

"Is that better?" she asks sympathetically.

All I can do is nod.

"We forget our emotions are so linked to our bodies," she tells me in that same even tone. "Hunger, thirst, exhaustion, sickness. All of these things can magnify a bad mood. When you next feel upset or out of control, try to make a mental checklist. Have I eaten today? Have I slept? Caring for the body is caring for the mind."

"Um," I say. "Ok."

I still feel weak, shaken. Perhaps it was the heat. Or the ice cream. I close my eyes and hear her moving around me, pulling out a chair.

"You've come because you want something to wear," she reminds me. Her voice is strange. There's an accent there somewhere in the click of the consonants but it's unplaceable. Sometimes I think it's Irish and then it shifts, and I think South African or Russian or maybe even somewhere else completely, like Minnesota.

"I have," I say. "I need to feel more… me."

"And who's that?"

I don't know how to answer. After a moment, she takes pity on me.

"How about this – tell me what you'll be doing in these clothes."

Disorientated, I forget to lie. "I'll be disposing of something."

"Of what?"

"Lulabelle," I admit. She considers this and then nods. Her silk shirt is tightly buttoned at her wrists and neck but when she tilts her head to one side, I see the faint straight line of a scar below her left ear.

"I see," she says calmly. "So, you need an outfit worthy of an assassin."

"An assassin," I echo. Is that what I am? I try out the label, and I think I like it. I feel my ego swell to fit these new parameters. Assassin. "Yes, an assassin."

"You need something practical then," she says and then seeing my reaction she laughs and shakes her head. "Alright, not too practical. But you must at least wear trousers. And flat shoes."

"Not too flat," I warn.

She watches me with cool eyes. I can't work out if they're grey or green or blue. It's hard to look at her directly. I look at her hands instead, the neat dry clasp of them on the wooden tabletop.

"It is a mistake to sacrifice comfort for aesthetic," she tells

me. "We are only as useful and capable as our outfits allow us
to be. We must choose our clothes carefully and then forget
they exist. We must move through the world unconstricted
and without limitations. A necklace that chokes will consume
our attention. A shoe that pinches will only hold us back
and make us unhappy. An itchy jumper can ruin a pivotal
moment."

She hesitates for a moment. "It's not often in my line of work
that I am given the opportunity to indulge in practicality."

"Not too flat," I say again, but I hear my conviction waver.

She watches me for a moment and then she nods with a
faint smile.

"Just as you like. How about the colour? White perhaps – an
angel of mercy?"

I shake my head. "Difficult to clean."

"Ah," she says. "You don't wish to make a statement of your
violence."

"I need to keep a low profile."

"Something classic then. A suit."

"No tie," I say, but I'm warming to the idea.

"No tie. And no label if they ask." Her voice has a hint of
pride. I feel a sudden joy in my chest at her approval. I hope
that we agree on more things. I decide to stay quiet and listen
carefully so that I think of something else to say that she'll like
to hear.

We talk for a while about the type of fit and the material and
all the while she is moving, bringing out a rack of suits, and
shuffling through it with her strong supple fingers, urging me
with light feather touches to my back and shoulder to stand
and undress.

For a moment I am flatfooted and alone in front of
the mirror, wearing only Lulabelle's underwear. I can
hear the woman moving in a backroom and I realise that
I have forgotten what she looks like completely. Again, I
have the impression of the echoing stone hall, the smell of

pomegranates. Grey veils shifting without a breeze in the corner of my vision.

What is this? It feels stranger than memory. Like deja vu perhaps. I wonder if some chemical is being released into the air, like supermarkets pumping out the smell of baking bread. I don't feel drugged. Perhaps the hitchhiker would know. Perhaps this is a normal and everyday state of mind.

When the tailor returns, the fitting begins.

I choose black fabric, the darkest she has, even though she warns me it will drain my complexion. As she moves around me, tightening this and pinning that, she keeps up her steady stream of advice.

I must always wear sunscreen, she tells me, and use an SPF lip balm if possible. If I wear jewellery it should be in a way that accentuates my most attractive features. Gold flatters me and silver doesn't. If I am having trouble sleeping then I should blink my eyes rapidly for a full minute before bed in order to tire myself out. What I wear is meaningless if my body is not clean and my teeth are not brushed. I should always say please and thank you without exception. If I'm caught in a riptide then I should swim parallel to the shore in order to escape.

I try to take all of this in but it's difficult. It's too much, I can't keep up. I keep trying to catch sight of her in the mirror. Her hair is held up, I cannot tell its length. There are lines on her face but a firm strength to her arms as they move in endless, complex patterns around my body. She could be anywhere between twenty-seven and fifty-five.

In order to avoid looking at her or the painting behind her, I look at myself.

Slowly, I am beginning to take on a distinct form. My limbs are four jutting dark lines. My shoes click with a glossy little heel. My shoulders are a square; my face is a circle balanced on top of them. When at last she steps back, the only hint of chaos left is my hair, tangling over the smooth fabric.

"You should tie it back," she tells me. "So it won't get in the way."

Until now I have been limp and obedient under the barrage of her commandments. At this though, I shake my head.

"No," I say. "I think I like it like this."

"They'll know who you are," she warns, but for the first time she smiles.

Giddy at this sign of approval, I end up telling her everything that has happened to me so far. Or at least I mean to. Instead I get caught up by my frustration at the automatic car.

"It's not fair," I complain. "What's the point of giving me a steering wheel that does nothing? It's a hunk of junk."

She is silent and after a moment, I say again, trying out the words under my breath, "A hunk of junk."

I don't know what I'm expecting her to say. I want her thoughts on it. I want her to say something that will make me understand why I'm so upset by this. Maybe I want her to tell me how to fix it.

"You should never be rude to inanimate objects," she says, with an incredible gravity. "It reveals how you treat those who you think of as less than human. If you are rude to a computer, you will be rude to an animal. From there it is a small step to being rude to a child or rude to a waiter in a restaurant."

I wait, expecting something more to follow but it never does. As I wait, I hear a buzzer ring.

My second target, here to pick up her dress. I remember all at once, my reason for being in this room.

"I should leave. You have your job to do," the woman says and steps backwards. I think for a moment she will disappear into the painting and I panic, reaching out to grasp at the cuff of her shirt.

"Wait," I say, hearing my voice crack at the edges. "Tell me please, how should I do it?"

Her face is a valley of strange mists but for the first time, I see that her lipstick has bled just slightly into one corner of her mouth.

"Kindly," she says. "You must try to do everything with kindness. If you must do it at all."

"I must," I tell her. The buzzer rings again and still, we do not move.

"It was nice to meet you, Lulabelle," she says and puts her strong hand on mine to gently detach it from her shirt. "I'll be thinking of you."

It's the first time someone has called me by that name and it feels wrongs somehow. Like I shouldn't answer to it. But I don't have another one to give her.

The buzzer rings.

She moves away from me, over to a thin metal panel on the wall.

"Come in," she says into the speaker and presses a button.

I look at her helplessly in my black suit.

"My name is Marie," she says. "You really should try and ask people's names. It's important."

With this parting advice, she leaves through a door I haven't noticed before. I want to call after her, ask if that's a first name or surname. But it's too late. Behind me there's the sound of a throat clearing unhappily.

I turn and Lulabelle is standing there in a doorway, hip tilted slightly to one side. Up close her outfit is almost unbearably tasteful. The only thing that throws it off is a cheerful yellow silk scarf tucked under her chin, covered in little dots.

"Oh," she says, when she sees my face. "It's you. What do you want?"

Be kind, I thought. I must try to be kind.

"Lulabelle sent me to…" I say and then I swallow. "To tell you that you're doing a great job. She's proud of you."

"Is she?" the Portrait asks, unimpressed, and stifles a yawn. "God, I'm so tired. I've been walking all day."

"Sit down," I say. "Have some water."

"I don't need your permission," she says rudely but sits down at the table anyway. I think about asking her name but that would be stupid. What does it mean to be kind?

I see her reach up to adjust her yellow scarf and inspiration hits me.

"That's nice," I say, touching my own neck. "I love the polka dots."

Her face lights up instantly and she smiles for the first time, wide and toothy. She doesn't look much like Lulabelle when she smiles.

"Do you really?" she asks and then lowering her voice, she looks up at me from under her eyelashes like she's sharing an intimate secret. "You know I picked it out myself. I had to fight for it too. Lulabelle hates polka dots."

"It was a good choice," I say, even though I know now that yellow is unflattering to my skin tone. "You look really lovely."

She blinks twice and goes a little pink. I reach under my suit to find the cute little leather holster that Marie had found for my gun.

"Well, thank you," she mumbles and then looks away, over at the painting. "Hey, what do you think of this–"

She doesn't finish the question. The gun gives a little jerk in my hand and then she's slumping into the chair, like a tailored dress crumpling to the floor.

As I leave, I catch sight of myself in the mirror and I practice a smile. Marie was right. It does feel better to be kind.

CHAPTER THREE

The Empress

She sits in the garden on a throne of red pillows, a crown of stars resting on her head. A life of tasteful luxury and graceful wealth. The corn rises up before her, golden and adoring. She smiles and the world smiles with her. Endless abundance.

Outside in the alley, the paparazzo is leaning against a steam vent.

"She in there?" he asks me.

"Yes," I say. "But she's dead now."

"Ah, shit," he says, his face darkening. He pats his trouser pocket for his cigarettes but when he pulls out the carton it's empty.

"You can still photograph her, can't you?" I ask and pull out my own, which are nestled in a little silk lined breast pocket next to my tarot cards. "Want one?"

"Thanks," he says, even though he makes a face at the Lucky Girl brand. I wonder if male cigarettes taste differently to female cigarettes.

When the end is lit, he puffs out a mouthful of smoke and says, "You can't show a corpse in magazines. The ones I work for anyway. Shouldn't you be leaving?"

"Why?" I ask, stepping a little closer to hear him. The traffic sounds are louder now. Bubble City is shaking itself awake.

He just points up the alley on the street I can see the flashing blue lights reflected in the shop windows. It's not the police. They wouldn't have come so quickly and they wouldn't have come at all for a Portrait. I hear the sound of a van door sliding open and then the click of heels.

I blink and see a flower, spreading yellow and white petals in the dark. Mitosis. How did they get here so quickly? Did Marie call them? She doesn't owe me a thing but still, the thought is deeply upsetting. I thought we got on well.

The paparazzo has started walking away, deeper into the alleyway, cigarette smoke trailing over the shoulder of his cable knit.

"Hey," I call out and when he doesn't turn, I jog to catch up. "Hey, wait."

He doesn't stop but he looks back at me and takes a questioning drag.

I was intending to ask him for directions but then I hear voices from behind me and I clamp my mouth shut and draw back against the wall.

"In here?" a woman's voice asks.

"Yeah, should be. There's another one active nearby though so keep your eyes open."

"Where the hell is the driver? I'm not dragging around a corpse in these shoes."

"Don't call it that."

I am keeping myself very, very still. I wish I had cotton wool for my ears. Just the sound of the engineer's voice makes me want to step out into the light. The paparazzo is saying something. With an effort I turn my head to him.

"What?"

"You need a lift?" He's watching me impassively.

There's a clank as the gate to Wellsprings opens. I nod.

At the other end of the alley we have to squeeze past a jagged metal fence and a long line of industrial bins overflowing with fabrics and stinking of chemicals. There, nestled beneath a fire escape, is his scooter.

"I'm scouting out a party in the Hanging Gardens," he says, popping open the seat compartment and pulling out a helmet. "Does that work?"

"Sure, sure," I say, looking over my shoulder. I think of how the Portrait looked when I left her. Marie could patch up the clothes if she wanted. There was no blood to ruin them after all and I had only left a small hole. I hope I left her in a dignified pose.

I realise the paparazzo is giving me one of his long scanning looks. "Hey. You look different. Who are you wearing?"

It takes me a moment to understand. I look down at my dark suit, and then I remember what Marie told me to say.

"I don't think it has a label," I say. He arches an eyebrow, visibly impressed; then he looks slightly puzzled, looking at me again; then shakes his head, his face clearing.

"Hop on," he says. "I don't have a helmet for you."

"That's fine," I say and clamber onto the back. "I don't need it. What's your name?"

"Call me Velázquez," he says dismissively and then, "You have to hold on tight."

I place one hand gingerly on the back of his jumper. Under the baggy clothes, his body is smaller than I expected. He's the first person I've ever touched. The hitchhiker's hands were too sticky.

Velazquez feels warm through the thick and scratchy fabric. He smells like strange tobacco smoke and convenience store pastries. For a moment I almost feel like crying. Who did Lulabelle hold that smelled like this? Or was it the pastries themselves, pastries eaten before pastries became expensive, before they became artisanal, before they became forbidden? Warm and eaten out of brown paper bags on the street. I think I remember this. Everything was new to her once too.

Without warning, he revs the engine and we pull out sharply. The transition from stillness to motion is startling and I have to hold on very tightly to keep from falling off.

He weaves through the traffic with an exhilarating speed

and frightening intuition. I can't tell which turn he will take or how each obstacle will be avoided. After a while I give up and press my head into his shoulder, my heart performing a series of stuttering acrobatics in my chest. Even then I can feel our speed from the way the wind grabs greedy handfuls of my hair, my clothes. He is shouting something to me over the noise of the rushing wind, but I can't hear it and the only sound I can make in response is a thin wavering laugh that's quickly snatched up and borne away in the rush.

I can't tell how much time passes when we finally come to a halt. The sky is tinged pink and purple overhead. I have to detach my limbs one by one; my fingers are locked into claws around his waist.

"Thanks," I say, and clamber, wobbling, from the bike.

He shrugs it off and I try to steady my vision to look around. I see a long street stretching off on either side, dark and quiet. Lulabelle has never been here before. There are a few people huddled in doorways, but otherwise it looks abandoned. Rows and rows of windowless grey apartment buildings. As I watch, the streetlights begin to flicker on, creating infrequent pools of grimy yellow light in the deepening twilight.

"What is this...?" I ask suspiciously. "I thought you said there was a party."

"There is," Velázquez says and laughs at my expression. "You're looking the wrong way. In this neighbourhood you don't do this..."

He swings his head slowly from side to side in a long drawn-out no. I reach for my gun.

"...you do it like this," he says and tips his head back, as far as it will go, his eyes staring up to heaven.

I keep my hand on my gun, but I copy him, craning my neck. There is a click in my neck. I see it. I see it all at once.

She has been here – but she's never bothered looking at it from this level.

Above us ten, twenty, fifty stories above our heads is another world. Every window is ablaze with light; blinking emergency blue, soft seeping irradiated green, pulsing red and flashing epileptic white. Between every building gold and silver cords are strung, as if some gargantuan kaleidoscopic spider has built its nest there up among the high rises. Now I am looking up, I can hear the sound floating down. The thump of bass and screams.

"What is this?" I ask in a whisper. A rush of vertigo comes over me, but I can't look away; I blink rapidly instead and see polka dot after-impressions on the back of my eyelids.

"The Hanging Gardens. The upper echelons, baby," Velázquez says. "But this is nothing. It's only nine thirty. They're still gearing up. You know..."

"What do I know?"

"You're supposed to be there tonight. The word is Lulabelle Rock is on the guest list."

I raise my eyebrows and consider this. If it's a Portrait then this will have been a lucky short cut. I don't have my binder but I'm sure it won't matter if I go out of order. And if it's not, if it's the real Lulabelle then...

"Okay, I'll stick around," I say. "Are we going up there? For the party?"

"Are you crazy? We can't go up there. Do you know what kind of security they hire for these things?"

"Why are we here then?"

"For the good seats," he says cryptically and cuts the engine.

The good seats turn out to be code for a dripping, smelly alleyway just across the road. There, we perch on garbage cans and he begins the laborious process of caring for his camera.

Bored, I kick my feet against the trashcan until he tells me to stop. I take out my tarot cards and flick through them, having to squint in the dim yellow light from a window above. I arrange them in order and then shuffle it, trying my hand at pulling random cards from the deck. A tower struck by lightning. Five men fighting with sticks. Seven cups floating in the sky filled with dragons and snakes and ghosts. I wish I had paid more attention to the hitchhiker. I wonder where he is right now, if he's found his master.

Night falls as we sit there and a chill begins to creep up my legs from the cold lid of the trashcan. I begin to think that no one is coming. I'm wasting time here.

Just as I am about to give up and go find a bus to take me to the car park, guests begin to arrive. At first, they come in slow drabbles, pulling up in dark cars and hurrying nervously past the dark-suited men and women who have appeared from nowhere to stand by the doors.

"Losers," Velázquez says dismissively beside me. "Nobodies."

"How do you know?" I ask.

"They're on time."

For these people, he doesn't bother raising the camera. A little later the crowds grow rowdy. The guests trip out of limos in high heels and fur coats, brandishing open bottles of champagne. These guests are noisy too, calling out to each other in screeches, bellowing over the blare of the music from car radios. A fight breaks out. A few of them smoke in the entrance to our alleyway, but they either don't see us or don't care. They mutter to each other and I hear snatches of it (I wish Caroline was coming, Are you ready? Give me a moment.)

An elegant man in a silk coat is looked over and turned away without explanation. Watching him walk back into the dark, his face impassive, I lean over and nudge Velazquez.

"Why did they do that? I know him – his face is plastered up all over the fashion district."

"He's a Portrait."

"So?"

"A knock-off Portrait."

"How could they tell?" I crane my head to look for him but he's already gone. "They didn't shine the light in his eyes."

Velazquez shrugs. "You just can. Up close. He's lucky they didn't call out a van to get him."

Unsettled, I sit back down next to him and hug the suit jacket in tighter around me.

A line begins to form. The bouncers settle into their crossed arms, eyes deadening.

"You don't want her picture?" I ask when I recognise an up-and-coming musician in a neon jumpsuit. Lulabelle had appeared with them once in a talk show where the gimmick was that the interviews were conducted in a bouncy castle. The up-and-coming musician had refused to take off her stilettos.

Velázquez shakes his head dismissively. "Small fry."

It takes another hour before the big shots begin to swan in. Their arrival is mostly unannounced. Some try to hide themselves in groups or under big trench coats, like detectives in noir films. Others step out of their cars with arms outstretched, pupils dilated, autograph pens at the ready. Mostly though, they glide through the crowd with an impossible kind of dignity. When they smile it's gracious and they wave with their elbows tucked tightly to their sides. Lulabelle was taught to wave like this to ward off any jiggling of arm flesh. Watching them I feel a twinge of sympathy in the bones of my wrist.

Lulabelle belongs over there, in the throng, but here I am, watching from this alley. She would find this all ridiculous. I feel her disgust sitting like a ghost on my shoulders. Besides me Velázquez clicks away like a busy little bug. My stomach grumbles and for the first time, the smell of warm pastries wafting off him makes me resentful.

Preoccupied by this, I almost miss her arrival.

She almost stumbles coming out of the limo but at the last moment, catches herself on someone's arm. Straightening up, she turns, and I hear Velázquez sigh in contentment, the shutter clicking.

For a moment I see her, as he does, perfectly framed. One elegant hand rests on the roof of the car. She's standing very tall and straight. Her eyes are rimmed in deep green and they look away, beyond us, to some distant shore. She's wearing gold tonight, a long shimmering dress that brushes the dirty pavement. Her hair curls around her face, in a big creamy cloud.

I feel so proud of her at that moment. She looks regal. Ethereal. Maybe it isn't pride. Maybe it's homesickness. I hop off my trash can.

"Well," I tell Velázquez. "It's been fun. See you around."

I can feel his eyes on me as I cross the street and join the crush of people, and I wonder if he's jealous that I can cross over the divide while he's stuck there in the shadows. It's twenty paces at the most but still I feel a shift come over me. By the time I reach the other side I am no longer a watcher but an active participant.

"Lulabelle!" I call out and she turns to me, slow recognition dawning on her face. She smiles and raises her hand in greeting. I see the unblemished palms and a strange mixture of relief and regret settles in my gut. I wonder which Portrait this is. I don't like the idea of going out of order.

"Darling!" she says and embraces me. She reeks of strong perfume. There's no sweat underneath it; she could be a strip of sampling paper. "Oh, I'm so glad to see you!"

"You are?" I ask doubtfully.

"Of course," she says. "You've come to replace me, haven't you?"

Before I have a chance to answer, an eager young man pushes out of the crowd and calls Lulabelle's name. We both turn but he only has eyes for her. Next to the gold dress I must fade into insignificance.

"Oh my god, it's really you," he gushes. "I can't believe it. I can't. Is it really you?"

"Yes," the Portrait lies warmly, clasping her hands to hide her palms. He probably knows but she's letting him pretend. "It's me."

"I'm your biggest fan," he tells her sincerely. "I've watched everything you've ever been in. Even the commercials. I've even seen your school play. You were amazing. You're always amazing."

"Thank you so much," the Portrait says and places a hand on his shoulder. He looks like he might faint and his eyes dart down at it spasmodically. "You know, that really means so much to me."

"I just want you to know..." the man says and for a moment he grapples with the enormity of what he's trying to say. "That I love you. I really do."

"I love you too," the Portrait says softly. "I'm so happy to have met you."

The man lets out a long sigh of happiness. They smile at each other. The noise of the crowd seems to dim and for a moment I can almost see a faint halo of light surround them.

Then someone shifts, the line moves on and they are torn apart. Lulabelle takes my arm and pulls me into the building. We are shuffled through a dark and flashing corridor and herded with a press of people into a lift. Someone presses a button and in a claustrophobic stifling rabble we begin our ascent.

The Portrait and I stand shoved into a back corner. All I can see are shoulders and the backs of people's heads. Someone elbows me and I push back, setting off a ripple of angry murmurs.

"Hey Lulabelle," a man yells over the crowd. "What was that creep saying to you?"

"He wasn't a creep, Raymond, you insufferable little prick," the Portrait snaps, head swivelling in the direction of the speaker. "He was a fan."

The invisible Raymond lets out a harsh guffaw but says nothing more.

"Sorry about that," the Portrait murmurs to me.

"Don't be," I say. I'm equally enraged.

The love of a true fan is a very precious and beautiful thing. Not to be taken lightly or disparaged. This thought is inherited from Lulabelle but it evokes so strong an emotion that it might as well be my own.

In the crush, I feel a hand slide its way down the small of my back and onto my ass. It squeezes; very quickly, so hard it's painful. I yelp and the hand withdraws.

"What is it?" the Portrait asks, brown eyes wide.

"Someone just grabbed me," I tell her. I wish I could move or reach for my gun but there are too many people.

"What?" she says, outraged. "Who? Slimeball! Show me and I'll tell the bouncer."

I can't turn but I jerk my head in the direction of the hand. "Behind me."

She looks and then her angry expression evaporates, leaving a blank mask in its place.

"Oh," she says tonelessly. "Actually, don't worry about it. It's not worth it."

"What are you talking about?" I say feeling betrayed. I twist until I see who grabbed me and then I turn back, mouth shut. Lulabelle has met him before.

The Portrait and I avoid eye contact for the next sixty floors and then, on the ninety-sixth floor there is a ding and we are spat out.

The party is a din, an utter mess. People twist together and spiral apart; the light bounces around them but it's too dark to make out any faces in the gloom. Music blares but from every direction something different is playing: disco, jungle and bluegrass, blues and bedroom pop and death metal. Some people are attempting to dance to the cacophony, but their progress is impeded by others sitting cross-legged on the dancefloor playing cards. Through the crowd I see a ping pong table where a pair of angelic twins are giving each other easy serves.

We step out into the bustle of it all, clutching at each other for support.

"What were you saying?" I yell. "About me replacing you?"

"What?" she calls back. "What did you say?"

I try again but I am drowned out by a lethal combination of Chopin, dubstep, and the pop of champagne bottles. She takes my arm in a firm grip and drags me through the crowd to the wall-to-wall glass windows. Bubble City stretches out below us, a glittering black monument.

This close to the glass, I can feel the chill rising from its dark surface. We lean our backs against it, teetering on the edge of the 1,250-foot drop. We can finally hear ourselves think.

"That's better," she says. "Now we can hear ourselves think."

"I haven't come to replace you," I say quickly, to get it out of the way.

"Oh," she says, and then to my horror, her green smeared eyes begin to well up. "Oh."

I stay very still, feeling uncomfortable. There is a torturous drawn out pause where she struggles to compose herself. Her lip quivers, her eyebrows struggle to keep their place. At last she lets out a ragged breath and regains control. I didn't know we could cry but maybe it's necessary for an actress like Lulabelle. It must be saline solution.

"Do you have any idea," she tells me in a low voice. "How long I've been partying?"

"No."

"Five months now," she says in a broken tone. "Five months of dancing and small talk and high fucking heels. Five months of living off canapes and martini olives. That's no way to live."

"Months?" I ask incredulously. "Not continuously?"

"Almost," she says, staring bleakly into space. "Sometimes, between 5AM and 10PM, I have time to check into a hotel. If there isn't a pool party to go to, or a rooftop brunch. If there's an unoccupied closet I can catch a few hours of sleep. I like coatrooms the best. You can crawl underneath the fur coats and make a nest for yourself. I once spent two days in a coatroom that way, until they found me."

"Who's they?" I ask, horrified. "Is Lulabelle having you followed? Are her bodyguards here?"

"No," she says miserably. "Just her friends. They love me too much, you see. They can't get enough of me. I can't give them enough... Oh god, here they come now."

She straightens up with a carefully concealed wince and fixes a brilliant smile in place.

"Darlings!" she cries out joyfully and spreads her arms wide.

Two women emerge from the crowd with matching white smiles, calling her name. As the three of them theatrically embrace, I notice that none of them have any lines on their palms. They smile at me vaguely but aside from one murmur of appreciation for my suit, I am irrelevant. Soon a crowd has formed and then, between one moment and the next, the Portrait has disappeared.

I think about diving into the scrum to follow her, but at the last moment the memory of the hand sliding down my lower back stops me. I decide on a drink instead, a strong one.

I snag something tall and fruit-studded off a passing waiter and wander for a while along the window, taking slow sips. The drink is lagoon blue and incredibly strong. I enjoy the way it blunts my senses, makes the flashing lights turn hazy and hypnotic.

I pass a couple staring out into the night, wrapped around each other protectively.

"...do you ever think about the city as a living creature?" the taller of the two murmurs to his companion.

"It's a beast," the shorter one agrees. "A monster."

A little further on I pass two friends in unbuttoned tuxedos, looking grimly out into the black. "This town," one says to the other, "it tears you up inside doesn't it?"

After eavesdropping on the third or fourth such conversation, I grow bored and slug back the last of my drink. I feel pleasantly drunk now. The tips of my fingers and toes are tingling nicely. I pass a buffet table laden down with food. The centrepiece is a giant swan with outstretched wings. It looks as though the feathers were stuck back on after it came out of the oven. A man in a metallic domino mask is picking at it with a fork, scraping out a cave between its ribs.

He sees me looking and tilts his head. "Don't I know you? Weren't you murdered this morning?"

"You're confusing me with someone else." I turn away, my stomach twisting.

I fight my way through the crowd and finally find the Portrait, sitting half passed-out in a plant pot. She is slumped among the green fronds, eyes lidded. By her side, a man is telling her with great enthusiasm about Kierkegaard's idea of the leap of faith. When I glare at him, he shuts up and wanders off to find someone else to educate. He casts a puzzled glance over his shoulder as he leaves and I see him sizing up the two of us side by side. We must look like a two-page fashion spread. Dressing for business and pleasure.

"I didn't come to take over for you," I shout into her ear. "I came to get rid of you."

For a moment I'm not sure if she registers my words, then slowly her eyes open, her spine stiffening.

"Well, why didn't you say so?" she says happily. "That's almost as good! Maybe even better."

"You wouldn't rather just stop?" I ask. "Have a rest?"

I'm not sure why I ask. It's not an option I can give her. I mark it down to curiosity.

"I've tried rest," she says. "It's just one long nap in a hotel room. After a while you get bored of the room service and daytime TV and you start to miss the party, even if your feet hurt. Waking up and falling asleep over and over again; it's exhausting. Just once, I'd like to close my eyes and not worry about when I'm going to have to open them."

I watch the coloured lights play over her face and then I nod. "Alright. How would you like me to do it? Shall we find a cloakroom?"

She tilts her head to one side and then I see a thought occur to her.

"What about this," she says. "You get a glass of champagne and watch the west window. If you don't see me go past by the time you finish, then you can come up and push me off the roof yourself."

"Why do it like that?" I ask, baffled.

"Why not?" she asks. "If this is my last party then I want to make a big exit. Give them something to talk about. No one ever remembers who attends these things. But they'll remember me."

"Okay," I say with a shrug. "Hold on till I find some champagne though."

In the end I can't find any, so I get a whiskey sour instead. She waves goodbye and then I wander over to the west window. I watch her make a final victory lap around the room and see for the first time the full extent of her powers. She moves from group to group like she's dancing; taking a shot, smiling at a story, leaning in to kiss someone beautiful on the cheek. Somewhere to the west of the buffet table, she stops and tells a final joke. Before they've finished laughing she's slipped away.

I turn to the window. The music is still pounding, someone jostles me and a little of my drink sloshes onto my hand. I look for a napkin to wipe it off and almost miss the golden blur plummeting past on the other side of the glass.

She looks like a shooting star.

I wait for a moment for someone to scream, but no one seems to have noticed. Maybe someone did scream, but the sound was lost in the music. I sidle up close to one of the couples by the window, but they only have eyes for each other now.

"I can't stand it," one of them is saying in a low passionate whisper. "I can't stand to see you with him. It's driving me crazy. Why can't you tell him? Tell him tonight."

"I can't," the other one says, "You know I can't."

I don't stick around to find out why. It seems like a private conversation and besides, the cocktails have started to give me a headache.

I find my way back to the lift and ride it to street level. Alone this time, it seems to take much longer.

On the way down I think about the way I'd left the previous Portrait in the dressing room at Wellspring. When she'd stopped moving, her joints had stiffened up almost immediately; I'd seen the parts where they had fitted her together. It was amazing really, how fast that shift had happened. By the time I'd left, the colour had already been leeching out of her eyes. I could have worn a white suit after all; there wasn't any blood.

At the door to the building, I hesitate. I can hear shouts and screams from outside, the sound of someone sobbing. I realise the Portrait must have fallen directly onto the line of people waiting to get in. I hope she didn't fall on her greatest fan. My mind baulks at the thought of the mess.

"Is there a back way out?" I ask a bouncer. She points me in the right direction and by the time I exit the building I am almost running. I don't know why. There's no rush after all.

CHAPTER FOUR

The Emperor

The throne where the emperor holds court has been carved out from a lump of solid stone. Behind him is the mountain range, ancient and impenetrable. His face is stern and below it is a long white beard that suggests an authority as old as the rock that surrounds him. Beneath the finery of his red robes, he is dressed for battle.

I have to take two buses to find my way back to the spiral lot where I left my car.

In both, I am the only passenger. It feels strange to sit alone on the plastic seats, surrounded by the detritus left behind by busy commuters. There's trash lying in the aisles and, on the second bus, a small puddle of vomit. If I close my eyes, I can still smell them, all the busy people rushing to work and back to home and then out again to restaurants and nightclubs and cinemas. On the first bus I wonder about the people who've sat in my seat before me. I wonder how they passed the time; if they read or listened to music or just looked out of the window. By the second bus I find the thought of it disturbing. Unhygienic. I wonder what diseases they were breathing out into the air; and what else they touched with their sticky fingers. I sit very still and try to hold my breath. After doing this for a while I discover I don't really need to breathe at all.

It would probably be best to keep in the habit, just in case it upsets people.

At the final stop there's a poster for Medea on the wall of the bus shelter. Lulabelle, bloody and haunted, looks back at me, a dollhouse clutched in her bony hands.

Truly horrific, a quote promises. Genuinely hard to watch.

The release date is getting close. It reminds me I don't have much time.

I give her a small wave but my heart's not in it. When I turn away I see a yellow car has turned onto the street behind me. It's going very slowly, almost crawling, passing in and out of the shadows cast by streetlights. When I turn and walk away I hear my footsteps echoing down the street, nervous and quick.

It's a relief to find my car sitting where I left it. Inside it's clean and orderly. In here I can adjust the temperature and humidity and if I want, the music. In here I have my A4 binder.

I spend a while sorting through it. There were twelve Portraits this morning. Now there are nine. The first two were in order but I have to hunt for the one at the party, skim reading in the low light.

I find her near the back of my notes.

Registration Code: PROCKL78960813
MODIFIED TYPE (enhanced: 'CAT EYE')
LOCATION: Variable, consult dashboard.
CHECK UPS: Weekly (wear and tear)

Killjoy, Lulabelle has scribbled next to her number. Needs to learn how to have fun. The word fun is underlined three times.

Got brunch girl and the clotheshorse. Ran into the party girl early, I type out in the console. That's three down.

The response is so slow I almost give up on it before it comes.

Try and stick to the running order.

"Oh shut up," I say out loud and exit the chat.

It's getting late now, nearly 1am, and I feel reluctant to continue. Do I need to sleep? I think about the Portrait in the gold dress, curled up in fur coats. I see her falling in a cloud of sequins. It would be helpful to know the limits of my own capabilities. I wish the Viking had included a manual.

As a makeshift alternative I get out the tarot cards again and look at the card marked 13. The Death card. It's comforting somehow.

It makes me feel like I am fitting into a pre-established pattern. I feel inevitable.

With renewed confidence, I look at the next Portrait's file. It's just two lines on an otherwise blank page. Her code and the address to a downtown office. I recognise it immediately. It's the office of Lulabelle's agent, Spencer Mandrill. When I try to picture him, I just see a big white smile floating in the dark.

Spencer's hilarious, Lulabelle's scrawled below the address. Don't trust him. Keep the file in the glovebox.

Spencer's address is pre-set in the car's navigation system. With the press of a button, I'm on my way. Almost as soon as we leave the bright lights of the parking lot, I feel something like exhaustion setting in, pinning my limbs to the car seat. My stomach makes an audible growl, tugging at my guts. I wish now I had been brave enough for the canapes.

I spend the journey with my eyes closed, the seat tipped back as far as it will go, holding my nose and tipping my head back to swallow mouthfuls of Fruel. I drink two and chase them with a selection of painkillers I find in the first aid kit.

By the time we reach our destination, I am somewhat restored.

Spencer's office doesn't look like an office at all. It looks like a fairybook castle.

White walls, an imitation drawbridge and a scattering of turrets, the thing sits like an ugly wisdom tooth in the middle of all the other glass cube offices around it. I have a vague recollection of the story behind it; something to do with an eccentric casino magnate. Spencer used to tell Lulabelle the magnate hanged himself in the highest turret. Once a bedroom with a tiger skin on the floor, now Spencer's office.

I look for the window and see it's the only one with a light shining. For as long as Lulabelle's known him Spencer has kept strange hours.

I buzz at the door and while I'm waiting, I knock on the ornate archway around the door frame. It has the hollow 'bock' of cheap plaster.

The door opens and I step out onto red carpet and watch my glossy shoes sink down into the fabric. I don't need to look where I'm going. Lulabelle's made this journey so many times before. These feet belong to her too and they know where to take me. I take my steps mechanically, left, right, pause. Passing the murals of simpering Greek goddesses with perky showgirl bosoms, I reach the overlarge central staircase and start to climb. The layout of this place is impressively impractical for an office and with my footsteps muffled there's an eerie empty silence to the place. It takes me two corridors and another spiral staircase until I reach the frosted glass door with the letters Spencer Mandrill, Talent Manager.

He owns the whole building, but this is the heart of it. Every other floor is filled with rooms of furniture wrapped in dust covers. I only know this because Lulabelle is a snoop.

I wrap my heavy, blue-tipped hand on the doorknob and let myself in.

Inside the room, which is an odd half-moon shape, a frail little redheaded secretary sits behind a large oak desk. At the sound of the door, she peeks up over the top of her desktop computer and gives me a tired smile.

"Hello, Ms Rock," she says. "Spencer's expecting you. You can go right through."

"Thanks," I say and brush past her quickly without stopping.

Her thick glasses, her limp hair, the exhausted slump of her shoulders under her cardigan; I don't like to look at her.

On the other side of the next door is another room, another desk. This one is twice as large and made of brushed steel. It looks like something out of an industrial kitchen, a butcher's chopping block. It could be a sacrificial altar in some ruined temple. There are no computers on it or papers or wires. Just a fountain pen in a stand.

Sitting behind it with his back to a large round window is Spencer.

"Baby!" he says when I come in. "You look like a million bucks!"

He stretches out his arms but doesn't get up, so I have to edge my way around the desk to lean in and give him a kiss on the cheek. Just as my feet knew where to go, my body remembers this. I wonder if the disgust is Lulabelle's or mine. I try and rush it and not inhale, but still I get a lungful of his heady cologne as my lips brush his dry skin. He tries to put a hand on my arm, but I pull away quickly and pretend not to see him reaching.

"Hiya, Spencer," I say quietly. "Sorry to come by so late."

"Is it late?" he asks. "You know I don't keep a clock in here."

"It's just gone half two," I say and then, because he still looks puzzled, "02.30 hours."

"Oh shit, that's nothing," he says, waving his hands. "I do my best work at this time. Hell, I've been up for thirty hours straight already and I'll keep going for another forty."

"That's not healthy, Spencer," I say, perching myself on the wickedly sharp edge of the desk.

Spencer lets out a bark of a laugh and waves his hand again. "I'll sleep when the city sleeps. Take a seat, doll, let's chat. You want a drink? Coffee, whiskey, juice? I have tomato. I think I have pineapple. Hey, you look hungry. Let me get you something to eat. You want some fruit? A pastry? I think I can even rustle up a sandwich. You like meatballs?"

"No, thanks Spencer. I'm fine," I say, moving back around to place myself gingerly in one of the overstuffed armchairs facing the desk. I sink into the cushions and then when I look over at him, I have to tilt my head back a little to see. I'm low down but the armchair is so big that I feel like a child, swinging my heels just a little over the floor.

I watch him as he buzzes the intercom and rattles off a long order of refreshments. He looks just the same as I remember. Or at least I think he must. A carefully maintained middle-aged man with salt and pepper hair that curls just a little under his ears. From the waist up he's impeccably dressed in buttoned shirtsleeves and a half-Windsor tie with a subtle blue stripe. Below that, sweatpants and socks. From where I'm sitting, I can see his feet under the table, kicking and stomping in a silent little tap-dance. For as long as I've known him, Spencer has never been able to keep still.

The socks are patterned with little oranges, sliced in two. Out of the left one, one hairy toe protrudes from a hole. The nail is long and yellow; it wiggles at me like it's saying hello.

Spencer finishes his order and takes his finger with a flourish from the button. He looks up at me sharply and looks for a long time, his hands flat and upturned on the table in front of him, like he's trying to prove to me that they're empty. The lines that criss-cross them look like spiderwebs.

"What a nice suit. Looking sharp, kid," he murmurs. "Who…"

"I don't think it has a label" I say.

He looks a bit puzzled, just as Velasquez did. Then he smiles fondly. "No kidding," he says. "Just look at you. So smart."

I try to bear the looking impassively but eventually my nerves fray. "Lulabelle told you why I'm here?"

"Oh yeah," Spencer says in that same fond voice. "She told me all about her little plan. What I'm wondering is, do you know why you're here?"

I frown and shift uncomfortably. "To get rid of the others."

"Uh huh, uh huh," he says impatiently. "But why? Did she tell you why?"

"Because of her movie," I say. "She needs the publicity."

He just smiles sadly, saying nothing. After a moment of squirming, I have to look away. I look behind the desk at the window that I've never seen unshuttered. When that proves unsatisfying, I look at the movie posters. The curved walls gives a faintly crowded feeling, like I'm being peered down at. Spencer has always made a point of displaying them, even the terrible ones from the start of Lulabelle's career, where she would play the barely seen teen daughter or nagging girlfriend. In most of these early posters, she isn't even present. The later ones you begin to see her creeping into the frame, sidling from the corner until she looms front and centre, in extreme close-up.

"Fine," I say, giving up at last. "You don't think it's because of the flop?"

"I think that Lulabelle loves to obsess over nothing. The kid's a true artist – she worries too much. The movie's fine and if it isn't, who cares? I have five more projects lined up after it. She's a hot property. She's just getting started. She can take a few punches."

"So?" I ask. "What are you saying?"

"So, why make you? Why wipe out the others? Don't you want to know? Aren't you just that little bit curious?"

We watch each other coldly. There's a knock at the door.

"Yeah?" Spencer shouts, without breaking eye contact.

The secretary enters, tottering under the weight of a tray piled high with bagels, doughnuts, ham sandwiches, a pot of coffee, tall sweating glasses of orange juice, small pots of assorted jams, crackers and three types of cheeses, a sushi platter and, balanced precariously between her shoulder and neck, a large wooden bowl of fruit. She takes two staggering steps and then somehow manages to make it to the desk.

Spencer makes a meal out of watching the feast being

prepared, exclaiming over each new dish, and testing every apple for bruises. When at last it's all set out before him, he touches the secretary's waist to pull her down and whisper in her ear. She nods and leaves and when she returns she's carrying a large unopened bottle of champagne and two flutes.

"Shall I leave it here?" she asks.

Spencer shakes his head with a little flick, like a horse bothered by a fly. "Open it up, doll. Hell, get yourself a glass. This is a special occasion."

"Thank you, Spencer," the secretary says quietly.

She takes her time popping off the cork, easing it out in careful wincing little movements. When it pops, she jumps, even though she must have been expecting it. Spencer watches her closely as she pours out two frothing glassfuls. I wonder if they're sleeping together. I hope not.

Spencer must have forgotten he offered her any because he dismisses her after that. She doesn't remind him and when she closes the door behind her, I imagine a hint of relief in the way the lock clicks shut.

"Well," Spencer says grandly when it's just the two of us again. "Look at all of this, huh? Go ahead, dig in."

"Thank you," I say, not moving. "But I told you before, I'm not hungry."

He knows I'm lying but he doesn't argue, just shrugs, and tucks a napkin under his chin. "Suit yourself."

He eats ravenously, tucking the food into his mouth in a steady mechanical process, the muscles in his jaw twitching furiously as he chews. He looks like a train driver shoving fuel into an engine. I'm tired of this. I want to be done.

"I do want to know," I say. "Please tell me. Why does she want to get rid of the others?"

He smears cream cheese on a bagel, tops it with a hunk of fleshy pink salmon and puts the whole thing into his mouth.

"Cus fawshuns chinj fisjt," he says, chewing with his mouth open.

"What?"

He swallows and says again: "Fashions change fast kid. What was new is now old, etc., etc. It used to be trendy to have Portraits. Everybody who was anybody wanted one. They all got those vats installed, started popping them out like rabbits. But that was a while ago. Now it's all about exclusivity."

"What?" He's trying to talk while chugging orange juice and his words are garbled, distorted.

"Exclusivity," he enunciates. "Less is more. To be in short supply – that's hot, that's sexy. Everybody wants to be an individual."

"Do they?" I ask coldly. I feel disappointed somehow. I don't know what I was hoping to hear – some secret maybe. This new information changes nothing, nothing at all. It doesn't make my quest any more or less noble. It's just what I was made for. It doesn't matter where the car wants to go or if it likes the view once it gets there.

"Of course they do," he says, and then gives me a sly grin. "Even you. All Portraits do."

I shake my head. I don't understand.

"Maybe you haven't got there yet," he says, wiping his mouth with his napkin. "You're what, a day old? It usually takes a little while, but yeah, it'll happen. You betcha. You want to be Lulabelle Rock forever? Or do you want to be something just a little bit different? Special. Unique?"

"It's not a question of if I want to be Lulabelle Rock or not," I say. "I am her. She is me."

But even as I say it, I'm thinking polka dots.

"It's the biggest flaw in your design," Spencer goes on. "Otherwise you're perfect! People, we age and change and gain weight and lose it and get sore joints. The minute we stop growing we start dying. Our lives rise and fall like waves on an ocean. But you – you're crystallised. You're a frozen moment in time. Portraits don't change, you know? You don't get sick. I don't know why you girls aren't happy. I know I would be."

I am silent. I don't want to look at his eyes, so I look at his big toe instead.

I hear a soft wet noise as Spencer takes another bite of melon. "You give yourself a name? I know some of the other girls have. Belle. Lou. Prudence, of course. I call mine Lulu."

"I don't know what you're talking about."

"You will."

"Look," I say, suddenly frustrated and tired. My head hurts. I can smell the coffee and I badly want to take a California roll but some instinct tells me not to accept anything from him.

It occurs to me suddenly, that the food might be a test. "Why are you telling me all this?"

"Just thought you deserved to know," he says and then he leans over the desk full of food towards me. His tie trails in the pot of cream. "Have you thought about what's going to happen when they're all gone?"

"No," I say flatly. I think about shoving a wedge of cheese in his mouth, so that he can't say anything else.

"I just wanted to tell you that you have options."

"Options?"

"At the end of all this, there's going to be one Lulabelle left. Who do you want it to be?"

I sit very still and when I speak, I try to do it very softly. "What are you saying?"

"You know what I'm saying," he says and pushes the glass of champagne across the table to me. "You're a smart girl. Drink up."

"Why do you care?" I ask. I don't pick up the glass.

"I'm just setting out your options. I'm your agent, that's my job."

"You're Lulabelle's agent," I say slowly, shaking my head.

He cocks his head to one side. "That's you, isn't it? Didn't you just tell me that?"

His empty hands are laid out again on the table. His smile is very calm but underneath the steel chopping block, his big toe is twitching in excitement.

"Did she tell you not to trust me?"

"I should go," I say. "I have a job to do."

"Do you see this?" he asks and without looking, he points behind him at the wall at what looks like a framed certificate. I can't make out what it says but I can see the embossed flower in the heading.

"Yes."

"You remember when that was signed? Do you remember the tests? The interviews? Try hard."

I rifle through Lulabelle's memories until I find it. The day spent in the Mitosis building out in the countryside. The offices had been open plan. There were beanbags, a coffee nook and table football. They had made her take test after test.

"I remember."

"It's a licence. That piece of paper guarantees your existence. And do you see the signatures?"

Vaguely. "Yes."

"I've signed it too, right under the part where it states that she is not only mentally and physically fit to make you but also financially viable. You see that?"

I nod and he sighs and sits back in his chair. The ergonomic supports squeak a little in protest.

"Lulabelle didn't pay for you out of her own pocket you know. The studio has a vested interest in Portrait technology. Lulabelle is an investment for them, you understand? And there are a lot of things that the studio wants that I've protected her from. You know what they're excited about right now? A showcase. They want to take one of you and put them behind glass, right next to Lexie Byce and Kitamura Hina and all their other top shelf brands. Museum of the living dolls. "

I stay very still and keep my eyes trained on the certificate. I am thinking of Lulabelle's memory of the Mitosis office. The employee who had told her that their first big order was for Portraits of child actors. They weren't, he had explained, subject to the same limited hours on set.

"I said no, of course," Spencer says, his voice suddenly soft. "I just want you to know. I'm not the bad guy here. My number one priority has always been Lulabelle. It's my job to protect her. And you, by extension of that. You're her legacy, you know that?"

He watches me for a moment and then sighs. "Alright, I'll let you think about it. Shall I call her in?"

"No," I say. "You stay here. I prefer to do this alone."

He throws up his hand in defeat. "You're the client. You won't even let me say goodbye?"

"I'll ask her," I say, standing, "if she wants that."

I leave him there with all his food. From each wall, a dozen Lulabelles watch me go.

On the other side of the dividing wall, the Secretary is typing out an email.

"Is it happening now?" she asks, looking up at me through her glasses. "Would you mind if I just finish this up?"

"Of course," I say. "Take your time."

I have a seat on the small sofa. There's not much to look at in the office except an old map of Bubble City on the wall. There's something off about it that I can't put my finger on and after a while I find it so discomforting that I pick up a magazine instead. Inside there's an article about the destruction of the rainforests. In the time it takes for the Secretary to send her email, I learn that it can take up to ten minutes for a raindrop to fall from the canopy to the forest floor. There is a large glossy photograph of a strawberry poison dart frog on the other page.

There's the sound of someone clearing their throat and when I lower the magazine, I see the Secretary is standing above me. The fluorescent lights make a gingery halo around her head.

"I'm ready now," she says. "Are we going somewhere?"

"Would you like to go somewhere?" I ask.

She hesitates and then shakes her head. "No, here is fine."

I tap the cushion next to me and she sits down. I think about how to do this. It doesn't feel like the others. She knows what's coming and, unlike the last Portrait, she doesn't seem very happy about it. She doesn't seem exactly unhappy either. She just looks tired.

"Can I ask?" I say, gesturing awkwardly at her glasses. "Are they?"

"They're clear glass," she says and takes them off with a sigh, folding them into her jacket pocket. "Spencer just liked the aesthetic."

"You've been alive for a long time," I say awkwardly. "You must have seen a lot."

"Yes," she says distantly. "Quite a lot."

"Was it, um, nice? Your life?"

She shrugs. "It's good to keep busy."

I take out the gun and make sure there's a bullet in the chamber. "Well, here goes."

She closes her eyes.

I put the gun to her head and I'm about to pull the trigger when a thought occurs to me. I lower it slightly.

"Hey, Spencer... he said you go by Lulu, right?" I ask. "Did you pick that?"

Her eyes open in a blaze and for the first time, I see a flash of real emotion cross her features. "No. That's what he calls me. My name is Lulabelle. That's always been my name."

"Me too," I assure her, a little taken aback. "But you don't ever want to be different?"

"I am different," she says firmly. "I can use Microsoft Excel."

I make a small humming noise to myself and think about it. "Alright then. Any last requests?"

"Yes," she says and when she looks over at me her brown eyes are very warm, even behind the glasses. I realise suddenly that she hasn't blinked once in all the time we've been talking. "Don't leave me here when I'm dead. Take my body with you."

"All the way down the stairs?" I ask doubtfully. "Where after that?"

"I don't mind – just not here. I'm not heavy."

"Well..."

"Somewhere nice. Please?"

I relent. "Alright. I promise."

She nods and then her eyes widen. "I almost forgot. Wait a moment."

She gets up and goes over to her desk, rummaging around in the drawer for a moment. When she comes back she's holding an letter opener designed to look like a small silver dagger. I watch her hold out her left hand and slide the blade of it underneath her thumbnail.

"When you disable me Mitosis receives a signal," she says, without looking up. "This is how they can collect the decommissioned Portraits. The parts are expensive to make."

I stay silent, watching her hands.

"By doing this you can disable their link," she says. "They can't track you or work out your status. But it's considered damage and therefore you're liable to be decommissioned if they find you."

There's a click from her thumb and when she looks up at me I notice her earrings for the first time. They look like lopsided little fishing lures.

"How do you know all this?" I ask her.

"I read all the emails," she says and then when she smiles, the earrings shake. "Industry secrets. Remember your promise?"

I nod.

"You know," she says. "I chose blueberry."

CHAPTER FIVE

The Hierophant

The hierophant sits between two tall pillars wearing a robe of three colours and a tall crown. One hand holds a sceptre and the other is raised in blessing or, perhaps, forgiveness. At his feet are his devoted acolytes and a pair of keys that seem to promise an unlocking. An unlocking of chains. An unlocking of mysteries.

Spencer must have been waiting for the gunshot because the second it's over he pokes his head through the doorway.

"She didn't want to say goodbye?" he asks.

"No," I lie. I had forgotten to ask. "She said it would be too hard."

"Oh well," he says cheerily, stepping into the room. "I suppose it's better that way. I hate to see a woman cry."

Standing in his socks he looks down at her, chewing absently at a piece of celery in his hands. Her glasses have fallen onto the floor and, without really knowing why, I pick them up and slide them into my trouser pocket.

"It happened so quickly," Spencer says sadly from behind me. "I wish there had been just a little more time. If only Lulabelle had given me some more warning. Lulu could have stuck around to train the new secretary at least."

"Sorry."

"Not your fault, babe," he says and then his eyes light up.

"You sure you don't want some of that champagne? I can't finish the whole thing by myself."

"No, really. I'm fine." I stand up and look at the body for a moment wondering about how to do this. In the end I stoop and pick her up in an awkward fireman's carry. I wobble at first but when I gain my balance I realise she really doesn't weigh much at all. Even so, I'm surprised I manage. I suppose I have Lulabelle's personal trainer to thank for that.

"You're taking the body?" he asks. "What the fuck for?"

"This is standard procedure," I puff. "Can you get the door?"

He doesn't move and for a moment I see something dark and ugly flash across his face. Then in the next moment, it's gone and he's smiling again, wide and toothy.

"Sure thing," he says and then he's opening the door with a little bow and waving me through. "Try not to get any of that fluid on the carpets, will you? I don't have anyone to call the cleaners anymore."

He trails behind me to the stairs and holds out a hand to block my way before I can take my first step down.

"Here," he says and holds out a small scrap of paper.

"What is it?"

"My number. At some point you will want to call me. You'll know when."

"I have your number," I say stubbornly. "In my car."

"Not this one. No one in the world would have this number but you."

"Not even Lulabelle?" I ask, my back starting to ache.

"Especially not Lulabelle," he says and then his voice drops. "I'm serious here, sweetheart. There will come a moment when your hands are at risk of getting dirty. Really dirty. When that moment comes, you'll know. You don't have to be alone out there."

Bent underneath the Secretary's weight, I can't reach out for it. He hesitates and then comes closer, so close that I can smell the cream cheese on his breath. He carefully tucks the number into my breast pocket. I want to push him away but my grip on the Secretary is already growing precarious. He winks again and steps back quickly and holds up his thumb and pinkie to his ear like a telephone.

"Don't forget," he says. "I'll be there. Night or day."

Two floors down, I close my eyes and take a deep breath. I feel sick with the smell of the food, with the scratchy feel of the Portrait's hair against my cheek. It feels like plastic fibres. She's becoming more doll-like by the minute.

"Do you think she always feels like this?" I ask the Secretary. "After meeting him?"

She doesn't reply.

When we reach the car, I stow her in the boot.

"What do I do with you now?" I ask her. She looks a little cramped, so I take a moment to arrange her limbs into a more comfortable position.

When I'm back in the driver's seat, I check the time. 3.24. The green letters blur and swim in my vision. There's a brand-new inspirational quote for the day.

BE YOURSELF. EVERYONE ELSE IS ALREADY TAKEN.

"Okay," I say, staring dumbly at the dashboard. "Okay, what now?"

I catch my own eyes in the rear-view mirror. They look bleary. I put my hand in my trouser pocket and wrap my fingers around the hard edges of the glasses. When I put them on my face I see the secretary looking back at me, tired and frightened.

"I'll keep my promise," I tell her and for a moment I think I see a face behind her in the rear window, peering in from the outside, pale and angry, with lips drawn back over its teeth.

I whip my head around but when I look back, I can only see my own reflection in the dark glass. I toss the glasses into the back seat and scrub my hands over my face to wipe it clean.

"Don't be stupid," I say and then, "Shh. Shut up."

I don't want to get into the habit of talking to myself.

I pick up the binder and flick through brusquely, wondering if I should be putting big red crosses over each Portrait I've dealt with. I don't have a pen though, not in any colour. It just keeps going, on and on. Eight more Portraits to go. When this is all over maybe I'll have a chance to rest. Even the Partygirl had to sleep sometimes.

When I try to picture what sleep would feel like all I can think of is sitting on Lulabelle's balcony, watching the sun's reflection on the glass table.

The next Portrait, PROCKL78960313, has a few pages of information, the most so far. She lives in an apartment in Rocher du Saint, the closest thing Bubble City has to a historic centre. She goes out walking most mornings, she buys groceries at a little organic family-run market on the corner with a modest monthly allowance. She has a subscription to the local newspaper. She buys most of her clothes second hand. She is sloppy at recycling. For all this information I have no idea what function she actually serves. There is no loopy green note from Lulabelle.

I plug in the address and spend the half hour journey catching snatches of fractured hallucinatory sleep. The streetlamps flash in and out of vision. At a red light I see a long striped tail disappearing around a street corner. I turn the radio up to stay awake. A woman is singing about storms and teacups and how much she misses someone.

The car takes me to a neighbourhood with wide tree-lined streets. When the car stops I turn off the music, interrupting the singer mid-lyric. There's no one around and the streetlamps seem softer here, more golden. Rocher du Saint is built on the only natural hill in Bubble City and for once there is nothing towering over me, no skyscrapers or roads. The buildings are mostly brownstone and only go up ten stories at most. I feel myself growing taller.

I feel safe leaving the Secretary in the car here. This doesn't seem like a place where a corpse would be found. The stars are beginning to wink out above me and the birds are waking up in the branches overhead. I wish they would stay sleeping.

At the door to the Portrait's apartment building I am faced with my first real obstacle: the buzzer is broken. I press it maybe twenty times before finally registering the handwritten notice informing me of this fact. Sorry! The note says next to a smug looking smiley face. I scowl at it. Written in blue ink, not green, but I would recognise Lulabelle's handwriting anywhere. After all, it's my handwriting too.

There's a fire escape in the alley. When I stand on my tiptoes, I can only just brush the bottom rung with the tips of my fingers. I huff and puff at this for a while and try a few jumps before giving up and trying a different approach.

It takes me a long time and a lot of coaxing of the navigation system but eventually I get the car parked in the right place. From there, it's fairly easy to hop from the roof to the last rung of the ladder. This feels like the sort of thing an assassin would do. Lulabelle played a hired killer once, back when she was starting out. It wasn't much more than an elevated extra role. She was one of ten actresses, all wearing venetian masks and fishnets, and most of them ended up being decapitated in the final fight scene. For having this as my only experience I think I'm doing pretty well.

The Portrait lives in the loft of the building. That's only ten floors up but the metal I'm clinging to shrieks with every movement and I have the unpleasant feeling that the only thing holding it in place is force of habit (and maybe rust). Somewhere around the fifth floor a sudden wind rises; the platform sways and when I grab at a railing, it crumbles away to a red dust in my hand. I look down and see the drop spiralling away from me. I resolve not to look down again.

It occurs to me that I don't know if I feel pain. Maybe the fear of it is just inherited. It doesn't make me any less scared.

When I finally reach the building's roof, I roll myself gratefully onto its flat, solid expanse and lie for a while, staring up at the sky. I can see clouds now, the same soft grey-pink of a jaybird's feathers. There were jaybirds where Lulabelle grew up. I think they must have been jaybirds.

I realise that I have never seen a jaybird in my life, only in a distant memory. Lulabelle's memory. Giddy now with fatigue, my eyes begin to sting when I think about it.

I make another resolution. Stop thinking about it. I decide I will never think about jaybirds again. The sky is pink and grey. No need to romanticise it.

I clamber to my feet with a wince. Up here on the black asphalt, the world is made up of aerials, satellite dishes, vents and chimneys and skylights. The towers of the fashion district and Hanging Gardens look far away from here, as distant and colourful as the northern lights.

The closest skylight is just a few paces from me. In the dark it glows, soft and buttery. I walk over and peer down through the smeared glass.

I can't tell the dimensions of the room from here, but I know it has high ceilings because of the dizzy feeling I get when I see the drop. I can see a white sheet spread on the floor, covered in dark smudges. I can see the jutting edge of what could be an easel and a corner of canvas. I see a hand outstretched and, in it, a paintbrush.

One of the skylight's panes of glass has a latch; with achingly slow movements, I pull back the bolt and ease it open. Why have a skylight that opens from the outside? It feels like I'm opening a birdcage.

The opening is just large enough to fit through. I lean out over the edge and look down. From here I am directly above her. All I can see is the top of her head. Her bleach job needs a touch up. In fact, her hair has more dark roots than platinum curls at this point.

I think maybe I'll just shoot her from here. It will be easier that way. Quicker. I pull the gun from my breast pocket and find her in the sights. I hold my breath.

And I wait for a moment… and I wait…

She tilts back her head and looks at me.

My finger goes lax around the trigger. I nearly drop the gun through the gap.

"Fuck," I say, low under my breath, heart racketing in my chest. It's not just the shock of being seen, there's something else, something wrong about her eyes.

"Hello," she calls up. "Do you want me to get you a ladder?"

I open my mouth and then a moment later, I close it again. She waits patiently and then I realise what's wrong. Her left eye is like mine, a deep dark brown. I know that eye intimately. I have looked at it in the rear-view mirror for the entire day that has been my life. Lulabelle has seen it in mirrors for thirty-five years before that. I have seen that eye in the face of the Clotheshorse Portrait I shot in Wellsprings. I have seen that eye smeared with glittering green eyeshadow on the Partygirl. I saw it behind the thick glasses of the Secretary. I know the eye on the left very well. I know it tired and teary and bruised and I know it chemically dilated and I know it hangover-bloodshot and above all I know it as a brown eye.

The eye on the right I don't know at all. The eye on the right is a stranger to me. The eye on the right is blue.

"Yes please," I say at last. "Thank you."

There is a lot of fumbling as she sets up the stepladder. It takes a while to put it in the right place and after that it's just a little too short. I have to squeeze my way through the frame and when I do there is a sickening moment where I am hanging, legs windmilling in empty space, unable to tell where I am or where she is or where we are in relation to each other. I feel a moment of panic in which I realise that if she wanted to, she could very easily take the opportunity to kill or maim or at the very least hurt me badly.

But she doesn't. A steady hand grips my ankle and guides my foot to the top.

I clamber down and when I'm finally standing before her, jelly-legged, she pats me on the shoulder sympathetically.

"Drink?" she asks. "I'm having one."

I nod dumbly and when she turns away, I am finally able to look at her. She's a little shorter than me, because I'm wearing shoes with a small heel and she is barefoot. Her hair is messy, like mine. We are both wearing white business shirts, but mine was made for me and hers is oversized and badly buttoned and what's more, it seems to be a man's shirt. Beneath it she's wearing striped pink pyjama bottoms. This entire outfit is accessorised with paint; blotched on her front, smeared up her hands and wrists, flecked into her hair. She smells of it too. Chemical and sweet.

I watch her back as she pads away from me across the hardwood floor. The layout is open plan and the kitchenette is tucked against the west wall, but it takes her a while to reach it because the loft is so outrageously large.

Glancing around I can see it looks something between an artist's studio and a torchlit cavern. In the lamplight I make out a kitchen table on one side of the room, a large spreading sofa and rug on the other. In one corner is a bed; or at least a collection of soft things that together resemble something like a bed. Two doors, one slightly ajar and spilling out antiseptic white light.

Once my eyes have travelled around the edges of the room, they come to the centre of it. The abstract wooden scaffolding of the easel and ladder side by side on the white sheet. Next to them, is a grand piano. It's such a beautiful and large thing that I wonder why it was the last thing I noticed. The piano reminds me of a stallion. I don't know why.

I'm still puzzling over it when something cold bumps against my hand. When I look down, it's a crystal tumbler filled with amber liquid and a soggy torn up slice of orange.

"Sorry," the Portrait says, still holding it out. "I thought you would take it."

I do, mechanically. It's a lot heavier in my hand than I thought it would be. Condensation begins to pool in the webbing between my thumb and index finger. I mumble something like thank you.

"I know this is rude to say to people," the Portrait says. "But you look very tired."

"I don't need to sleep," I tell her but when I look over, her face is shimmering like I'm seeing her through the heat rising off a highway.

"Why not?"

"I'm a Portrait," I say. "We don't need it."

"Who told you a stupid thing like that?" She blinks at me with her brown-blue eyes. "I sleep all the time."

"It's nearly four AM," I point out. "You aren't asleep now."

"I'm crepuscular," she says. "Like a rabbit. I suppose they said you didn't need to eat either."

"No, they gave me those smoothies."

"Fruel?" she asks, tilting her head to one side. Now the blue eye is lower than the brown.

"Those are disgusting. Eat with me – I was just about to grill a steak."

"You aren't a vegetarian?"

She's turned back to the kitchen but now she gives me a confused frown over her shoulder. "What? Why would I be? Was that in my file?"

"No," I say, confusing myself now. "It's just I thought... Like a rabbit..."

"I think you need to sit down," she tells me, pulling out a stool by the kitchen counter. "Before you fall."

I sway in place and look down at the drink in my hand. The ice cubes jostle and clink against the ragged flesh of the orange.

One of the legs of the stool is slightly too short and I have to concentrate very hard to stay balanced. The Portrait moves around the kitchen, taking out a covered plate from the fridge and a bag of pre-tossed salad.

"Mustard?" she asks me.

I shake my head again, feeling wary. "We don't like mustard. We haven't liked it since we were five."

"I tried it again actually, last year. It's pretty good. Want some?"

"No." I feel almost angry that she suggested it.

"How do you like your steak?" she asks me, fetching down a heavy saucepan from a rack on the wall.

"You know how I like it," I mutter darkly, not sure what she's playing at. She grins over her shoulder at me, as if I'm being endearing. I'm not trying to be endearing.

I scowl down at my drink, more bothered than I should be by the quick flash of white teeth. To cover my nervousness, I take a quick gulp. It tastes nothing like the smooth cocktail I had at the party. It is somehow both too watery and too strong, too bitter and too sweet. I gag a little and as I do, I see again the golden blur falling past the dark window. I take another drink and this time I don't care about the taste.

"You know why they gave you the smoothies, don't you?" she says, rooting around in the fridge. "Fruel is owned by Mitosis."

"I thought it was made for us specially. Isn't it... isn't it what powers us?"

"They imply that but it's not actually true. We can run off anything. Dog food, diesel, grass if we eat enough of it. It's a very efficient design."

"I'm sure that there was something on the label..."

"They word those things very carefully. The legalities surrounding our existence are very complicated. Why do you think they always have lawyers riding around in those vans of theirs?"

I didn't realise she was a lawyer. I was too distracted by the engineer.

"How do you know these things and I don't?"

"I've been around longer... and Lulabelle told me about it," the Portrait says, dumping the salad leaves into a bowl. One clings to her hand and she shakes it off onto the counter.

"You talk? A lot? Are you close?" I ask, feeling a surge of resentment.

"A little," she says and then she winks her blue eye at me. "I think I'm her favourite."

She laughs like this is an inside joke, but I stay silent, watching her closely.

"Why?" I demand. "Why you?"

"Well…" She pauses, thinking it over. "I suppose I'm useful to her."

"We're all useful. That's the point."

"Useful for her peace of mind, I mean. You know why she made me, don't you?"

"Of course," I lie. "Lulabelle's told me all about it."

She doesn't look up from where she's mixing dressing, but she smiles again to herself, like I'm being very charming.

"Well, let me remind you anyway," she says. "Lulabelle made me for a very specific purpose. My job is to sit here in this apartment and practise all of the hobbies she doesn't have time for. I paint, I make music, I sew. Sometimes I even write. That's why I exist. To create. Constantly. Endlessly. And if one day, I turn out to be good at woodwork or crochet or haikus, then Lulabelle will know that she has a hidden talent."

I try to wrap my mind around this and for the most part, I fail. I take another drink instead. The bottom of the glass is sludgy with sugar and scraps of rind.

"I think," the Portrait goes on. "That she's afraid of devoting her energy to the wrong project. Or missing out on some undiscovered potential… That's why she's fond of me, I think. I'm like a diagnostics test on a computer. I tell her who she is."

"Why decommission you then?" I ask snidely. "If you're so amazing?"

She frowns at the salad and then seems to decide that it's been sufficiently tossed. "Well, I've been alive for a while now. I've tried most things out. I mean I never got around to glassblowing I suppose, but I'd have to install a forge and I don't know if the building superintendent would be happy with that."

She turns away to fetch two plates and cutlery. There's something so dejected in the set of her shoulders, that my resentment fades almost immediately. I try to remember what Marie told me. Be kind, be kind, be kind.

"What were you painting?" I ask, trying very hard. "When I came in?"

Deftly, she lays the steaks side by side in the pan. The moment they touch the hot metal and oil they begin to sizzle, and the air fills with the smell of blood and salt. My nostrils twitch and there's another painful twist in my stomach.

"I was painting an eye," she says and even though she has her back to me, I can tell she's smiling. "It's part of a series actually."

"A series of eyes?" I ask, and then, slyly: "Brown or blue?"

"Any colour," she says, shrugging. "Lots of them. The colour isn't important. It's the emotion that matters."

"What do you mean?" I ask, but then she says the steaks are ready, and it's a long time till she answers, what with the serving-up and turning-off of the stove. By the time we're sitting across from each other at the kitchen counter and tucking in, I've already forgotten my question. I'm more concerned with trying to chew the steak which is hard and rubbery on the outside and almost cold at its centre.

"This is my technique," she says abruptly, making me choke a little on my stringy mouthful. "I pick up a mirror. A small hand mirror, so small that all I can see is my eye. And then I look into it and think of a very specific emotion. And then I paint it. Do you want something to wash that down with?"

I shake my head but that lodges a piece of steak in my windpipe and in the end, I'm coughing so badly that she gets up and pours me a large glass of water from the tap.

"What kind of specific emotions?" I rasp out at last, eyes watering.

"Well, the piece you interrupted is going to be called The Realisation That We Cannot Return to Childhood. The one before that was Seeing a Wild Animal in the City While Walking Home Drunk. The other day I thought of the next, but I suppose I'll never do it now. It was going to be Finding Something You Lost in Exactly The Place You Thought It Would Be. I was inspired by my keys."

I wonder if she knows that she's fallen into the same intonation that Lulabelle uses for explaining her latest projects in interviews. I hum and take another bite. "Will you put the title next to the painting or let people work it out themselves?"

"Oh, they'll never be exhibited," she says and then gives an odd laugh. "So, you're finished now. Are you ready to kill me or would you like a nightcap first?"

I look down at the remains of my unappetising cocktail and dinner. I feel comfortably full and warm.

"Maybe a coffee?" I ask and then, remembering Marie, I add, "Thank you. Is it difficult, painting?"

"Only the beginning, where you're looking at the blank canvas. A blank canvas is a big responsibility. Go sit on the sofa, you'll be more comfortable." She stands up and starts to collect the dishes. "I'll bring it over when it's ready."

I stand up and try to cross the room. Every step sends the room spinning around me in new and confusing revolutions. In the centre of the room, I steady myself with one hand on the piano.

"Don't you think it looks like a horse?" I ask her. "A thoroughbred."

"Did you say something? Hold on, the kettle's boiling," I hear her call out.

"Maybe it's the way the light's reflecting," I say, tracing my hand over the glossy surface. "Like it's been well-brushed. But also, it looks like it wants to be played…"

"You're mumbling," she says. "Do you want sugar?"

"...like a horse wants to be ridden." I say and then I frown and wonder to myself, does a horse want to be ridden? Does a piano want to be played?

I am suddenly afraid the piano will bite me or kick out, so I lift my hand and quickly retreat to the sofa. I sink down into the pillows and they're so soft that I keep sinking, until I am almost fully submerged in brown corduroy and colourful loose-knit shawls.

"Take your shoes off if you're going to lie down," I hear her say, but the day, my short eventful life, has caught up with me all at once. I don't think I will ever be able to move from this position. I think I might decompose where I am.

It's getting very hard to keep from nodding off by the time she comes over with the coffee but something is nagging at the back of my mind.

"I never told you," I say as she presses the cup into my hand.

"What's that?"

"I never said that I was here to kill you. How did you know?"

She looks at me for a moment and then her shoulders relax. "Someone sent me an email."

"Oh." I'm too tired to understand this. My eyes are dry with the effort of staying open. I try and widen them manually but still they keep slipping, heavier and heavier with each passing moment.

"Sorry," I say around a yawn. "This is really unprofessional."

"That's alright," she says kindly. "Go to sleep. You can kill me in the morning."

It's already morning, I try to say, and it's true, already the dawn is draining those deep pools of shadow. But as I watch the light creep in, the four walls of the loft crumble and fall away completely, and I realise that I have started, quite by accident, to dream.

CHAPTER SIX

The Lovers

Naked under the sun, the lovers stand side by side in paradise. Hands outstretched but not touching, the man watches the woman as she watches the angel that looms over them, blessing the union with blood red wings. Two trees, one burning and the other heavy with apples. A serpent is winding its way up the trunk.

I wake up the next morning to find that she's taken off my shoes. I lie on the couch for a while, wiggling my socked feet around. It feels nice. The first time I woke it came slowly and left me with a headache. I don't remember being pulled from the vat and unplugged from the machines. I only remember the pink spot on Lulabelle's white dressing gown.

This way of waking, all at once and fully, is wonderful. I amuse myself for a moment by pretending that this here, right now is the moment of my birth and that I have done nothing wrong, nothing bad, ever, at all, in my whole life.

It's a strange thought to have. What have I done wrong?

"Good morning," a voice says. "I put your coffee from last night in the microwave for you."

I open my eyes and see the blue-brown eyed Portrait looking down at me.

"Where are my shoes?" I ask her.

"By the door," she says. "They're very nice. I like the heel on them."

"Do you?" I ask groggily. "They're not very practical. Someone told me clothes should always be practical. That you should put them on in the morning and forget about them."

"That's no fun," she says. "Clothes are like costumes. They should make you happy."

I sit up and take the cup she's holding out. It's so hot that the porcelain burns my fingertips but, when I take a sip, the coffee itself is lukewarm. It doesn't taste very nice. I watch the Portrait carefully over the dark ripples. The paint-stained shirt is gone, replaced by red jogging shorts and a shirt that informs me that 'It's Always Taco Tuesday Down At the O.K. Corral!'.

I'm still trying to process this cryptic message when she tilts her head to one side and smiles at me. All at once, I find it hard to think of anything at all.

"I was just about to make lunch," she tells me. "Do you have time to eat it before you kill me?"

I remember the toughened steak and noxious cocktails from the night before and I frown doubtfully. "What are you making?"

"Omelette," she says. I relax. Omelettes are the only thing that Lulabelle can cook. They're difficult to fuck up.

I think.

"Alright then," I tell her. "I can wait till after that."

She nods and disappears from my field of vision. I stay where I am for a moment, drinking my rapidly cooling coffee. A thick woollen blanket is pooled on the ground; I must have thrown it off in my sleep. The knit is uneven and dotted with gaps. When I stand up, I take a moment to fold it, placing it carefully back on the sofa. It's a rose pink and, when I lay my hand on it, very soft to the touch.

Looking around, I wonder what time it is until I see a cat clock on the wall with eyes and a tail that moves in time with the seconds. It feels familiar. Did Lulabelle have this clock as a child?

Eleven-thirty. The loft is filled with sunlight, streaming in from the skylight and the large, sloping windows that stretch across the south facing wall. Outside I can see the tops of trees, a spray of green against the hazy city skyline. I can see two spires poking up, the curved roof of a temple, a minaret. Rocher du Saint is a strange place. Older than anything else around it but overshadowed, almost forgotten. I reach for Lulabelle's memories of it but they're scattered and infrequent. I get the sense it didn't mean much to her.

Last night I dreamt of leaving Spencer's office.

I dreamt that I had to carry the Secretary down two hundred storeys of a rickety fire escape. She had grown heavier and heavier until at last I realised she wasn't the only body on my back, that the golden Portrait had been stacked on top of her and the two other Portraits on top of that. I tried to shake them off, but four sets of arms gripped at me; forty fingers scratching at my face and pulling at my hair.

On the other side of the room, the Portrait that is still alive, the Artist, moves around the kitchenette, humming along to a small transistor radio balanced on the refrigerator. The song is about the devil. I take my time walking over, stopping to look at the artworks hung on the wall.

In the daylight, I can see why the Artist laughed when I talked about exhibiting them. I don't know much about art, but even I can tell that they are uniformly terrible. The perspective is skewed, the colours are garish, and technique laughably sloppy. Every choice made in their execution was the wrong one. The eyes, and I can only guess that's what they are, peer out from every wall like lopsided balloons. Teary, bleary, and bloodshot, the loft is an optician's nightmare.

"Do you only paint eyes?" I call over, not looking away from one particularly ugly specimen that looks like it might have caught an infection.

"Right now I do," she says over the sound of the saucepan sizzling. "For a while it was clouds. And keys before that."

There are other artworks too: a squat, half melted clay statue of what could plausibly be a tiger. A handful of embroidery hoops nestle on the piano, unspooling quietly. I wonder if this is the real reason Lulabelle likes her so much. Just by existing, this Portrait confirms that Lulabelle has made the right choices all along. No wasted potential here.

The piano is still there, but in the morning light it's just an instrument. I'm drawn to it anyway. When I sit down on the stool, my hands drift to the keys. Without thinking much about it, I play the first few bars of something.

"You must remember this," the Artist says over my shoulder. My hands falter and I look up at her.

"I don't," I say. "I don't know how I know this."

"No," she says. "That's the name of the song."

I shake my head. "I think it's called As Time Goes By."

"How do you know that if you don't remember?"

I frown at the piano and try to play a few notes. Now that I'm concentrating I can't do it anymore. I try to play a scale then give up.

"I don't think my memories are working," I admit quietly. "I used to think that I knew everything Lulabelle did. But now I'm not so sure. It's all very confusing."

The Artist is silent for a long time and then she says, "Come and eat."

I sit down at the table and she puts a plate in front of me. The omelette doesn't look particularly appetising but it doesn't look burnt either. When she's not looking I give it a surreptitious sniff. It seems edible enough and I decide to risk it.

"Orange juice?" she asks, and then her eyes widen and she snaps her fingers. "Bald men! That was it."

"What was?" I ask, holding out my glass so she can fill it.

"What I used to paint. In between the keys and the clouds. I knew I was forgetting something."

"Why?"

"I was interested in the, uh," she twirls a finger at the crown of her head. "The formations. I've always felt that bald patches were very expressive. Like a second face, just on the top of the skull. What about you?"

"I don't know if I've ever really given them much thought," I admit and she smiles and shakes her head.

"No, I mean what would you paint?"

I put down my knife and fork and chew slowly, considering. All I can think about are elevator interiors and my car, but I don't think that would be very interesting.

"I don't know," I say. "Birds."

She hums around her mouthful of food and points her fork at me as if to say good choice.

"Jaybirds," I blurt out, feeling buoyed up by a sudden, strange expansion in my chest. "I would paint jaybirds."

"What about ducks?" she asks me, sounding serious. "Do you like ducks? There's a park near here, with a lake. You should go. They have swans too."

I'm nodding and then I remember the buffet table and my smile falters. I put down my fork.

"That would be nice," I say. "But I don't think I'll have time for that."

As she washes the dishes, she enquires politely after my work. I tell her that I have eight Portraits left, including her.

"So, I'm fifth," she muses, scrubbing thoughtfully at the frying pan. "Is that number significant I wonder?"

The question makes me think of my hitchhiker and unthinkingly I blurt out, "That makes you the Hierophant."

"The what?"

I take out the cards and lay them out to show her on the tabletop and she comes over to stand behind me, drying her hands on a towel. The Fool, the Magician, the High Priestess, the Empress, the Emperor. The fifth card is the Hierophant in his big pointy hat.

"Hold on," she says, leaning past me with one hand on the table. "That's six cards."

She's close, hair just brushing my shoulder, and I shift away, made strangely on edge by the proximity.

"Yes," I say and tap the fool with my blue finger. "But this one is numbered zero."

"So, what's a hierophant?" she asks, picking up the card and squinting at it. "A pope?"

"I don't know," I confess. "I didn't learn all the meanings."

She considers it for a moment, first upright and then upside-down as if that will reveal some hidden clue. I'm very aware of her presence next to me but I don't want to look over. Finally, she puts it down and straightens up. My shoulders relax slightly.

"Hierophant," she says, slowly and luxuriously. "I quite like that. So what are you?"

I pick out the card and show her. She looks at it with an unreadable expression.

"Hmm," she says after a moment. "I suppose that fits."

"It does, doesn't it," I say, feeling pleased. I'm glad she sees it too. There's a pattern here, a sequence. Pre-ordained, just like my ring binder. I hope she understands that. For some reason, it's important to me that she understands.

She's silent for a moment and then her face brightens. "Do you want to hear a poem I've been writing?"

I hesitate, wondering what time it is. I really should be going.

"Alright," I say. "But just a small one."

She smiles in obvious relief and then spends a long time searching around in the clutter of the loft for the scrap of paper she wrote it on. I get the sense that she doesn't receive a lot of visitors. I sit on the arm of the sofa, putting on my shoes and then wander over to look out of the window. It's not the best view in the city, nothing like the Party Girl's wall to wall panorama. I can see a parking lot and a billboard advertising a new kind of fridge that can design meal plans for you. Most of the street is hidden by the trees from up here but I can still make out the morning traffic through the foliage.

I'm trying to make out the lettering on a coffeeshop when I see the yellow car parked at the curbside. At first my eyes slide over it but then I notice the figure leaning against the hood. Whoever it is is wearing a red baseball cap and sunglasses but there's something about the way they're posed, something about the crossed ankles and fingers starfished on the metal… it's familiar somehow, like something I've seen on a movie poster.

They turn their head and even through the glasses I am momentarily convinced they're watching me back.

"Aha!" the artist calls out, so loud it startles me.

I turn away from the window to see her holding up a scrap of loose paper she's pulled from the piano stool. "I found it. Are you ready?"

I nod, feeling itchy. I can still feel eyes on the back of my neck.

"It's called 'Love Is A Fish'." She clears her throat:
Love is a fish and I am the fish
I'm twitching on my slimy white belly
I'm a flash of silver by your feet
I'm in the deep cold breathing in the dark
I'm breathing it out again
I love you and I'm dangling on the wire
Hook ripping through my cheek.

When she's finished, she looks over at me expectantly. I try to school my features into an expression of careful consideration.

"Hmm," I say. "It's interesting."

She visibly deflates. "It's trash, isn't it? I thought there was a good chance it was trash, but I wasn't sure."

"Is love really like that?" I ask. "It doesn't sound very nice."

"No," she says gloomily. "It doesn't, does it? I don't know, really. I'm just guessing. I've never been in love."

"Me neither." We watch each other across the room. I am very aware that we have run out of ways to procrastinate.

"How close are you to finishing your painting?" I ask.

She frowns, a small line appearing between her mismatched eyes. "It needs another coat. But I'm nearly there."

"Well, what if…" I swallow and realise that I'm nervous. "What if I come back to you later. To give you time to finish? You'd have to promise not to go anywhere."

Her face is very still and calm and for a moment I wonder if maybe she hasn't heard me, doesn't understand.

"Alright," she says at last. "I'll wait here for you. It shouldn't take too long."

"No," I agree and then look down at my plate, the yellow smears of oil and egg on my knife. It actually was a good omelette.

Walking out to the car, I realise I've left my tarot cards spread out on her kitchen table. I am torn for a moment, wondering whether to go back and get them, but in the end I don't. I'll be back soon anyway. Maybe the cards will remind her of me while I'm away. I'm humming as I climb inside and start up the engine. I think it's the song from the radio.

The file is lying out on the passenger seat and I frown at it. I was sure I had left it in the glovebox. Distracted, I don't remember to look for the yellow car until after I'm halfway out of the city.

The next Portrait lives high up on the southside of the valley and goes by the name of Prudence Anderson. This fact, so starkly typed, is deeply unsettling to me. Prudence is married to a man in real estate and her two children attend the local school. Prudence teaches drama at an afterschool club for teens, and sometimes does voiceover work for the local radio station. Prudence is a pet owner. Prudence is involved in regional politics. Prudence was once pulled over for reckless driving but talked her way out of a fine. Prudence has a prescription for anxiety medication which she rarely uses. Prudence is a member of the PTA and the gym and two different book groups.

On and on this information goes, pages and pages of her life. In deranged block capitals Lulabelle has scrawled: I

HATE THIS DUMB BITCH. TERMINATE WITH EXTREME
PREJUDICE.

The t in extreme has been scored through with such force
as to rip through not only the top page, but the one beneath it.

It's a beautiful day outside so I roll down the window a little
to feel the breeze. There's a sour taste in my mouth and I think
maybe I should buy a toothbrush. Or at least some deodorant.
I'm beginning to smell. The song from the radio is still going
round my head.

"Six, six, six," I whisper. I've already forgotten the rest of
the words.

As we climb up the side of the valley, the tall buildings give
way to houses with neat, chemical green lawns and orderly
driveways. The south side of the valley is less star-studded than
the north but there's just as much money on display. You can see
in the land itself, the way it's been sculpted into artificial flattened
tiers. The road is a long slow zig zag to the top; by the time the car
is turning onto the Portrait's street, my ears are popping.

The neighbourhood we arrive at is identical to the
neighbourhoods stacked below and above it; a featureless
suburbia of neat lines and semi circles. As I step out onto the
eerily clean pavement, another car pulls up on the other side
of the street. Like mine, it is sleek chrome. I watch as a black
man in a blue suit climbs out and lights up a cigarette.

We regard each other warily across the expanse. I know his
face from somewhere, but it takes me a moment to recall that
he co-starred alongside Lulabelle three movies ago. The Man
She Tried to Forget. It was a modest hit. He played the titular
Man I think, but beyond that I've forgotten everything about
him. He makes smoking look good but when I pull out my
own pack and try to mirror him, I cough at the first inhale. He
smiles and shakes his head.

I look away from him, embarrassed and drop the cigarette
half smoked. After stubbing it out with my sensible heel, I
walk over the buzzcut grass to the front porch of the house

which is grey and pillared and very boring. I think the style is neo-eclectic, which is to say it feels faintly fascist. It's just gone one-thirty.

According to the binder, the Portrait who calls herself Prudence should be home alone.

The doorbell is a discreet silver button. I press it and a chime rings out that reminds me of a dentist's office.

"Just a minute!" Lulabelle's voice calls from inside.

I look over my shoulder and see the man in the suit has finished his cigarette and is walking down the path to the house across the street. Absently, I press the button again.

I am still craning my head round to look at him when the door in front of me is wrenched open by a brunette woman in dungarees. She looks harassed and sweaty.

"What?" the Portrait snaps. "You can't wait five seconds?"

"I… um…" I trail off and in the end I forget what I was going to say. Her appearance has thrown me off completely. She stands there, hands on her hips, watching me coldly. I'm suddenly very aware of how I must look in my slept-in clothes and unbrushed hair. I'm pretty sure the fluid from the secretary's wound has dried into a sticky mess on my shoulder.

"Well?" she says at last. "Did you just come here to gawp?"

"Is that…" I begin and then try again. "Is that our old nose?"

She rolls her eyes and pulls me inside. When I am safely hidden away from the neighbours, she locks the door in two places.

"I guess you'd better come sit down," she says, without enthusiasm. "I'll get you some iced tea."

I follow her to an immaculate white and cream living room, dominated by a velour couch and flatscreen television. The two objects stare each other down across the room, both obscenely large and devoid of life.

"Sit," the Portrait tells me, pointing at the couch. I perch gingerly by a stiff ornamental pillow while she pulls down the shades.

"Are you hungry?" she snaps. It feels like an interrogation.

I shake my head meekly. She sniffs and stalks off to the kitchen, presumably to fetch the tea.

While she's gone, I look around the room. There isn't much to see. Four white walls and a rubbery houseplant in the corner. It's frigidly tasteful. It reminds me of Lulabelle's villa.

The Portrait comes back and thrusts a large glass clinking with ice into my hands. It's so cold it hurts to hold, but there's no place to put it so I sit where I am with it held awkwardly in my hands. She stands over me with her arms crossed. I notice she doesn't have a glass herself.

"I thought you had children?" I say.

"I do." She frowns. "Did Lulabelle tell you that? I knew she was checking up on me. That bitch."

"Where are their toys?"

"Upstairs. They have a playroom. That way only one room in the house gets messy."

I nod slowly. "Do they know you're a Portrait?"

"No," she says and then holds up her hands, fanning out her fingers.

I see the glint of a wedding ring but more than that, I see the lines. They spread in a delicate web over the skin of her palms. The lifelines cut very deeply – I wonder what the hitchhiker would read on them.

"Plastic surgery," she explains. "Very difficult work. Technically illegal. But Lulabelle – that fetid hag – she spared no expense. Unlike the rest of you, I'm not off the rack. I'm tailored. Did you know I'm the only one of us who can bleed?"

"That was in your file. How do they do that? Is it dye?"

"Probably. Tricky work these custom alterations," she says smugly. "My husband, my kids… To them I'm just a normal person. Prudence Craggs. Carter by marriage."

I have to hold on very tightly to the glass in my hands to keep myself calm. Her foot is tapping nervously on the ground.

Fidgeting. One of Lulabelle's bad habits. I try tapping my fingers on my leg but it doesn't come naturally.

"I don't know how you can use that name," I say softly. "I don't understand how you can bear to use it."

"Why wouldn't I?" she asks, letting out a quick brittle laugh. "It's who I am. It's who you are too. And Lulabelle, even if she doesn't like to think about it. She can't bleach away everything. Why are you so afraid of it?"

"I'm not afraid, I just don't understand. Don't you want to be Lulabelle?"

"I did once," she says and looks away from me, out through the shuttered windows. "But my husband knows me by my childhood name. You remember John, don't you?"

I don't and then I do. Of course, I do. How could I forget? He and Lulabelle grew up together in that boring little nowhere town. They used to ride bikes together, go wading in the streams and talk about... everything. They used to talk about everything, things I can't remember.

I can't remember how Lulabelle had felt about him, but I remember the way he looked when he smiled at her. I know how much she had watched him, for years and years and later, when they were much older, I remember the way she had kissed him. It had been in the same shady grove that had been their clubhouse as children. They had both been standing in the cold water and they had kissed for so long that Lulabelle's bare feet had gone completely numb.

When Lulabelle left to make it big in Bubble City, John wouldn't come out of his house to say goodbye. I remembered the way she had cried on the bus, all the way there.

"I remember John," I say softly. "So this is why Lulabelle made you."

"She was a coward," the Portrait who calls herself Prudence says. "She is a coward. And greedy. She wanted the career, but she couldn't bear to let him go. I was one of the first she ever made. She got me to take her place and then because she's a liar, she never told him I was a Portrait. She's made me a liar too. I had to tell him I was the real Lulabelle and the one making movies was the fake. And I'll never be able to tell him the truth. It would hurt him too much. But I could forgive all of that if only she wasn't so fucking jealous."

She closes her mouth with an audible snap and takes a long inhale through her nostrils. When she starts talking again it's in a low whisper.

"She can't bear to see me with him. I know she hires men to follow me. I know she's probably rigged this place with cameras. I know she sits and watches us and wishes she were me. And I know why you're here. You're here to decommission me. Because she can't stand it anymore. Because she never could. Because she's a cowardly, greedy, lying, jealous, murdering loser."

Throughout this tirade, her voice has been rising steadily until at last on the final word, it reaches a crescendo. I feel frozen, pinned down. I desperately want to put down the iced tea, which has been getting heavier and heavier, but I don't know where to put it.

The Portrait's gaze swivels and scans and finally homes in on my uncertainty with all the speed and accuracy of a missile targeting system.

"What?" she snaps. "You think I sound paranoid?"

She does, but she's also right, at least about why I'm here, so I shake my head.

"A little bit ungrateful maybe," I venture and when her eyes narrow, I rush to explain myself. "Don't you think you're lucky to have all of this? Don't you love Jo – your husband? Your kids?"

"I adore John," she tells me, tears welling to her eyes. "He's my guiding light. My partner in everything. He's my rock, my soulmate, my one and only. And I like the kids almost as much."

"I didn't know we were able to reproduce."

"They're adopted. Legally, of course, they're Lulabelle's. You knew that, didn't you, that we can't have children of our own?"

"Legally or biologically?"

"Either. Both. And when she dies they'll be motherless."

"And do they love you?"

"Of course they do. Why wouldn't they?" She sinks down next to me on the couch and puts her head in her hands. "Oh god. What will they do when I'm gone?"

"I'm sure they'll be alright," I say, still looking around for somewhere to put my glass. Very carefully I place it down on the carpet, leaning up against a leg of the couch. "Do you have insurance?"

"That's not what I mean," she says wetly, muffled into her hands. "I mean, what if they forget me? What if they stop loving me? What if they move on and never think about me anymore?"

"Don't you want that?" I say and she begins to sob noisily.

I pat her on the back. "Well, they might do those things anyway, even if you don't die. When they grow up and move out or if John gets bored..."

"Of what?" she snaps. "I'll never get old or saggy or grey haired. I could be perfect forever."

"Well, then it had to end at some point anyway," I point out. "He would have worked it out eventually. And then what? He would hate you."

She glares at me through the tears.

"You're not her," I remind her, trying to be as gentle as possible.

"I've spent more time with him than she has. I know him better."

"That won't make a difference. What was your plan anyway? Were you going to start tattooing wrinkles on your face?"

She looks like she's about to start crying again and I reach out and take her hand.

"Listen to me," I tell her. "If it's all going to end anyway, why not control the narrative?"

She looks down at where our hands are linked. In a small voice she says, "I don't mind dying. But..."

"What is it?"

"I can't bear the idea of them going on without me."

An idea occurs to me. "What if... What if we gave you an exit they would never be able to forget? An exit they could never hope to understand."

"What do you mean?"

"I mean a murder most foul. Unsolved!" I'm warming to my theme now. "Unsolvable!"

"You think?" she asks me hopefully, looking over with a damp, mascara-streaked face. "They won't move on?"

"How could they?" I say kindly, patting her back with more confidence now. "You'll be a saint to them – an icon! Untouchable. They'll think about you forever. They'll never escape you. You won't even be human to them. They'll never have to see you make mistakes or be stupid or cruel or embarrassing."

"If my death was a mystery..." The Portrait has begun to perk up, her eyes widening. "If no one knew why it happened – maybe I could leave some clues scattered around my body..."

"They'll be obsessed!" I say. "They'll lie awake at night trying to find your killer. But they never will. You'll haunt them."

"I think I have some things upstairs," she says and jumps up. "Come and help me choose what to wear!"

I sit on the bed in their tastefully decorated oat coloured bedroom while she tries on outfit after outfit. We consider funereal black, her meringue of a wedding gown, a slinky cocktail dress and briefly, nothing at all. As she gets more excited she flings clothes onto the bed. Some of them fall over my lap, sparking a hazy memory of past dressing rooms. In the end she settles on a beautiful peach-pink summer dress on the basis that it will set off the blood beautifully. I think of what the Artist said about costumes and I make a note to tell her about this when I see her again.

After that she rushes around the house, rifling through her clothes, and opening all the drawers to find suitably cryptic items to lay around the corpse. She suggests tearing out a page from the newspaper and clutching it in her hand. I suggest she underlines significant passages in the Bible, but she hasn't got one. We consider the flowers in her back garden but when we look them up, none of them have particularly interesting meanings. I suggest she writes a code on the back of her hand instead, a random string of letters and numbers.

Under the pretence of helping, I take the opportunity to snoop. I find a picture of their wedding day and spend too long looking at John's face. It's strange how much he hasn't changed. He looks exactly the way Lulabelle remembers him. The two of them look perfect together. Like a set of matched dolls.

Going through their shared wardrobe, I wait until Prudence isn't looking before pressing one of his shirts to my face. It smells faintly of laundry detergent. I don't know what I was expecting. I can't remember how he used to smell.

I'm trying to find a crucifix from an old Halloween costume for her when I find the closet on the landing halfway up the stairs. I pull the cord of the single exposed light bulb and it takes my eyes a moment to adjust before I realise I'm looking at a shrine.

I know immediately I have found something I shouldn't. I freeze in place, listening. When I hear her humming coming from the bathroom on the landing above me I know I only have a moment.

The light swings above my head; the shadows twist and contort. From every poster, every DVD case, every signed photo and ghost-written memoir, Lulabelle looks back at me. A line of little dolls on the back wall stand to attention with stiff plastic arms and dandelion puffs of blonde hair. They're all there, assembled in chronological order: the one-eyed astronaut, the troll hunter, the robot gardener. I see merchandise for films stretching back years, magazine covers I had forgotten existed. None of the eyes seem poked out and there are no threats scrawled over the walls, but I still feel intensely uneasy. I turn off the light and close the door very carefully. It's not so much disturbing as highly embarrassing for everyone involved.

I find Prudence downstairs, arranging herself in an artful pose on the couch cushions. One hand trails to the floor, loosely clutching a single card, the queen of hearts. Her eyes are closed, and her makeup is freshly applied. She looks beautiful. An image to carry for a lifetime.

She cracks one eye open when I come near.

"Dothg soogmy in the fae," she says.

"What?" I say. "Take the pearls out of your mouth."

She spits them neatly into her palm and looks up at me. "I said don't shoot me in the face. Aim for my heart. And try not to get any red fluid on the couch – we just had it re-upholstered."

"Okay." I take out my gun and hesitate. "Can I ask you something?"

"What is it?"

"Is there a famous actor living across the street? I think I saw him on the way in."

"Oh, Bert," she says and then frowns. "I don't think he's an actor. At the last barbecue we had, he was telling John about working in risk assessment. But he might be in hiding. A lot of people in the suburbs are."

"Really?"

"Oh, yeah. Mobsters in witness protection, detoxing celebrities, disgraced politicians. Our next-door neighbour is a war criminal. I googled him at the PTA bake sale."

"What about you and John? Why are you here?" I ask. "I thought he would never leave the countryside. Didn't he say that once?"

I frown, trying to remember. Cold feet, the shadows on the stream, John's chin moving soundlessly around the words as he holds Lulabelle's hands. I will never leave the countryside.

The Portrait shrugs. "He did say that. Once. But all the jobs are here. You go where the money is. Are you ready?"

I nod and reluctantly steady the gun.

"You know," the Portrait says softly. "I'm glad she sent you."

"Really?"

"Better the devil you know."

This phrase sounds familiar. It takes me a moment to remember it was the name of one of Lulabelle's first movies. She played an angel.

I lick my lips nervously and think about where best to shoot. In the heart perhaps, as she suggested– that's symbolic but will it kill her quickly, or will there be a lot of thrashing and splattering? She's the only one of us who bleeds. I wonder if this is why Lulabelle hates her.

I realise suddenly that I don't want to do this. Not because I'm fond of her – I don't like this Portrait much. She scares me in her intensity, with her brown hair and old nose. Perhaps she scares the real Lulabelle too.

I don't like her, but I don't want her to die either. But what's the alternative?

"Oh wait," the Portrait says, sitting up and spitting out the pearls. "Is that a car in the driveway?"

I lower the gun and look to the window, and that's when she lunges at me, pulling out a kitchen knife from underneath the throw pillow. The snarl on her face is rabid. I stagger back and let off three shots without thinking.

She's dead by the time she hits the ground. I stand over her, breathing heavily before I try and arrange her body in the agreed position. I wonder if she meant all along to kill me or if she hadn't made up her mind till the last second. I wonder if the iced tea was poisoned. It's spilt now, all over the white carpet, a spreading sticky brown stain dotted with little chunks of ice. It's such a shame. It's not the only casualty. The sofa is stained now too.

I'm glad there aren't any family photographs up on the walls watching me. With extreme prejudice, Lulabelle had requested. I wonder if the mess I've made of the upholstery will satisfy her.

"Sorry. And sorry about the furnishings," I tell Prudence. "But your face is fine."

I try and haul her up into a dignified position but even if it's not real, her blood feels horribly warm. I wonder if normal people have so much of it.

There will come a time when your hands will get dirty. Spencer was right.

I am shaking by the time I leave the house. While I was in the house, the clouds must have been gathering because the sun is hidden and the temperature has dropped. I feel like throwing up and the sensation strikes me as incredibly unfair. If this is what I was made for then it should be easy for me. Like breathing.

The dashboard is lit up as I climb into the car, and a tinny version of Für Elise is playing through the speakers. I set a new course and after a moment's hesitation, accept the call.

It's Lulabelle at the end of the line, her voice a flat nothing. "Is it over?"

"Yes."

"Mitosis are on their way. I would leave now. They're not very happy about you and my legal team charges me for every phone call they get about it."

"Why are they unhappy? I thought you said that this was a loophole. That you were allowed to do this," I say, starting the car and peeling out.

"Mmm well there's a preferred process," Lulabelle says and then, switching tracks. "So, what did you think of her?"

"She was a nailbiter. And a fidgeter."

"Hmmph."

"She said she was one of the first Portraits you ever made."

Lulabelle snorts. "That's one way of saying it. She was the second. She's always getting ahead of herself."

"Who was the first?"

There's a pause and then Lulabelle hums, disinterested. I can almost hear the shrug over the line. "I don't remember. Maybe that one who does the paintings. I get you all mixed up. You talk to Spencer? Did he try and sell you on that horrible living museum thing?"

"He mentioned it."

"You know I would never let that happen, don't you?" she says in a rush. There's an edge of something almost desperate in her voice. "I wouldn't do that to you. To any of you."

I don't really know what to say to this. After a moment Lulabelle clears her throat. When she speaks, her voice is clipped.

"Anyway. You're not doing too badly so far. Keep it up." With that she hangs up.

It never rains in Bubble City but a thin yellowish fog has rolled out over the city below. As the car descends it gets soupier. I can still see the red lights of the car ahead of me in the distance. I follow the glow of them for a while but when we reach the floor of the valley, he turns right and I go left.

CHAPTER SEVEN
The Chariot

A warrior rides out from the city in a chariot of stars. The black sphinx and the white sphinx that pull it wear no bridles or reins. The charioteer must drive them forward through force of will alone.

My next destination is the lobby of the Apollo Hotel, but first I need to make a detour.

The fog has thinned by the time my car parks itself outside the gates of Martyr's Park but, when I step out, the air wraps itself around me, damp and grey. As I pop the boot of the car, I regret that I never asked for anything thicker than a suit jacket at Wellsprings.

The Secretary is where I left her, curled up with her curls falling over her face. In the time that she's been in here, her hair and eyes have become almost completely colourless. She looks like an unpainted doll.

"Sorry that took so long," I say. "But I think you'll like it here. I heard it has ducks."

It takes some manoeuvring but I manage to lift her onto my back, piggyback style, with her head lolling over my left shoulder. She's not heavy, just stiff and unwieldy and cold. We set off through the gates and up a gravel path lined with rose bushes; a passing dog walker gives us a strange look.

110

"Too much to drink," I say, rolling my eyes affectionately. "Bottomless brunch."

He looks like he wants to say something, but then his Shih Tzu tries to pick a fight with a fast-food wrapper, and in the resulting chaos the Secretary and I slip away. I lean forward so that my hair covers my face. I don't want to be recognised. The thought of ending up like the Portrait at the bus, starving and filthy with autographs shoved into my face, is never far from my mind.

The mist is thick enough to make my hair feel damp in minutes. Only the hardiest of Bubble City residents remain. The park can be beautiful, I know – and if I didn't then there would be a thousand films to remind me. Lulabelle's starred in a handful of them. When the sun is shining the park sits on top of Rocher du Saint like a green velvet hat. At the peak of the hill you can stand in the cool shade of the martyr's statue and see the whole city laid out for you, buffet style.

Today though, there's not much to see but grey. The trees that fringe the park loom overhead, rivalling the skyscrapers in the distance. I feel eyes on the back of my neck and imagine packs of feral squirrels staring down at us from the branches, sharpening their claws. A few runners pass us, jaws clenched, straining in Spandex. A lone busker is too busy packing away his trumpet and counting the money in his hat to pay us any notice. By the time we climb up to the ornamental lake at the foot of the martyr, the fog has thickened to the point where the hill feels more like an island floating in a smoky sea. I watch the mist snake around a family of four as they picnic on the wet lawn, and almost lose my footing. The Secretary's cool cheek rests against mine and I shudder, trying to jostle her back into position.

We pass a shuttered ice cream stand, and then a tiny boathouse by the water where a man sits in a lawn chair. His nose protrudes from a thick scarf and woollen hat pulled low on his brow.

"Rent a rowboat?" He calls out and I shake my head.

"She gets seasick."

"Suit yourself," he says mournfully.

I'm panting for breath by the time we reach the water's edge. I set the Secretary down on a suitably remote bench. Her head lolls back like a drunk, a sleeping vagrant. When I'm done arranging her limbs, I take a moment to sink down next to her. The bullet hole wound is exposed on her white blouse and so I try to hide it with her cardigan. If she bled then it would look like a carnation or a rose in her buttonhole. As it is, it's just a breaking point.

"This isn't bad, is it?" I say, looking over my shoulder at the lake. I can't see any ducks yet. Someone has taken up the boat owner on his offer and as I watch they carve a slow and stubborn arc across the water.

Behind him on a raised platform is the vast bulk of the statue, her face lost in the mist. An information board informs me that the thin trickling spring that feeds into the lake is the only natural source of water in the city.

"Shame about the weather," I tell the Secretary. "But I guess you won't feel the cold."

There's a rustle from the weeds by my feet and I see the flash of a beak. I look over at the Secretary and smile. Then I feel stupid.

"It's stupid really," I say, watching as the duck climbs out onto the pathway, shaking out its wings. "But I can't help feeling that you shouldn't be dead."

The Secretary doesn't have anything to say to that.

"Or even that we had talked a little bit more before I... Well, before it happened. You knew a lot more than me, I think."

I don't really know how to explain it to her. It's not jealousy, even though I would like to understand things, like industry secrets and fingernail chips and whatever it is that Spencer is really planning. Perhaps it's more that it feels unfair. Unfair that she spent all that time learning to understand things just for me to come along and make it all useless.

But that's how it had to go I guess. Like Lulabelle said – no point crying over spilled milk. I wasn't capable of crying if I wanted to. I wasn't made that way.

The rowboat has drifted closer to the shore. The rower seems to be having some trouble with a swan. I watch the struggle for a while. When the boat turns, I stand up and walk a little closer to the edge, trying to peer through the mist.

"Hey," I call out, cupping my hands around my mouth. "Hey, don't I know you?"

It takes a while for the boat to make it to the shore, mostly because the swan seems reluctant to give up the chase. The captain's face is made all the more frantic by the heavy dark eyeliner. He seems to have lost his black leather jacket somewhere in the struggle. Underneath it his arms look very skinny in ripped black mesh and a rather faded black band shirt. I wonder if he misses the heat. He doesn't seem to have been provided with any kind of robe or pointed hat, which is a shame because they would have kept his head dry.

"Can you help me," he calls over when he's close. "There's a rope."

"Toss it over," I say, and then in an undertone to the Secretary: "Don't worry. This will just take a moment. We go way back – I gave him a lift too."

He throws the rope limply towards shore and I start forwards to catch it. His black nail varnish has chipped down to the cuticle. But then again, so has mine by now.

"Rough day?" I ask as I pull the boat to shore. He clambers out ungracefully, tripping over his own long legs.

"I was sent out here to practise augury," the hitchhiker says, looking faintly green. "Which I'm usually really good at! But the birds in this place must have something wrong with them. They're so mean."

"Augury?" I ask him.

"Fortune telling. You can tell a lot by watching birds," he says, sitting down on the bench and running a hand through his dyed hair. "The sounds they make, the flight patterns the..." He frowns, seeming to have just noticed the Secretary. "Is she ok?"

"She's dead," I say. "What kind of birds did you have back home?"

"Uh... Crows and owls and... Did you – did you kill her?" He is blinking very rapidly.

"Yes, but it's alright," I say, going over to the Secretary and gently holding up one of her palms so he can see. "She's like me."

"Oh. Okay," he says, but scoots a little way down the bench from her. "Is this the work you had to do?"

"Part of it," I say, before dropping to a whisper. "But keep that to yourself, okay? Or I'll have to kill you too."

"Um..."

I smile. "Just kidding. That would be illegal."

His shoulders relax but he gives me a strange look. "You seem different from last time we met."

I shrug. "A lot can happen in a day."

"Yeah," he says, watching his boat knock gently against the shoreline. "This city is strange, isn't it?"

"Is your teacher nice?"

"He's incredible. He has so many books and he's even more talented than I thought, and he says I have a lot of potential. He..." the hitchhiker deflates and begins to fiddle with his rings. "Well, he talks about his divorce a lot."

I reach over and pat him on the shoulder before I realise I haven't washed my hands yet. The hitchhiker sees Prudence's 'blood' at the same time I do. He does a bad job of hiding his grimace.

"Sorry," I say. "Well, it was nice seeing you again. But I'm on a tight schedule."

"Wait," he says, looking startled. "Are you just going to leave her here?"

I look at the Secretary. She said that she wanted somewhere nice.

"Do you think she would have liked it here?" I ask the hitchhiker.

"I don't know her," he says and then pauses, considering. "Would you like it?"

I think about it and then look around at the mist and the water and the trees.

"It's a bit much isn't it?" I say, nodding at the statue. "Why did they make it so big?"

"Maybe they felt guilty."

I raise an eyebrow and the hitchhiker looks surprised. "Don't you know the story? They were lost in the desert–"

"Who?"

"I don't know – people. The first ones to settle here. I think maybe they were running from something or maybe they just wanted to start a new place to live. But anyway, they were dying out there in the desert and this woman lead them here. She told them there would be water and when there wasn't they killed her. Her blood turned into the spring. That's why she's the patron saint of travellers."

"Well it seems like she wasn't leading them to water. Maybe they were right to kill her. Maybe they should have found a better place for a city."

The hitchhiker shrugs. "Well she's also the patron saint of fools. And stitches."

"Stitches?"

"Well when she appears – and that's only happened a few times according to my master, she's... Well, sewn up. They cut her into pieces you see after the miracle. They thought that she would turn the whole valley green."

"Did she?"

"Doesn't look like it, does it?"

I consider this for a moment and look down at the secretary. "Patron saint of fools?"

"That's right."

"Maybe she'll look after us then," I say and then narrow my

eyes, considering. "I think if it was me... I'd like to be in the boat."

We hoist her weight between us. The water rushes over my feet and it makes me think of John. Is he home yet? Are the children with him? Why am I thinking about these things?

The hitchhiker is reluctant to touch her so I'm the one who crosses the Secretary's hands over her chest. When I think she's ready, I crouch down with one hand steadying the boat and look critically at her. Lying there nestled in the boat she looks like a marble statue. The rain is falling in her clear and sightless eyes. I try to close them but the eyelids are stiff now, uncooperative. In her suit she could be a still from a black and white movie, the only patch of colour the little blue feathers on her fish lure earrings.

"It's a shame we don't have flowers for her hair."

"Very Shakespearean," the hitchhiker mutters behind me. He's watching the walkway for people. It's sweet, really. Country bumpkin. He doesn't know that it would only take a moment to explain and then no one would care. At worst they might try and get an autograph, or take some kind of trophy. Even reflected celebrity has value.

They probably wouldn't be interested in the Secretary. Lulabelle Rock is a blonde bombshell or nothing at all.

"She only did Shakespeare twice," I tell him, still studying the Secretary's face. "Bianca and Perdita. But she wasn't very good. She kept forgetting her lines." I glance at him. "That's a secret by the way. I might actually go through with killing you if you tell anyone that."

He mimes zipping his mouth shut.

"Never Ophelia," I say with regret, and then I kick her away from the shore. The boat glides smoothly over the surface of the water, parting the mist. The duck follows in its wake, like a funeral procession, then loses interest.

The hitchhiker sighs. "I'm not going to get my deposit back for that."

To cheer him up, I buy us both a coffee from the ice cream stand. The hitchhiker takes his with cream and talks the woman behind the counter into giving him extra sugar packets. I give him mine too. The coffee, black, burns pleasantly and for some reason it makes me think of the Artist.

"Can I get an ice cream too?" he asks and with an effort I stop myself from telling him about her.

"Sure."

At the last moment I get myself a pastry. It comes in a warm paper brown bag.

"I meant to tell you," he says when we part ways at the gate. "We're going to see your movie tomorrow."

I look at him blankly for a moment before I remember. "Oh. Medea? Is that out already?"

I feel a spike of panic. Everyone on my list was meant to be dead by the premier.

"My master has tickets to a preview. He got them from some producer he did a job for."

"A job?"

The hitchhiker looks uneasy, licking sombrely at his ice cream. "He did some kind of ritual for them at a... well, at a party."

"What kind of party?"

He shrugs and I give him a sidelong glance. "Is that what you're going to do?"

He takes a mournful sip from his coffee and we watch a squirrel scale the gate, nose twitching. "Maybe."

"Don't watch the movie," I tell him. "You won't like it."

"He's a big fan of yours," he says and then he looks at me accusingly. "I didn't realise you were so famous when we met."

I chew my pastry for a moment and think about saying, I'm not, I never was.

It's good, buttery and sweet, but I don't know if it tastes the same as the one Lulabelle had all those years ago.

"Do you have a pen?" I ask instead and then when he pulls

one out of his many pockets, I scribble Lulabelle's signature on the back of the empty paper bag.

He thanks me, folding and placing it very carefully in his breast pocket. I get a strange feeling in my stomach watching him. It's strange to write your own name and have it feel like forgery.

There are a thousand fake signatures floating around Bubble City. Even if the handwriting is replicated perfectly down to the last dot on the i, they're all worthless if they aren't the real thing.

"Well, I'll see you around I guess," he says and then hesitates, leaning in closer to hiss. "You need to be careful. I think someone is following you."

"What? Did you see them?"

"No but I felt them. Back in the park. Someone has very ill intentions."

I flick a glance over to the park gates. Beyond them the greenery is full of shadows. For a moment I think I see a flash of platinum hair through the leaves.

"Okay," I say, forcing my eyes back to the hitchhiker. "I'll be careful."

He smiles and pats me on the shoulder awkwardly. When he's halfway down the street he turns back and gives me a wave. I wave back.

When I turn on the car the radio plays automatically. I sit there for a moment, drinking my coffee and listening to the soft layers of string. When I'm finished, I crumple up my pastry bag and shove it into the empty cup. After stowing it under the seat, I pull out the file.

The binder on my next target is very thick – this Portrait seems to lead a busy life. The appointments listed for this week alone take up five pages. I skim through a few passages en route.

13:00 Lunch with BP at the Astoria. Laugh at jokes.

13:45 Stroll in Hopfgarten with MEW. Argue loudly.

14:00 Meet ZQ for bubble tea. Put your hand on shoulder and giggle.

It continues in the same vein, pages and pages of itemised hours. Lunches and coffees and shopping sprees and malls and funfairs. Occasionally the same initials crop up more than once, but for the most part it seems to be an endless list of social calls with a revolving door of socialites. For most of them there is a line or two of instruction. Throw drink, link arm, smile (no teeth). Glare, make a scene, flirt with waiter. Sometimes these instructions are not so specific.

The word improvise crops up occasionally, usually with a mood attached. Improvise friendly, I read. Improvise aggressive. Improvise flirtatious.

The reason for the itinerary becomes clear on the final page, where, in a relatively restrained hand, Lulabelle has written: gossip, scandal, intrigue, etc. Spencer and the other agents worked it all out. It's a network. V complicated. I sense in this brief fragment a shrug. I wonder if Lulabelle knows who all the initials belong to. I doubt that she cares.

I'm on the road when the music stops and two voices start discussing the news of the day. There's a war going on somewhere and prices are rising and the electric storms are coming more frequently, but I'm not really paying attention until I hear them say Lulabelle's name.

I fumble for the controls and turn it up just in time to hear, "...and that's how many now? Three?"

"That we know of, Jim. A spokesperson speaking on behalf of Ms Rock has made it clear that this is very much an ongoing situation. "

"And they've denied any involvement?"

"Looks like it. Sounds like someone out there has a vendetta."

"Now I heard some people online are speculating whoever it is that's doing this isn't actually targeting Portraits."

"You think they're after the real deal?"

"I don't think it's crazy to think this is a process of elimination."

"With her new film Medea premiering this weekend I guess

this means we'll be seeing a lot more security on the red carpet. Now, Jim, am I right that there is a theme to the dress code?"

"You're right on the money, Jolene – in true horror style the guests will be working with makeup artists to recreate some classic cinematic kills."

"I hear Kiki Lamont will be going headless in an homage to the classic 1967 film Antoinette–"

I switch it off.

By the time I reach the Apollo Hotel the Portrait is already stepping out of the lobby into the street. She hangs prettily on the arm of a tall man I recognise as a well-established comedian who is allegedly trying to start his own cult. She's wearing jeans and a t-shirt, and she looks casually, implausibly beautiful. The sun chooses this moment to emerge from behind the clouds and she's golden when she stands on her tiptoes to kiss his cheek. All I can do is watch from traffic as she climbs into an idling car and waves goodbye.

Her car pulls away. He waves, but she doesn't see. As my own car crawls past him in pursuit, I crane my head to see the palms of his hands, but I'm too slow. So, this is RK, I think. I wonder if all the initials are celebrities (or at least, the Portraits of celebrities) pawned by their publicists into the endlessly churning machine of the gossip industry.

The Portrait's car weaves in and out of view, but I know her destination (17:00 High tea at the Willow Rooms with AG. Start a fight) and for a few streets our cars move on a synchronised route. I am on a slight delay – she turns left, a moment later I follow. We wait at the same lights, we gather speed together, we slow at the same time. It's like a dance, where she leads and I follow, but also it's not really like that at all because neither of us is in control of what's happening. The cars are the ones in control, the ones in conversation, chirping silently at each other across the distance. Not every car in Bubble City is automated, but the ones who are like to talk.

I'm only three cars behind but I can't see her through the

tinted glass. If it weren't for the licence plate, I wouldn't be able to distinguish her vehicle from the rush hour traffic. It looks like all the other cars around us. It looks like mine.

They are all different brands, of course, and there is some slight variation in colour but they all give off an impression of uniformity. The way the light glances off all the metallic tones puts me in mind of a school of silver fish. It lulls me into a daze and maybe because of that, I almost miss the moment that the Portrait deviates from the established route.

By the time I notice that she has taken the wrong turn it's too late. She has disappeared down a side street while I am still driving resolutely forward. I press my face to the window just in time to watch her slide away.

I curse out loud and try to hit the emergency brake, but the car refuses to comply. I wrestle with it for a moment, trying to reset or at least slow its course. It wants a new destination, but I don't have one.

Turning at a junction, I see her car again, picking up speed two lanes to my left and five cars ahead. In desperation I tap a point on the map just up ahead and slide the speed control up to fast. Begrudgingly, the car obeys me, and we begin to swerve in and out of traffic, overtaking in slow painstaking inches.

For a while, the Portrait's car and mine seem to be on a parallel course. We are still heading in the vague direction of the Willow Rooms. I begin to wonder if maybe I was being too hasty, if perhaps this was just an alternate route.

Then, just as I am beginning to relax, the Portrait's car takes another unexpected turn.

"Fuck." I stab at the glowing map and the process begins all over again.

For the next hour, we tussle like this. It's an infuriatingly slow race: we obey every traffic law, show careful consideration to other drivers, and keep to sensible speed limits. The Portrait enjoys an easy ride. She could have set her destination to any address in the city. All she has to do is sit back and enjoy the ride.

As for me, in order to not lose her, I am constantly setting and re-setting my target. My navigation has been reduced to crude brute measures: north, south, east, west. Every inch of control I have has to be wrestled away from the car with tooth and nail. I hunch over the screen, sweating and frantic, eyes flicking between the map and the distant license plate up ahead. My fingers are curled into claws, ready at any moment to stab out some minor adjustment. There is no way to anticipate her movements. I can't plan or consider, only react.

I am quickly exhausted but I can't stop or even rest – she has deviated from the itinerary. Somehow I know instinctively that if I lose her, I'll never find her again.

At one point we are almost side by side on the road, gunning it down the wide avenues of Bubble City's antique district. We stop at a red light and I take a moment to brush the hair away from my damp forehead. Glancing at her car, I realise that she is watching me. The tinted window is rolled down and she appears in full technicolour, one elbow perched on the sill. Her electric blue nails click soundlessly against her car's chrome window trim, identical to mine.

She cannot see me, I remind myself, the glass that separates us is too dark. She can probably only see her own reflection.

Even as I think this, I watch her grin and lift two fingers to her forehead in a lazy salute. The light is still amber as she switches into drive and shifts forward minutely.

I sit there, frozen with rage, unable to look away. My face feels cold and stiff. I am so angry that for a moment I want to throw the car door open and pull her out onto the street. It's not just that she's laughing at me. It's not even that she knows that I've been tailing her, or even that she has evaded me so effortlessly, with such due diligence to the rules of the road. She hasn't even broken a sweat.

I'm angry because she's in control. I'm angry because that's not fair.

The light turns green and the Portrait's car eases away.

"Fuck, fuck." I mash the manual button, slamming my foot on the pedal when it pops out. An alarm goes off within the car, loud enough that pedestrians on the street look over in alarm.

"Shut up," I snarl. "Shut up, shut up, shut up."

I jerk my head up to see a single hand jutting from the Portrait's rolled down window. She's waving goodbye. I sob in frustration, stomping down hard on the pedal. The car beeps again, high pitched and whiney.

"Fuck you," I say and then my hand is forming a fist. As if from far away I see it drive down hard on the control screen. The first blow does nothing, but the pain lances up my arm. I ignore it and strike again. And again. On the third blow, the screen gives way, along with what feels like a small bone just above one of my knuckles.

The display cracks into a spiderweb. For a moment, the bright infographics fracture and then, with a faint pop, the whole screen goes black. My hand pulls away and my foot comes down on the accelerator like a counterweight. The car jerks forward in a sudden violent burst. The steering wheel clicks up into place and when I turn it, the wheels skid.

A warning alarm is going off from some panel and I laugh along with it, forcing the car ahead. I overtake the car ahead with ease, grinning as it shrinks in the rear-view. My hand throbs dully but in my joy I barely feel it.

The Portrait has a head start on me, but now we are on an even footing. Now I can be fast. I weave in and out of traffic, gaining speed all the time. I remember this Lulabelle's hair whipping in the wind as she wound her way along a golden coastline. Did she feel this too? This wild kind of joy; something almost slippery in my chest. The road comes alive to me as a series of obstacles, gaps, and potential pathways. I blare through a red light: their laws have no power over me anymore.

I swerve and I bully and I tailgate. I cut off a boxy driverless delivery truck at a junction and thrill to hear the automatic horn blaring after me.

When I finally reach the Portrait, I follow a mad impulse and overtake her. In the rear-view mirror I see her chasing me. The strict adherence to the rules is gone suddenly, as if somehow I've given her permission to forget them. We take it in turns, we dance around each other and all the time, we're going faster, faster, faster. My hand is stiffening up and when I use it to roll down the window it tingles oddly. The wind that comes through blows my hair this way and that, tangling in my vision until I can barely see the road.

The sky is orange and pink and as the Portrait and I race, so do our shadows.

In a darkened valley between two long rows of skyscrapers, we drive side by side. I look over at her and she's smiling at me. I smile back. All my anger has evaporated. Of all of us, she was the one to work it out. Why tie yourself in existential knots or stage tiny acts of useless rebellion? Fuck polka dots and mustard and old names. All this time, I just had to do what was most natural. Just do what feels good. Just drive a little faster.

"Thank you!" I shout.

"What?" she yells back, or at least I think that's what she says. Her mouth is open, but her voice is lost to the roar of the wind.

"Thank you!" I scream again. Her face screws up and her car veers dangerously close to mine.

Her mouth opens again. She is saying something to me. Something important. I am watching her face so intently, I see the exact moment where she loses control.

What happens next, I hear more than feel.

The sound of it is unbearable, giant steel fingernails dragging on the chalkboard highway. Our car fenders stop flirting and collide with a terrifying passion. I see my shock reflected in her face and then she is spinning away from me. The world flips like a pancake. Once, twice, three times. On the first roll, I smack my head hard against the steering wheel and then I am cushioned from the worst of it by a thick grey cloud. I am aware of the roof crunching in towards me but even as it presses in close, my vision tunnels away from it.

A black wave rushes up to meet me and before I can even suck in a breath, I am submerged.

Darkness.

For a too-brief moment I am swaddled in rough fur. Mink pelts, a sable coat, a lynx shawl. The closet door cracks open and a sliver of light falls over me. Go away, I tell the shadow in the doorway, I'm trying to sleep, let the party go on without me, but they just watch me silently and they watch and they watch–

When I come to, I feel a warm trickle make its way from the corner of my lip and roll downwards around my nose, up into the curve of my eye. I blink and see it splash onto the crumpled roof of the car. Clear and colourless. I blink again and realise I am hanging upside down. I think we have stopped moving but my body is telling me that I am still in motion. My swollen hand gropes blindly for my seatbelt.

A crowd has formed by the time I crawl from the wreckage.

It's hard to move because I'm clutching the grey ring binder so tightly. Hands descend on me, but I brush them away. I look up and the faces cluster over me, mouths moving but I cannot hear them. They grab at me again and this time I cannot shake them off. They pull me to my feet, away from the sting of broken glass and rubble. When I look over my shoulder I can see the way our cars have wrapped around each other in death. It's hard to tell what was mine and what was hers. A wing mirror is lying in the gutter by my feet, oddly intact.

The abrupt end to our journey has left us at the edge of one of Bubble City's invisible border lines. We had reached the end of the trendy neighbourhoods and little boutiques. If we had driven just a little further we would be under the canopy of the raised highways with their graffitied concrete pillars. For a moment I wonder if somehow we came up against a forcefield of some kind, an invisible wall. But no.

Just recklessness. Just another collision. She might have been the one to cause the crash but her death was inevitable the moment she saw me.

I'm really racking them up now. I didn't even mean to make it happen this time.

"Oh," I hear myself say. "Oh."

My ears are ringing so badly it's like my voice belongs to someone else. A Portrait of a Portrait. A copy of a copy. I pull away from the hands, take two steps toward the wreck and then I can't go any further. My legs are shaking and so I sit cross legged on the rough tarmac. The hands try to pull me up again, but I don't let them. I put the binder in my lap and curl over it.

I look at our cars – my car. It doesn't look like a thing that was ever functional.

"I'm sorry," I say, so softly I could be speaking to myself. "I'm sorry I shouted at you. I'm sorry I hurt you."

Another hand falls on my shoulder. I try to shrug it off, but it remains. Someone is crouching beside me. They smell of cigarettes and convenience store pastries.

"Hey," they say. "Get up now."

I look over and make out a blurry dark triangle of hair and a drooping moustache.

"Velazquez?" I mumble. "What are you doing here?"

"Chasing ambulances," he says and then, brusquely. "You alright? You're a mess."

I let him help me up, gripping onto the arm of his jumper. He allows it patiently and, when I've stopped swaying, he gently shakes me off so he can take pictures. We aren't alone in watching the crash site. A crowd has gathered around us. Out of the corner of my eye I see someone is pointing a phone at me.

"The other driver?" I ask.

He shakes his head.

"She's dead?" I don't feel any relief.

He nods. "You want to see a picture?"

"No," I say. "No, thank you."

There's a burst of sparks from the tangled-up wrecks and then a small fire bursts into being. The crowd murmurs appreciatively. Velazquez raises the camera again.

"You should be careful," he says, cigarette hanging in the corner of his mouth. "I hear you're turning up dead all over the city."

I keep my mouth shut and watch the car burn.

The sun is all but gone now and the flames are very bright in the twilight. The sparks rise up through the smoke. When I see the Mitosis van pull up I know I can't stay here. I clutch the binder tighter and lose myself in the crowd. Velazquez doesn't say goodbye.

"Hey," someone says as I push past them. "Aren't you that actress?"

I shake my head, mumble something and keep walking.

I walk for a long time. The further I get from the crash, the more people stare at me so I leave the main streets behind, disappearing into the darker shadows beneath the overpasses. When night falls in earnest and the streetlights turn on, I skirt around their edges, keeping close to the wall. When I pass a shop window Lulabelle looks back at me, haunted, a fresh cut oozing clear fluid onto her chin. My left hand is twisted strangely where it grips the binder. Her hair is a tangled sooty mess. She could almost be a brunette. That could almost be my old nose. I miss it.

I remind myself of someone. Maybe the Portrait at the bus stop, with her poor dirty feet. I remember wondering if we could feel pain. I know the answer now, but why? Why make us feel anything at all?

"What have they done to you?" I whisper, and then

immediately feel very stupid. It's not that the words are wrong, only that it's wrong that I should be the one saying them. I want very badly for someone else to ask me that. I want someone to touch my chin and tsk and say, oh no. You poor thing. Let's get that seen to.

If I were human they would sew me up and give me a cast. Maybe Mitosis could fix me if Lulabelle told them to. But why would she bother? I don't need to be pretty to get the job done. I'm so close to the end now.

When my feet hurt too much to walk, I sit in a sticky late-night café and drink gritty black coffee while I study the binder. The only thing to do is keep going. When the waitress comes over, I give her the last of the Viking's ice cream money and leave. The next Portrait on my list lives only three blocks away.

I'm not used to finding my way with street signs. It makes me slow, stupid. The damage done to my body wasn't terrible, but it slows me down. The neighbourhood I'm walking through looks as though it might have been nice once upon a time. The ghost of hopeful urban planning lingers in the little balconies and shared gardens. At some point though, the overpass must have built above it and then another and so now there's a canopy of crisscrossing roads above my head. These are places that Lulabelle has never been. I am officially off-road.

As it gets dark I pass signs that advertise clubs where you can meet Portraits of Marilyn Monroe, Esther Jones and Cleopatra (the last claiming to be created from DNA found at the long-lost tomb shared with Antony the Great!)

It's dark by the time I reach a neat little ten-story. There's a yellow car parked outside and roses planted in the garden. I have to press my face in close to one before I can smell anything but the stink of exhaust from the road above me. The scent makes me think of a perfume bottle with a crystal stopper. Fat lipped bouquets in Lulabelle's dressing room.

I press the buzzer and lean for a moment with my forehead against the door.

"Hello?" Lulabelle's voice asks.

"Hi," I say. "It's me."

In my head I see the Secretary drifting on the dark water. There's a pause and then the lock clicks open.

There is no lift, so I drag myself, step by step up eight flights. I make it by counting stairs. There are one-hundred and four. Six Portraits dead; six Portraits to go. Seventy-eight cards in a tarot deck. This last thought is comforting – not everything was lost in the crash. Somewhere in the Artist's loft, they are still spread out on a table. Maybe she looked at them while she ate supper. I wonder what she ate. I wonder if she's finishing the painting right now, while I am standing, quietly broken in this stranger's landing. I hope she's working slowly.

There is a green door in front of me with a welcome mat. I take a breath and knock. The only thing to do is keep going.

The door opens.

CHAPTER EIGHT

Strength

In a tranquil meadow, a woman dressed in white holds a lion by its jaws. She is wearing a crown of wildflowers and above her head is the twisting ribbon of infinity. The lion's teeth are sharp and very white, and its red tongue lolls out. They are watching each other carefully.

There are no lights on inside the apartment. I think it might be a small room. I think I see furniture and framed pictures on the wall but in the dark, everything is just a different shape of shadow.

One shadow, more substantial than the others, holds the door open for me.

"Come in," it says. "Sit down."

I limp past her into the dark and sink down onto a chair-shaped patch of darkness. The only illumination comes from the window, the glow of a streetlamp outside cut into stripes by the blinds. The carpet is divided into bars of light and dark, like a piano keyboard. As the Portrait moves towards me, I imagine the notes being played one by one, a stilted scale.

"I know who you are," the Portrait says softly. "I know why you've come."

"Can I..." My head hurts. "Can I have a glass of water?"

"No," she says.

I am too tired to look at her. I scrape some of the dried fluid off my chin, feeling the peel of it under my fingernails.

"I've been getting calls all day," she goes on. "You haven't been very subtle. Is that Prudence's blood?"

"Yes," I say. "Who called you? Which of the others?"

"Does it matter? We'll all be dead sooner or later," She moves around the room, brushing her hands absently over the door, the edge of the table, the bookcase. I catch glimpses of her as she moves into patches of streetlight, but there doesn't seem to be anything special about her. Platinum hair, white linen pyjamas, my mouth and eyes and nose. Just Lulabelle, like all the others.

"How are you finding the city?" she asks me. "It's a strange place, isn't it?"

"It's confusing."

"Have you noticed the strangest part yet?" she asks. "Have you looked at it on a map?"

The map on Spencer's wall. I realise now what was wrong. "Bubble City – that's not it's real name."

"That's right," the Portrait says. "Before the city was here there was just a large rock in the middle of the valley. One day they took her up on it and cut her into pieces. Her blood became cold sweet water where it touched the rock and trees grew up from the places in the valley where they scattered her body. Because of this they made her a saint and when they built the city they named it after her. This is why Bubble City has a different name on the map."

"Why are you telling me this?"

"I think it's important to know exactly where you're going to die."

My hand edges for the gun under my ruined jacket.

"Do you know why she made me?" the Portrait asks without moving.

I stay silent, thinking about the distance to the door. I don't know why she was made– I didn't take the time to read the file properly.

"Tax purposes," the Portrait spits out. "That's why."

"Tax purposes? What does that mean?"

"I don't know," the Portrait says bitterly. "Exist. That's all the instruction I was ever given. Once a month money is deposited in my bank account. Just enough to live on. I don't even own this flat. Do you know what it's like, to live ten years with no goal, no purpose? Nothing to do but watch daytime television and buy food and eat it. Do you know what it's like to spend your entire life bored?"

"You could paint," I whisper.

"What?" she snaps and takes a single step forward, into the light.

I see her expression; teeth bared, lip curled, eyebrows drawn together in a thick furrowed line. In the middle of all this contorted hatred, her eyes are glassy and cold, like marbles that have been left in the freezer.

"I want you to know I gave you the benefit of the doubt," she says softly. "I did my own research. I gave you time to reflect on your actions."

I stiffen in my seat. The way she's standing against the window makes her silhouette stark and clear. A yellow car parked outside.

"You're the one who's been following me."

She stays where she is. For the first time I realise why her stillness seems so unnatural. She hasn't taken a breath since I've come in.

I flinch back (too slow) and reach for the gun, but she lunges forward in one smooth movement, raising her foot like a ballet dancer to kick it from my hand. I turn my head to watch it skitter over the floor and in that brief second, she is on me.

There's a sharp explosion of pain in my left eye and stars bloom in my vision. Before I can even process what's happened, the second blow comes, an uppercut, knocking my head back. I gasp and then the air is immediately knocked from my chest by the third hit, a tight fist to my stomach. Blind, dazed and heaving for breath, I topple from the chair and onto the carpet.

"Fuck," I try and say. It comes out as a gurgled wheeze.

"You don't need to breathe," she tells me. "Grow up. Stop being so dramatic."

I sense her walking around me slowly and when I look up, her foot whips out and kicks me in the back.

I think I make a strangled noise. I think I spasm, but I have become unable to understand my body. The pain is like something alive, separate from me. It's an animal sitting on my back. I can't fight it or understand it. All I can do is curl in on myself on the carpet. I thought I knew what it was like to hurt before this.

Above me, the Portrait is talking.

"...did you know," she is saying, the words coming out in a thick vicious slide. "That we're built to last?"

Eyes streaming, I wheeze and shake my head against the carpet. I can't see her but I can sense her movements as she prowls around me with her sharp hands and feet. She crouches suddenly and I cringe back.

"We can be killed," she tells me, face pressed up close enough that I can tell for sure she isn't exhaling. "But we won't die. Unless someone kills us."

I shake my head again, face pressed hard against the carpet fibres. In this moment I would do anything to not be hurt again. The Portrait is speaking in a strange sing-song way that makes me wonder if this is rehearsed.

"I took classes, I studied and trained and practised. Boxing, Krav Maga, Russian Sambo. Aikido, Judo, I went to the rifle range, I lifted weights and even tried cross-fit. Do you know how many weapons I have hidden around this flat?"

The red fuzz of pain hasn't dimmed but it's begun to localise. My hand, my eye, my face, and stomach. These places are vulnerable, they have to be protected, but I can almost breathe normally now. I look over the horizon of the carpet and see the gun lying under the sofa.

"Sorry, I know I'm talking too much," the Portrait says and then she stops pacing and crouches down to look at me. The expression on her face is almost tender. "I don't talk to many people."

I wheeze at her and she frowns sympathetically.

"I don't want to hurt you," she tells me. "This is just survival. You understand that don't you?"

"...no," I manage to choke out.

"Maybe you don't," the Portrait says and reaches out to brush her fingertips over my chin. "Did you murder the others to survive? If you did, I think I could forgive you. But you didn't, did you? I don't think you've learnt about survival yet. Why did you do it?"

I don't know. Because Lulabelle told me to. Because of the grey A4 ring binder. Because I was given a gun and not a paintbrush. Because I'm number thirteen, the Death card.

"It's my purpose," I whisper. "It's why I was made."

She smiles sadly. "And do you want to do it?"

Does the piano want to be played? Does the horse want to be ridden?

"I don't know," I say. "No. Yes."

"What do you want?" she asks me. When she leans closer, I think for a minute that her right eye is blue. "Do you want to live?"

I swallow and then I try to roll away, towards the gun. My broken hand reaches out and then I scream as her foot comes down hard on my fingers.

"I thought so," she says, almost regretfully. "So you do understand then."

I look up at her. Standing over me with her back to the window, she looks like a monolith. Like a carved statue, ancient and unmovable.

"Get up," she says. "I've been waiting for this my whole life. I won't let you lose so easily."

Very slowly I pull myself up to my knees and then onto my feet. Hunched with pain, I am shorter than her even in my shoes with a heel. I cradle my hand to my chest and think about the tarot cards, still lying on the kitchen table. Will she know? I wonder. When I don't come back?

If I fail, then Lulabelle will just make another Portrait to take my place. When that Portrait looks down through the skylight with the gun in her hand, I wonder if she'll hesitate like I did. Maybe the Artist will cook my replacement a steak too. I hope she does. I hope that my replacement will be braver than me. I hope she will be kinder.

"Come on," the Portrait in front of me says. "Hit me. Try it. Fight, if you want to live."

I raise my hands but they're shaking and the left one is too contorted to make a fist. She laughs and then I swing. She side-steps deftly and then our fight begins in earnest. To call it a fight is too generous. Every move I make is fumbling, uncertain. I lash out wildly and she parries gracefully.

Soon though she gets bored. She starts to land little jabs on me, too quick to catch or counter. I can sense her frustration growing alongside mine. I'm not the fight she was looking for. I am no fun. I'm an old cat blundering after a piece of string. I can tell she's angry by the way she hits me. By the time I fall down I don't think she's enjoying herself at all.

"Stop," I gasp. "Stop, please."

"Is that it?" she says sadly. "After all this time? Is that all you'll give me?"

I look at the floor. It seems to circle in on itself like a whirlpool. I tilt forward, I am being sucked in. Be kind, I think. You must try to do everything with kindness.

"Others," I hear myself say. "Others will come if you kill me."

"And they'll be stronger?"

"Yes. And smarter." I close my eyes. There's a gritty feel to my mouth.

"She won't let me go, will she?" the Portrait asks, anxiously. "She'll follow me? Even if I change my hair and leave the city? Even if I kill everyone she sends after me?"

"Of course," I say brokenly. "She'll follow you to the end of the world."

The Portrait steps forward and from behind her back she draws a knife. It must have been tucked into her back pocket the whole time. Her other hand swings forward like a pendulum and grips the back of my head firmly, tipping it back so my throat is exposed. I think of the Artist looking up at me. I think of craning my head back to see the coloured lights. I try to breathe. This is what it must have felt like for the others.

The buzzer rings.

For a moment we both freeze in place, looking over at the door. It keeps buzzing uninterrupted, as if someone has their finger held down on the button.

The Portrait walks over to the window and twitches aside the curtain. I'm thinking about crawling towards the bathroom when she swears loudly. "It's those Mitosis idiots. Are they with you?"

I shake my head and she frowns, coming back over and kneeling down to touch my injured hand. I try to pull back but she holds it up to the light, turning it over so she can see the damage.

"I must have knocked out the tracker," she swears again under her breath. "They'll have seen the link drop. Can you get up?"

"You're going to let them take me?" Panic grips at my chest. "Can't you just kill me now?"

"It's not that easy," she says. The buzzer is still going and she runs a hand through her hair. All the icy calm of before is gone.

"Please."

She pinches her nose and then seems to reach some internal decision because she gets up and goes to the door.

"Come on up," she says into the intercom and then comes over and starts pulling at my arm. "Up you get. You can wait in my room. I'll get rid of them."

"But," I mumble. "The engineer…"

"I'll get rid of him."

She hauls me through a doorway to a neat little bedroom where she deposits me on the flower-patterned duvet.

"Just… stay quiet, okay?" she says and before she leaves, I catch her hand.

"Thank you."

She looks down at me with an unreadable expression. "Maybe she was right about you."

Before I can ask who, she's gone and the door is clicking shut behind her. It opens again a moment later and my binder is flung onto the bed where I scramble to gather it up.

Clutching it to my chest like a teddy bear, I lie there for a moment, staring at the painting that's hung over her dresser. It's of a wide, ambiguously emotional eye. It's not very good.

From the other room I hear a door opening and voices, muffled through the wood. Holding my breath I try and roll over to the far wall. There's a window there and beyond it, what looks like a fire escape. My hand is on the latch when I hear the sound of heels clip-clopping closer to the bedroom door. Dropping to the floor as soundlessly as possible, I'm rolling under the bed just as the lock clicks open.

"She's not in here." It's the woman's voice. The lawyer. From where I'm lying on the floor I see her shoes, the heels sunk deep into the carpet.

"How long has it been since your last check-up?" the engineer is saying from the other room.

"Three months." The Portrait's voice sounds dulled. Docile.

"And can you select a colour for me?"

The door is still open. The shoes turn away from me and

when the lawyer leans in the doorway, I see her hand come down and rub at her ankles. I put my hand over my mouth.

"She's gone," the lawyer says again, impatience edging into her voice.

"Come take a look at this," the engineer says and then the door is swinging shut.

I take my chance. Undoing the latch is easy enough; squeezing out of the window and onto the fire escape, less so. It feels like moving through molasses that somebody's mixed in with ground glass. Outside the wind catches at my clothes. Up here I'm almost level with the motorway. The lights blur in my eyes as I climb down, two twisting snakes of red and white stretching off across the city. Beyond them the great towers glow neon in the dark.

I have to jump at the last ladder and I land hard, the impact cracking through my knees. Struggling to my feet I stick close to the wall.

Waiting outside the building is the Mitosis van. I can't see a driver but it's dark. I stand there, weighing up my chances. I'm about to make a run for it when a taxi comes rumbling down the street and stops at the red light. I head for it in ungainly half limping run and open the door just as the light turns orange.

"I'm sorry," I say as I climb inside. "But could you just take me a couple of streets away? I don't have any money but–"

"That's alright," the voice from the front says. "I can do pro-bono."

Relieved, I slump into the backseat. Inside it smells very strongly of potato and leek soup and mothballs. As we pull away I turn back in my seat to watch the building entrance where a figure dressed in white is being escorted from the building.

I don't know why they would take her. I wonder if she regrets not killing me when she had the chance.

"Long night?" the voice from the front seat asks. "You look like you've been in the wars."

I nod miserably and close my eyes, letting my head fall back against the seat.

I'm not stupid. I know that this is dangerous. I know you shouldn't get into strange cars. I know that the driver could be another Portrait waiting to kill me, or Lulabelle herself or maybe the Viking, or even just another of the endless list of people who could hurt or kill me. People I haven't even met yet might want me dead. But my feet hurt. My hand hurts and my back, stomach and chin. If I don't open my eyes, then I am just sitting down in a warm place.

I want the world to be gentle with me, but I don't know if I deserve it. I've not been gentle with the world.

"How's it been going so far?" the driver asks me. "Are you nearly done?"

I open my eyes. I see the dressmakers faint smile in the rearview mirror, watching me. Her hands are firm on the steering wheel. I could cry to see her if I were capable. I'm so relieved I forget to be frightened or even wonder how she came to be here. Maybe I'm dead already and she's carrying me to the afterlife. It would be a relief, in a way, to know Portraits go anywhere at all.

"It's not going well at all. I crashed my car and lost my gun and I still have five Portraits left. And my hand hurts. And I've ruined the suit you made me."

"I'm sorry about that," Marie says and adjusts the speed slightly to let the car behind overtake. Something silver dangles from the rearview mirror. A sewing needle held on a long red thread. "It was a good suit. But five isn't that many. It sounds like you've almost finished."

"I am," I say. "And then what happens? Then what do I do when the mission is over?"

She smiles again and indicates in due time. "You find a new mission and start again."

I don't understand but I want her to be happy, so I nod. "Why are you driving a taxi? Don't you work at Wellsprings?"

"In the day," she says. "But I like to get out and about in the city. It's a different place in the dark. We're here."

She draws the car to a halt but leaves the engine running. I don't want to get out just yet. I wonder if I could ask to go with her. Do taxi drivers need assistants?

"Do you think…" I begin and then I have to clear my throat before I go on. "Do you think it's already too late for me?"

I watch the back of her headrest intently. I can only see the faintest outline of her hair. Her arms are bare and I can see the thin scars that encircle her arms, at her wrists and just below the joint of the elbow. They look like silver bracelets.

"I think that you should try and be on time as much as possible," she says. "It shows respect."

I try and think about this. It's not really what I meant. "Thank you. Goodbye Marie."

"Goodbye Lulabelle," she says, and I get out.

The taxi draws away almost immediately, and I am left alone, clutching my ring-binder, in a street full of trees. I take a few limping steps to my left and I am in a familiar doorway. My hand gropes for the buzzer. I try to press and hiss when my hand won't cooperate. My other hand finds the button.

Please, I think. Please.

I hold it for a long time, but nothing happens. My eyes come to focus on a handwritten note. It's hard to read through the swirling miasma. Sorry! Buzzer broken. I lean against it till my forehead is resting against the smug little frowny face. My eye hurts. I wish I were back in my poor dead car, driving out of Lulabelle's villa. That was my chance. I was brand new back then. The car was already en-route, but I could have changed the direction.

When the door opens, it's so sudden that I stumble and almost fall. Someone catches me before I do.

"Hierophant," I say and clutch tightly at the collar of her paint-stained work shirt.

She lets out a strange sigh and pulls back a little, eyes wide and mismatched. I don't let go of her. I think my fingers twisted in the cloth of her shirt are the only thing anchoring me to the world. She looks at my torn suit. She looks at the cut on my chin and my mangled hand. I feel her looking like almost a physical sensation, like cool water.

"Are you okay?" She brings one hand up not quite touching my eye. "That looks painful."

I don't want her to see my face, so I let my head rest on her shoulders. For a moment she stands very still and I think maybe I've made a mistake. I start to pull back and then her arms come up around my back. I turn my face into her hair. I want to laugh but it comes out as a kind of sob.

She holds me very tightly and we stand like that for a while in the doorway. I think that if I fell asleep right now, she would probably carry me upstairs, but I don't want to push my luck, so instead I just lean into her as she leads me inside.

Upstairs her loft is softly lit. The radio is still playing in the corner. I sit on the same chair where I had breakfast. There are still plates left out. While I stare at the congealing egg yolk the Artist disappears into the bathroom and soon, I see steam creeping around the edges of the doorway. The clock's eyes slide from side to side as the time ticks past. After a while, the Artist reappears.

"You could have sat on the couch," she says. "You don't look comfortable."

"I didn't want to get your blankets dirty."

"I don't care about that."

"You finished," I say, looking at the paint drying slowly on the canvas. Every last eyelash is present and accounted for.

"I went fast," she said. "I knew you'd be back soon."

"You didn't have to. You could have stripped the paint off and then you'd have even more time."

"Paint more every day and undo it every night?"

"Yeah," I say. If she's Penelope then what does that make me? One of the suitors loitering at her door? Or Odysseus, trying to find his way home? I wish I remembered more of the story. But Lulabelle had given up halfway through, bored.

"You would have caught on pretty quick."

"No," I say and then I have to look away from her.

She's silent for a moment. "I don't think the canvas would have cooperated."

She takes me by the arm to the bathroom. She helps me strip off the tattered dirty remains of my beautiful suit and then holds my hands to steady me as I lower myself by inches into the hot water. The heat is terrible, and I suck air past my teeth. A moment later, the relief comes, a bone deep relief that makes me sigh and lean back against the rim of the tub. It's large enough that I can submerge myself completely and so I do, dipping my head beneath the misty surface. When I come up, my hair is slicked back and coated in a thin layer of essential oils. Lavender, bergamot, clary sage.

"Hold out your hand," the Artist says. She sits on the edge of the bathtub, looking away from me, up at a small high window. This bathroom is full of plants. They hang from the ceilings in baskets. They are perched on every surface. With the dripping tap and humid air, it could be a rainforest.

I hold out my hand and she prods at it for a while before getting a clean cloth. After that, the only sound is the drip-drip of the tap and my occasional hiss of pain. The bathwater begins to cool and as the steam clears, I see that it's turned grey with dirt.

"The last Portrait knew I was coming," I say. "She was warned."

Her hand stills for a moment but she doesn't say anything.

"She said that she was called," I say, pressing my advantage. "By one of the others."

"Which Portrait was that?" she asks at last. "What number are you on now?"

"She was number ten."

"Strength. She called herself Belle," she says absently, and screws on the top of the lotion. "Did she talk to you about the saint?"

"Yes. I never knew that story before today."

"Lulabelle still doesn't – I think that's why Belle likes to tell it. How does that feel?"

"Sore," I say. "I didn't kill her."

The Artist pauses for a moment. "Hold on and I'll wrap the fingers up with some tape."

I shoot her dark looks from under my dripping fringe as she stands and begins to rummage through the cupboard.

"Did you know each other well?" I ask. "I saw your painting on her wall."

"Which one?" she asks, unconcerned. "What did it look like to you? Happy? Sad?"

I want to snap; they all look the same! But even though I think she might have betrayed me, I still can't bring myself to hurt her feelings, so I clamp my mouth shut on the words and settle for resentful splashing.

"It was dark," I say moodily. "I didn't see."

"What happened to her?"

"Mitosis took her away. I don't know why."

She hums, finds what she's looking for and then she sits back down. Her hands wrap around mine again, soft and strong. She's still not looking at me.

She hasn't looked at me for a while, I realise. Even when she was helping me undress. It makes me strangely angry. I want to say something awful or profound, to shock her into it. I don't know why she won't look. It's nothing she hasn't seen before. The small touches to my hand are so clinical, so irritatingly efficient. I want to pull my hand away but I can't, so instead I just sit there getting more and more frantic, trying to stay as still as possible.

When my hand is finally bound up, she puts it carefully down on the rim of the tub. I let out a sigh when she stops touching me; the relief is instant but so is the ache in my stomach.

"You probably shouldn't use this for a while," she says softly, looking down at it. "And don't get it wet; I don't know if the break makes you more susceptible to water damage. I'll see if I can find something. It's been knocked quite badly – the eye-socket is cracked but that might just be cosmetic."

She stands up and turns to leave, eyes still averted.

"Why are you being so nice to me?" I ask. "Do you think that I won't kill you? Is that why you're doing it? Because I will. You know I will."

She doesn't move, framed by the jungle and the open doorway beyond. The steam has curled the ends of her hair.

"I do know that," she says quietly. "I know you'll kill me."

"Don't you want to live?" I'm genuinely curious.

"I do," she says. I still can't see her face.

"Why won't you look at me?"

She turns around and when I see her face, I know why. I inhale sharply. Her blue eye blazes like a Bunsen burner. No one has ever looked at me like this before. I don't think that anyone has even looked at Lulabelle like this.

"You think I told her to hurt you?" she asks me.

"No."

"I didn't warn her, but I didn't warn you either," she says. "I knew what she was like. I've been sitting here all day, thinking that you were dead. Thinking that I'd killed you. The first time I met you I nearly did. I spent a long time waiting to meet you."

I shake my head and watch her get nearer. Everything in me is leaning towards the Artist as she approaches. Fighting against the feeling, I retreat into the water, until only my face is afloat.

She stands above me, looking down. For a nasty moment I think of what we must look like to a third-party observer. A woman staring down at her own reflection in the water. And then forcibly, I reject that thought. There is no third person here. There is no one looking at the two of us, only me looking at her, and her looking at me.

"The cocktail I gave you," she says. "When we first met."

"You drugged it."

"Yes," she says and then she falls to her knees beside the tub. I reach out with my damp arm and take back my hold on her collar, pulling her down, to the cooling water, to me.

CHAPTER NINE
The Hermit

The hermit travels alone and on foot through the wasteland. His cloak is grey and tattered and he clutches a tall wooden staff. The lantern in his hand holds a golden star, but still it only sheds enough light for the next few steps. In the dark he must place his feet carefully.

That night I dream of leaving Bubble City. I can hear the sound of a party happening behind me, laughter and voices and music, but I am too afraid to look, so I don't. As I walk, the roads rise up and tangle around me and then they become a rainforest. I stop and watch a drop of water fall from the distant canopy above me to the forest floor. It takes a long time because it keeps falling onto leaves and collecting with other raindrops which in turn split into new formations. It hovers for a long time on the tip of a leaf just above my head. My neck starts to hurt from craning up to look at it.

Here's a riddle for you, someone says. Is it still the same raindrop when it reaches the ground?

I look around for the voice and see a tiger sitting in front of me with its paws neatly crossed. Its wings are folded and every feather is a different shade of black. It ripples with the dappled light of the rainforest. It looks like the moon glancing off a midnight sea.

Hello, I say. Did you like the movie?

Not really, the tiger says. It was very depressing.

Not funny? No one laughed?

Maybe they did, the tiger says. I went to the bathroom for the worst parts.

I tried to warn you, I say.

The tiger rolls its shoulders, the muscle working under the fur, the dark wings bristling on its back. How's your work going?

Not great, I say. I think I've formed an attachment.

That'll happen, the tiger says and then looks up at the raindrop. I'm glad to see you anyway. I remembered another interesting fact about the number thirteen.

What is it?

The reason it's important. The tiger's tail twitches and lashes at the air, the wicked curve of its claws lazily retracting.

What?

Did you know there aren't twelve lunar months in a year? There's actually twelve point four-one.

How do you have point four-one of a lunar month?

You can't. That's the point. The calendar we made – it doesn't fit the pattern. You can't divide the natural world up so easily. It doesn't make sense.

I don't understand, I say. What does that have to do with thirteen?

Because – the tiger looks up with its huge unblinking amber eyes. Oh. I think you're about to wake up.

Wait, I say. Before I go. What's your name?

Simon, the tiger says, and the raindrop falls onto my forehead with a thunderous crash.

I wake up and lie there in the dark for a moment staring at the skylight up above. There's just the faintest smudge of pink showing through it. I still ache but it's a distant feeling. I roll over and nudge the Artist where she's snoring on the pillow beside me.

"What is it?" she asks muzzily. "You okay?"

"I wanted to tell you," I whisper. "I left my gun behind."

She looks at me blearily and her hand finds mine in the covers. "Do you want to go and get it?"

I think about it for a moment and then I shake my head.

"Go back to sleep," she tells me and I do.

This time, I don't dream of anything at all.

We wake up around noon and because we're both starving, we decide to order food.

"What do you like to eat?" the Artist asks me.

"I like sarsaparilla ice cream," I say but then I can't think of anything else, so in the end, she orders from about ten different places so we can work it out.

While we wait, we laze around in bed and watch the small television set balanced on the dresser.

"What do you think happened to her?" I ask as we watch a cartoon cat being hit with a frying pan. "The one they took away?"

"She'll survive. She's a survivor. They imprinted her that way."

I look away from the cat and his squashed face. "What do you mean?"

"Don't you know about this?"

"Imagine I don't."

The Artist stretches the long line of her body and puts her arms behind her head. I try not to be distracted. "We're most impressionable the moment after we wake up. There's about a 45-minute window. That's when we're given our instructions. Did a timer go off after Lulabelle talked to you?"

"I didn't realise it was a timer."

"Well it was. Pretty much everything you're told in that time is set in stone. Programming, imprinting, first laws… you can call it what you want but they're just instructions."

"Trust the engineer," I murmur and she makes an irritated sound at the back of her throat.

"That's from the little pre-prepared script Mitosis hands out. After she reads that Lulabelle sort of... improvises. The first thing I remember was being in the back of a car. Lulabelle was sitting next to me. She was telling me about a crayon drawing she made when she was six."

I stay quiet and wait for her to go on. I can picture it very clearly, Lulabelle looking out the window, the Viking's cool hands on the wheel in the front. The Artist, coming to in stages, staring at her knees.

"And she told you to make art?"

"She told me to make things. Whatever I wanted. I was lucky really."

"The one who fought me... Belle. She told me that they had only told her to exist."

The Artist nods. On the screen, a roasted chicken climbs out of the oven and starts dancing. "That's a hard one. But easier, for us. We don't die, you know."

"She said."

"If it wasn't for the addendum then we might be the only things left at the end of the world. Imagine that. A desolate wasteland... undead celebrities fighting over scraps in the ruins of Bubble City. Wait, pass me that notepad – I want to write that down."

"What's the addendum?"

She takes the notepad from me and pauses for a moment, looking down at the blank page.

"It's something they added later," she says. "After that big court case with Rishi Munzak."

"The musician?" I try and search back through Lulabelle's memories. "Isn't he dead?"

"Yeah, that was the problem. Before he died he made a bunch of Portraits. Tried to leave everything to them and his family contested it. And after the family won the case Mitosis had to put in the addendum to make sure it didn't happen again."

"How?" I think I know how.

"Well, when the original dies their Portraits are decommissioned. Automatically."

I think about this for a moment. The cartoon ends and is replaced by an advert for something called a BumbleB, a drone that can fetch groceries right to your door, delivering them straight from completely automated supermarkets. We watch as the drones fly down empty white aisles, collecting shiny red apples and slabs of thick steak.

"Where were you going?" I ask. "In that car. When you woke up."

"Here," the Artist says. "This building. This room. It didn't look like this back then of course. It looked a lot emptier. All it had was this bed and all these boxes."

"Empty boxes?" I see the Artist standing in the middle of all of them, the white walls, the sunlight and cardboard.

"No. They had... they had supplies. Art supplies. All sealed up in clear plastic. Paints and pencils and little tubes of coloured clay. And a canvas on an easel, already set up. Waiting for me."

"That must have been nice. Were you happy?" I look over and smile at her, but she is watching the television set as the bright colours flicker. There are points on our body where we are touching; my knee is on her thigh, her arm is underneath my neck, but I feel all at once that we are actually quite far away from each other. Then she turns her head and smiles back, and I think that maybe the distance isn't impassable.

"I wasn't happy," she says. "I was scared. I hated it. I spent two months in this bed, looking at the canvas."

I look over at the easel and picture it as the only thing in the room. Before the piano, before the comfortable sofa and misshapen figurines and lamps. The flat white plane of canvas must have glowed in the dark.

"I went to bed staring at it and it was there waiting for me when I woke up. We spent so much time looking at each other."

"Why didn't you paint something?"

"I tried," she says, sounding hurt. "I tried to. I got out the colours. I stood in front of it. But I didn't know where to start. Nothing was good enough. Nothing was worth saying."

"What happened?"

"I don't know," she says. "One day I just did it. I can't remember what but the paint smelt good."

"Do you still get scared sometimes? Of starting?"

"No," she says with an odd emphasis. "No. I like them best when they're empty. They can be anything. They can be a mountain or a castle on a cliff or a dream you had or some shapes that look good when you arrange them in the right way."

"Well," I say, thinking about it. "They can only be anything until you paint them. Then they're just one thing."

She shakes her head. "They can keep changing after that too."

Something about this conversation is upsetting but I don't understand why. I try and think about it for a moment but in the end I blurt out, "What do you do if you're halfway through a painting and you realise it's a mistake? That you got it all wrong? Do you stop?"

"No," she says. "I just keep going. Or try and paint over it. It's alright to make mistakes."

"But what if the whole painting is a mistake? Or terrible? And the more you work on it, the worse it gets?"

"Well yeah. That can happen. But what's the alternative? Just leave the canvas blank? Or leave it unfinished? It's hard to tell if it's good or bad till you're finished. And what's good or bad art anyway?"

I scrunch up my face to think about this and whatever expression I'm making must be strange because the Artist laughs and then, very casually, she kisses me.

It's strange just how quickly I've adjusted from no kisses at all, to earth-shattering kisses to finding kissing very natural. Or, at least, easier to slide into conversation. They still feel earth-shattering to me, but I'm trying hard not to show it and be very cool about the whole thing.

"What will you paint next?" I ask her. "Will you paint me?"

"A self-portrait?" she teases.

I scowl. "It wouldn't be that. You've got different eyes."

"You like my eyes?" she asks me and then flutters them for effect.

She's joking but I feel very serious. "I love them. They're beautiful."

"It's just a coloured contact," she says softly, watching me closely.

"I know," I say, even though I hadn't been sure until she said it. "But they make you different."

"Different from Lulabelle?"

"Different from me," I say and then, watching her from the corner of my eye, I say. "I like being different from you. I like that we aren't the same."

I'm worried that she'll be offended, but she just smiles. "Me too."

"Hey," I say, remembering suddenly what I had wanted to ask her last night, "Lulabelle told me you were the first one she made. Is that true?"

Before she can answer we're interrupted as the food arrives, all at once, courtesy of five bemused bike couriers. We take their brown wrapped parcels one by one with great ceremony and then we spread out all the food on the bedspread and settle back on the pillows. The Artist's plates have a willow pattern, and I heap on rogan josh and vegetable chow mein and crispy fried kapenta. I take a slice of pepperoni pizza too, on the Artist's insistence.

She watches me eat and every time I try something new, she asks me, "What about that? Do you like that?"

Over the next hour or so we work out that I like curries, especially the hotter dishes but not anything too salty. I prefer the consistency of broccoli to lamb, and bubble tea is delicious. When I say this, the Portrait looks ecstatic.

"Really?" she says. "I hate it!"

We smile at each other, delighted. After that it becomes a

game, to find out all the ways in which we disagree. We start with the food and move on from there to nature, to the city, to animals and music and abstract concepts.

"Blue," she says. "Beards. Pigeons. Luck."

"I like it," I say. "I don't like them. Pigeons I don't care about one way or the other. I don't believe in luck."

"I do," she tells me earnestly. "I do believe in luck."

At some point though, we get too full to eat another bite. The Artist gets up to clear it all away in little plastic boxes and I am left in the tangled sheets, thinking.

I know my time here is almost up.

The Artist must know this too because when she comes back, she sits down on the edge of the bed and looks away from me, up at the skylight.

"It's nearly seven," she says. "We've spent the whole day in bed."

"You've finished your painting," I say. "Will you start a new one?"

"Do I have time?" she asks me. I look down at her hand where it grips the white sheet.

"I still have four left, before I get to you."

"Well you better get going then," she says softly. "I'll get you some clothes."

She moves to get up and I lunge for her hand, clutching at it tightly. "Listen… if by the time I get back… if you were gone and I had no way of knowing where you were…"

"I'll wait for you," she says fiercely, looking over. "I promised, remember?"

I swallow hard. I don't know why she won't make this easy for me. I don't know why she won't run. I could chase her for the rest of our lives. They would be longer that way and even if we weren't together I would still get to see her sometimes. In the distance.

She shows me to her wardrobe and lets me pick out my own outfit. It feels a little like rummaging through a child's dressing up box. There are more scarves than socks and most of the clothes are covered in paint. Finally I find a pair of high-waisted jeans hidden behind what looks like a full-length velvet cloak. There are a few tiny insects embroidered on the back pockets; the way the stitching is coming loose tells me they're hand done. I pull on a white vest and a button up with a headache-inducing flower print.

I don't recognise any of the brands. I wonder if Lulabelle wouldn't recognise them either or if already I'm losing something of her. She would never wear a shirt this ugly. That makes me feel a strong rush of affection for it. When I finally look in the mirror, I look a little bit like a stranger, but more like the same person wearing different clothes.

The biggest difference of course, is the bandaged chin and hand. And, of course, my damaged eye. I turn my head from side to side, examining it in the mirror. The colour has bleached away in a rough stain that stretches from cheekbone to eyebrow. The iris itself is still brown which is a strange relief. Otherwise I would have matched the Artist.

It makes me a little sad to think of when I had first stripped naked and seen myself, fresh and new and untouched. The only thing that's remained a constant is the electric blue nail varnish. What's left of it.

As I look at the few scraps of paint still stubbornly clinging to my nails, a thought occurs to me.

"Why do you think they're blue?" I ask the Artist, who is standing behind me looking at my reflection. "My nails wouldn't have been blue in the vat."

"Maybe Lulabelle painted them for you after you were fished out. So you'd match."

I think about that glass table on the balcony and Lulabelle leaning over me in her white towel robe, turning my limp hands this way and that. Waiting for me to wake up so she could tell me about her movie. I shudder involuntarily.

"Do you have any polish remover?" I ask.

"No," the Artist says. "But I have other colours."

Thinking of the hitchhiker in his dark leather and eyeliner, I choose black. The Artist does it for me and does a sloppy job. The paint goes over my cuticles and smudges. She takes a long time, tongue sticking out the side of her mouth and brow furrowed in concentration. When she finishes, she blows on them so they'll dry.

"What do you think?" she asks anxiously.

"Perfect." I know it's time to leave.

I stand on the sidewalk outside, gripping my binder to my chest along with some money the Artist gave me for the bus. Already the afternoon is turning into evening and the birds are singing louder than ever. I take a deep breath of lukewarm air. The city smells good like this – when everything is soft. I think of how I'll never know what the inspirational quote for today would have been and it makes me sad, but not very much.

I'm just about to leave when the door opens behind me. When I turn, the Artist is there, looking a little frantic. She thrusts something out at me, a large tan jacket with some ratty looking wool around the collar and sleeves.

"Here," she says. "In case you get cold. I put your cigarettes in the pocket."

I put it on. It's heavy and smells like paint and strong dark coffee. It's a little too big so I roll up the cuffs. Because of my hand, the Artist has to help me.

"Thank you," I say finally because I don't know what else to say. "Thank you. I love it."

I look up and then very quickly lean over to kiss her. It's a nervous, misjudged kiss and lands more on her cheek than her lips but I can feel her smiling into it. When I pull back I feel very self-conscious so I duck my head, push back my hair. We are both laughing a little. I really have to leave now.

The next Portrait lives just a bus-ride away. On the way there, I sit at the back, by the window and leaf through her file.

Registration Code: PROCKL78960613
STANDARD TYPE (no deviations, cosmetic or otherwise)
LOCATION: Flat 3, The Tower, Shallot Street.
CHECK UPS: Yearly (low risk, sedentary)

Responsible for maintaining an online presence.
Note: **Do not touch the computer**. A team will be out to take over operations ASAP.

Be nice to her, Lulabelle has written, she's had a tough time.

This unusual display of compassion is both concerning and unwarranted. I don't even know what I'm going to do when I find her. I don't have my gun.

I have no idea what the system is. I'm still wondering by the time the bus drops me off at the corner of a retail park.

It was a long journey, and now that I'm here it hardly feels like Bubble City at all – at least no city that Lulabelle has ever walked through. In every direction are empty parking lots and mega malls with papered up windows and yellowing advertisements. Everything is under the shadow of the motorways above. It reminds me of a zombie movie Lulabelle co-starred in once. The ground is covered in litter and broken glass. I'm glad I'm wearing sensible shoes.

After walking for a while I pass a shanty town built in what looks like an old multistorey parking lot. I can hear music and see shadows moving behind strung up sheets of plastic. Someone in there has a tv set and, as I pass, I hear snatches of dialogue:

How did you find me?

The letters in your journal. That and a geography book. Your Elizabeth sounds lovely–

I think the scene must be over but then there is the sound of a scuffle and a man shouting, "Kill me and have done with it!"

Behind the parking lot I see my first signpost. Shallot Street. Maybe this was a real neighbourhood once upon a time. Maybe even a town of its own before it was gobbled up.

I'm expecting something impressive – if not a renovated castle then at least a high rise – but the Tower turns out to be an unimpressive three-story house, wedged in between a closed megaplex and what looks like the remains of a laser rifle arena. It's red brick and solid but shabby around the edges. A wheel-less bicycle rusts in the scraggly patch of grass outside. There are scraps of yellow ribbon tied in the chain link fence. The entrance has three buzzers, unlabelled. As I'm hesitating over which one to pick, I realise the door is slightly ajar.

Pushing it open I see a dark passage and a narrow flight of stairs. There's muffled music coming from somewhere within and a smell of garlic, strong but not unpleasant. As I make my way up the stairs the banister creaks and the music stops. I press myself against the wall but after a moment it resumes.

The stairway gets narrower further up. By the time I reach the top landing I can touch both walls without stretching out my arms. There's a light switch but when I flick it, the single hanging bulb stays dead. The only illumination comes from a crack of light running under the edges of the door at the end of the hallway.

This door too is unlocked and for some reason, this feels expected. She's waiting for me.

The room inside is empty. Small but very neat, with walls painted a pretty sage green. A large window on the west wall lets in the last dregs of the daylight. A comfortable sofa, a small bed in one corner, a polished wooden table with a vase of dried flowers. A calico cat is curled up asleep on the bed. As I watch, it takes a deep breath, the fur rising and falling. I wonder what it's dreaming about. I hear a mewing sound and I turn around.

Another cat is by my feet, looking up at me. This one is jet black. I crouch down, holding out my hand.

"Hello," I say. "Nice to meet you."

The cat regards me silently and then seems to come to some internal decision, stepping forward to sniff my hand. I smile and scratch it behind the ears where the fur is very soft and short. The first Portraits ever made were people's pets. Lulabelle read that in a leaflet while waiting at the Mitosis office for a consultation. I can't access the interview after but this memory is strangely clear in amongst all the sepia.

"Where's your owner?" I ask the cat, who blinks at me solemnly.

The kitchenette is small but well stocked. The cat's food bowl sits, overflowing on the floor by the sink. The fridge is covered in postcards with greetings from faraway places. Some of them (London, Monaco, Cairo) I recognise but most I don't. Lying on the counter are three envelopes. One of them is marked Molly and Sam (ground floor flat) and another is addressed to Lulabelle. The last has the number 13 on it. As I pick it up I feel a faint breeze ruffling the hair on the back of my neck.

The window opens onto a sloping roof and that's where I find her. Lying on her back, her eyes are open. The evening light paints pink and gold across the still blank canvas of her body.

I sit down next to her. When it becomes clear there's been no foul play, I take out my cigarettes and smoke one sitting next to her. If I squint I can almost make out the domes and spires of Rocher du Saint, far off in the distance past the skyscrapers. The valley walls seem higher than ever around the city.

"I'm sorry," I say but I don't really know what I'm apologising for. For not having arrived sooner, for not being the one to kill her, for not having offered to save her if that's what she wanted. For not being there to keep her company.

Maybe it's easier this way; she's taken the decision out of my hands.

I open the letter marked with my number carefully, being sure not to get any ash on it.

Hello Death,

I'm sorry I couldn't wait for you.

I've come to realise I don't need to exist anymore. The bots I've set up are capable of completely automated and highly responsive content creation. Unless someone pulls the plug Lulabelle will keep on living online for at least a decade.

With love,

The Hermit

P.S The downstairs neighbours will take care of the cats. If you're feeling helpful then could you please drop off the letter I've addressed to them?

P.P.S I hope you don't mind that she told me about the cards.

P.P.P.S The password to the system is INFELIX. That's the name of my cat (the black one).

I read it over twice before putting it back into the envelope and placing it carefully into the inner pocket of my jacket.

When I go inside I force myself to look at the far corner of the room. Unconsciously or not my gaze had slid over it the first time, retreated to the safety of the kitchen and the sleeping cats. This hatred isn't inherited from Lulabelle but it doesn't feel like mine alone.

The industrial desk, the three screens and two keyboards and headset monitor. Below the desk I can see a tangled nest of wires. They look like the roots of something twisted and awful. When I sit down at the desk and type in the password, I see the monitor flicker to life.

I watch as her ghost tweets about the price of a matcha latte. A photo appears on her public story. A white bikini, a blue drink. A moment later it comments on a favourable review of Medea. Excited for you to see this one guys!

Why did she give me the password? Did she just need

someone to bear witness? I didn't set anything in motion. Lulabelle will live on in this way. Immortal until the power goes out.

Or someone pulls the plug.

And maybe that's it. Maybe she was giving me a chance to fulfil my purpose. She was someone who took her job seriously. Maybe this is a nod of respect, one professional to another.

I sit there, thinking about killing her in this way and my gaze drifts away from the stream of images, up to the wall, where a single white sheet of paper is pinned above the desk. There's a poem written on it in blue ink.

I'm not scared of spiders
No matter what is said
There's no bite to you spider
Go softly where you tread
Look for us when you're weaving
You'll find us in the web
Don't be frightened spider
We're bound by silver thread

It's unsigned but I recognise the handwriting. The rhyme scheme is a little off.

I think I'll let her live this time.

CHAPTER TEN

The Wheel of Fortune

Suspended in a clear sky surrounded by fluffy white clouds is the wheel of fortune. A wise blue sphinx crouches on top of it and below it lurks the god of the dead, red and dog-headed. Winged creatures watch as slowly it begins to turn.

I'm petting the cat when the telephone by the door begins to ring. It's an old-fashioned landline, the kind with a coiled cord and the heavy receiver. I stand looking at it for a while and then on the third or fourth ring, I pick it up.

"Hello," the voice on the other end says. "Hello, hello?"

I know that voice.

"Hello Lulabelle," I say, making a face at the cat. "How are you?"

"Which one are you?" she asks suspiciously.

"Number thirteen," I say. "The Assassin. Death."

"What was that?" she asks. The line is very fuzzy. "Did you say she's dead?"

"She is," I say. "But I'm not finished yet."

There is a sharp crackle of static down the line and then Lulabelle snaps, "I know you're not fucking finished. If you were finished, I wouldn't have spent the last three hours calling every fucking phone number I know. Where have you been?"

"I got in a car accident."

"Are you broken? Is that why Mitosis keeps calling?"

"Maybe. How have you been?"

There's a pause from the other end and then she snaps, "Not good. One of them broke into my house."

"Why?"

"To kill me, you idiot!"

"Uh-oh," I say and move over the table to leaf through the binder. "Which one?"

There are only four left now. It's not the Artist, I know that.

"Does it matter?" Lulabelle snaps. "I need you to come and get rid of her for me!"

"Don't you have security guards?" I ask.

"Just get over here," she says. "And hurry."

"But I crashed the car."

"You…" she starts and then just sighs. "Oh, for Christ's sake. Just stay where you are, I'll send someone to pick you up. Jesus. I have to do everything myself."

She hangs up and for a moment I stand with the phone pressed against my ear listening to the dial tone. The black cat is rubbing up against my ankles again, so I put the phone back in the receiver and pick him up.

He mews at me and swipes out a paw at a lock of my hair. I wonder if he can tell me apart from his owner.

"I'd like to take you with me," I tell him. "But you'll probably be happier downstairs."

He mews again. I scratch him behind the ears and then, still looking at him, I pick up the phone and dial a new number. The card is dirty and creased now from being moved from jacket to jacket, but still legible.

Spencer picks up on the second ring.

"You found her," he says, breathlessly. "Where is she?"

"Found who?" I frown at the receiver.

There's a pause and then when he talks his voice is buttery smooth. "My mistake, I thought this was the dog walker. Third time this year my shih tzu's run off on him. Sweetheart, how are you? I can't tell you how happy I am you called. You sound hungry. How about I pick you up and we can go–"

"Tell me about the deal," I say. I keep my voice very quiet. "Please."

There's a moment of silence. When Spencer starts talking his voice is buttery smooth and practically vibrating with barely restrained excitement. There is a lot of effort being exerted on both sides of this conversation, I realise. For my own part I am trying hard not to hang up on him.

"It's simple," he says. "Really simple. You see, I love Lulabelle, I really do, but this new plan of hers, it's crazy. Fruit loops. I'm not saying that exclusivity doesn't look good as a PR stunt, but fuck, Portraits are too valuable to be wasted on something people will only care about for what? The fifteen minutes before the next story breaks? We only took thirteen samples, which, by the way, wasn't my idea. I tried to tell her we should expand the franchise globally. A Lulabelle for every city of every country in the world! Doesn't that sound like something?"

I stay silent. After a moment he picks back up, sounding a little more nervous.

"Anyway, now you're out of the vat, we're all out of spares. I was hoping she would keep a few tucked away just in case. What if there's an accident? This might sound harsh, but Lulabelle isn't a person. She's an industry. Do you know how many jobs depend on her continued existence? You don't kill the golden goose."

He leaves me a pause to speak but I stay quiet. After a moment he gives up and continues.

"Excuse my French but it's fucking selfish of her. To do it without asking me too. Not cool. I'm like a father to that girl. Also, maybe this doesn't mean much to you, but my new secretary is an idiot."

"What's the deal?" I say again. My fingers are getting white around the receiver.

"You don't like killing them, do you?" he presses. "The others. How many are left now anyway?"

"Four. Four now."

"Hmm. Not great but I can work with that. Here's the deal. If you work for me, you'll never have to kill anyone again. How does that sound?"

I am silent for so long thinking about it that he gives up on waiting for an answer and starts talking again.

"Don't you want a shot at being the new Lulabelle Rock?" he asks.

Do I? What does that mean? I don't even know what Lulabelle does all day. She isn't going to parties or making art or picking up kids from school or walking the streets of the fashion district wearing pretty clothes.

"What would happen to the others?" I ask.

"They would be on the backbench. In case of any accidents," Spencer says. "As insurance. You understand – it's just good business sense."

Maybe that means they would be squirrelled away in country villas. Or maybe it means the vats getting cracked open again. Home sweet home. I try and remember what that was like and I feel a rush of nausea.

"What if I wanted one of them to be free?" I ask. "Not insurance. What if I wanted one of them to keep on living in Bubble City?"

Spencer hums in thought. "Well… I guess it would be nice to get my old Secretary back. You've talked to this one? How does she feel about dyeing her hair?"

I hang up on him.

The phone rings almost immediately.

"Listen, listen," he says quickly. "Hold on, look. Just… Give Lulabelle a message from me okay? If you see her?"

"What is it?" I ask. I feel a nervous urge to hold the phone away from my ear in case it grows teeth and bites me.

"Just tell her to pick up the goddamn phone okay? Tell her

to remember who made her. A deal's a deal. Just..." He sighs. "Just tell her to call me back. Okay? And don't forget what I said about the moment–"

I hang up.

I stand for a while looking at the phone and then I go downstairs, taking the letters and closing all the doors carefully behind me. As I pass Sam and Molly's door I take extra care putting their letter through the slot.

Down on the pavement I watch for headlights. I am struck with a sudden wild thought. If I went upstairs right now and climbed back out on that roof, could I save her? Was there still time? The thought is irrational but still I feel the urge to turn around.

But I don't. I just wait and wait and feel every second go past and then finally a dark car pulls up and it's too late.

When the door opens, the Viking leans out and says, "Get in."

"Hi," I say when I'm in the car. "Did you miss me?"

"It's been three days. Why are you taking so long?"

"I had to work everything out myself. It's not... it's not easy."

For a moment I think I almost see a flicker of something pass across the Viking's face. But when he speaks, his tone is brisk.

"You should have had an escort. The early Portraits Lulabelle made were chaperoned."

"By whom?" I say snidely. "You?"

"Yes."

I struggle to know what to say to that as the car pulls away. It's driverless and the location has already been set. It seems the Viking has nothing else to do but be disagreeable.

"Well," I say at last. "I'm nearly done anyway."

"You've been wasting time," he says gravely. "And because of that, Lulabelle nearly died."

"When the Portrait broke in? Your security team couldn't handle her?"

"We can handle her just fine. She's currently restrained."

"Then why do you need me?" I ask petulantly and put my shoes up on the dashboard.

"You know only Lulabelle can kill a Portrait," he says and narrows his eyes. "New shirt?"

"Then why doesn't she?" I say, looking away from him, out of the window. I think I see a fox moving in an alleyway as we shoot past.

I've come to terms with the fact I'm effectively a gun, created to be pointed at people. Still, I would rather know exactly whose finger is on the trigger. My brief conversation with Spencer is still going around my head. Why does everything have to be so complicated? It all seemed so clear when it was just a list.

"She's very sensitive. She hates violence," the Viking says straight faced. I twist in my seat to shoot him a look, but I don't think he's joking.

When I reach for the display screen, he pushes my hand away.

"Ow," I say, even though he didn't do it roughly.

"What are you doing?"

"Looking for the inspirational quote of the day."

"Hmm," he says, clearly not believing me but bringing it up for me anyway. When I lean in, he warns me, "Look with your eyes, not with your hands."

ONLY DEAD FISH GO WITH THE FLOW.

"Huh," I say and after that we maintain a brittle silence. I try to think about the deal and whether or not I should have taken it but for some reason I feel sure I made the right choice. Maybe I should be trying to save the lives of the others at any cost, but the thought of working with Spencer makes my stomach turn. At least this way I'll only be dealing with Lulabelle. Better the devil you know.

And there's no one I know better.

I'm expecting to leave the city and the thought of it makes my stomach churn. Already I am mentally counting the miles that stretch between the villa and the Artist's loft. But when we reach the city limits, the car turns its nose away from the desert and swerves sharply to the left, towards the star-speckled hills that overlook Bubble City on the southern side.

We climb steadily up the long looping roads, past dark unmarked gates and discreet little mansions. Higher up, I recognise a few barred driveways from Lulabelle's memories. The Z-listers are long behind us. We're now somewhere in the middle of the alphabet: the ageing soap opera actors, the social media personalities, the outrageous reality stars.

When I press my cheek to the cold glass window and squint, I can just make out the distant twinkle of lights along the high ridges of the valley. The steadfast C's, the iconic B's, the impossible A's. Those mansions are so inconspicuous that they barely exist in the material world. But we won't be going that far up. Lulabelle, for all her vast and complex multitudes, is a second tier Olympian at best.

We make three more hairpin bends before we turn in at one of the shadowed driveways. A security guard shines his light in the window, nods to the Viking, and then the gates are drawing back to let us through.

"You have your gun?" the Viking asks. The driveway rolls out in front of us, swept clean by headlights. I feel like I am being squeezed down the neck of a boa constrictor.

"No," I say.

"Where is it?"

"I left it under a sofa," I tell him, scraping black nail polish off my cuticles.

"And the car?"

"Crashed it."

He sighs and then takes his own gun from its holster. "This one has a kick. So be careful."

I roll my eyes but when I take the gun, I'm surprised by its weight. I feel the sudden drop of déjà vu. Am I really going to use it? The car stops before the feeling goes away.

"Lulabelle is waiting for you by the pool," the Viking tells me.

"You aren't coming?"

He shakes his head. "She asked for you alone. Good luck."

"Did you get attached?"

He turns his head to look at me. "What?"

His bushy beard is lit up blue in the light from the dashboard. "To the ones you chaperoned. Did you get attached to them? Who were they?"

"It was only one of them actually." He looks surprised that he's answered the question.

"That's not what you said."

He's silent. I can't help but press my advantage now I have an opening. Who was the first anyway? Prudence?

"Did you take her out for ice cream? Did you make her pick a flavour too?"

He shakes his head but it doesn't feel like a no. "I'll see you later. Don't forget: the gun has a kick."

When I get out I leave the door open just to be irritating.

The house is only one story high but still it seems to loom over me as I stand in the driveway looking at it. I think it might be ranch style, but you couldn't imagine any horse being happy here. Nearly everything is made of glass and in the dark, it glitters like a wet eyeball. An old-fashioned front porch is wrapped around the house like a bow. I know from memory that it will lead around back to the lagoon swimming pool. As I creep around the outer folds of the building, over the creaking wooden boards, I think about luck.

The Artist believes in luck. Perhaps because she's an artist. If I believe in anything, it's unluckiness. I think I could believe in coincidence. If I tried. Maybe even optimism, if only more in principle than practice. But luck doesn't mean anything at all. A person or a thing or a number can't be lucky. It's not a trait, like being happy or sad or having blue eyes or brown.

Being unlucky, though, that I understand. You can't mix up unluckiness with fate, because who would be destined to fail? You wouldn't design a piano so it couldn't be played. That would be dumb.

It wasn't luck that made me able to eradicate every Portrait I've come across so far (with one notable exception). That was, after all, the point of me. It wasn't luck that brought me to the Artist. It was my grey A4 ring binder. But to fall in love with her? That would be very unlucky.

For me at least. It could be very lucky for her if she takes advantage of my fault and uses this time to escape. It could still be lucky for her. As someone who believes in luck, she will hopefully understand this.

The pool casts an unearthly blue glow over the palm trees and surrounding rocks. By the pool's edge is a deckchair, occupied by a heavy dark shape that sags and pulls the fabric taut. Standing by it is a tall shadow. I think they might be talking, but the sound of the artificial waterfall covers any noise.

I think about hiding in the dark and waiting for someone to reveal themselves, but I'm tired of intrigue. I want to get this over with.

"Hello," I say and step forward. The shadow straightens up and turns and becomes Lulabelle, barefoot in a Pepto-Bismol pink tracksuit with her hair pulled back into a ponytail.

"Thirteen," she snaps. "Finally. I hope that thing is loaded."

"I hope so too."

She splutters but I ignore her and wander over to look at the figure in the deckchair. A Portrait looks up at me, rope cutting into her wrists, mouth gagged and eyes bulging. As I watch she tugs against the restraints.

"What's with the gag?" I ask. "Which one is she anyway?"

"I don't know." Lulabelle snaps, crossing her arms huffily. "Does it matter? Just kill her."

"I'd like to know. If I don't then I'll get confused," I say, trying not to sound frustrated. I'm doing my best here. She could at least pretend to care.

I hold out the binder and Lulabelle snatches it from me with her electric blue talons. She flicks through it impatiently and then jabs at a file. "There. That one."

I take my time reading it over, partly because it's too dark to read easily but mostly because it gives me a perverse little thrill to watch Lulabelle sigh and fidget and tap her feet impatiently on the tiles.

"I don't understand," I say finally. "It says here that she lives with you. How did she break in?"

Lulabelle sucks in a sharp breath and her nostrils flare. "She doesn't live with me. She lives in the gatehouse. It's a completely separate property, it just has the same address."

"Why does she live so close?" I ask, re-reading the brief, cramped paragraph. It's sparse and to the point.

Lulabelle's eyes flicker out over the surface of the soft blue water.

"She's my stand-in. On set. Only in emergencies, of course. I need her close, so we can rehearse together. Are you finished? Can we move on?"

I lower the binder and take in the sight of Lulabelle in her tracksuit, her hair pulled back very tightly from her face. Her blue talons clench and unclench on a magenta sleeve. I look down at the Portrait, who looks up at me and grunts. Her hands flex and unflex where they are bound to the lounge chair. Her hands are palm up, clutching at the air. There's something beseeching in the gesture. Distracted by this, it takes a moment to understand what I'm looking at.

Very carefully, I tuck the gun under my armpit, making sure the safety is on first.

"Oh, don't–" Lulabelle says, but I've already tugged the gag from the Portrait's mouth.

"Why do you have lines on your palm?" I demand.

"I could have told you that–" Lulabelle starts but the Portrait, looking livid, cuts her off.

"That's the Portrait," she snaps, spitting slightly with the words. Her mascara is smearing and her hair is falling in her face in wild hanks. She strains towards me and the deck chair shudders forwards. "That's the Portrait you idiot! I'm Lulabelle! Shoot her!"

"Oh great," the tracksuited Lulabelle mutters. "Now we're going to be here all night."

I look between them and sigh. I wish I had never picked up the phone. I can't help but feel this is something they could have worked out between themselves.

I pull up another deckchair and make Lulabelle – the other Lulabelle – sit down. I'd feel easier if she was also restrained, but I can't see any rope and I doubt she'll help me look. Neither of them seem to appreciate my attempts to be impartial.

"What are you doing?" Lulabelle snaps. "Untie me!"

"Shoot her!" says the other Lulabelle. "Stop fucking around!"

"Look," I say, trying to be reasonable. "Let's all try and calm down and we can work this out together. Can you both please hold up your hands?"

They do so very sullenly, the tied-up Lulabelle with some difficulty.

I look between them. Four identical criss-crossed palms. They're both looking at me with two identical scowls.

"Tell me something only Lulabelle would know," I say, and then I shake my head. "Wait, no. Stupid. Tell me why you both have lines on your palms."

"She's an actress," they say almost at the same time and then they glare at each other.

"You first," I say, pointing at Tracksuit Lulabelle.

"She's an actress," she says. "I told you. She stands in for me when I need it, so she has to look and feel realistic. It's surgery."

I feel a headache building behind my eyes. I really can't be bothered to deal with this. It's too complicated. It's too late at night.

"So, one of you is a Portrait," I say slowly. "And you do all of Lulabelle's acting."

"Not all," they both object, one a little faster than the other.

"Just small stuff mostly," says one and the other nods.

"Stunts."

"She's my stand-in."

"She does the nude scenes."

Watching them carefully, I continue. "So that Portrait, whichever one it is, is exactly like Lulabelle in every way. Physically and mentally. And you do the same things, right? Basically."

They both stay silent, refusing to be baited.

"Look," I say. "I'm just going to untie you because this is ridiculous. Maybe we could go inside and talk about it over a beer," I add hopefully. I've never had one but I've been seeing ads for them all over the city and I'm excited to try.

I put the gun down carefully on the tiles by the deckchair and start to work at the knot. The bandages on my hand make me clumsy and I'm still picking at it when Tracksuit Lulabelle launches herself from the deckchair, knocking it over with a clatter.

The fight that follows is distinctly unimpressive.

We both scrabble for the gun. Tracksuit Lulabelle has the drop on me but, unlike the last Portrait I fought hand to hand, she seems to have no martial arts training at all. I don't think she's ever been in a non-choreographed fight. I, on the other hand, have actual combat experience, which is to say I've been beaten up pretty recently.

She lands a blow on my swollen hand and I pull her hair in retaliation. She tries to kick me, but her feet are bare and I drive my boot against her blue-painted toenails. Her shoulder catches me in the solar plexus, as if by chance, and as we collide I have a sudden flashback to my night with the Artist. The Tied-Up Lulabelle is yelling something, but it sounds more like criticism than encouragement.

I think we're both on the edge of giving up and tapping out when the gun goes off between us.

Which one of us pulled the trigger I have no idea. Together, we fall back onto the tiles. For a moment I think that I have been killed. My head lolls to the side and I look across the faint ripples of the pool. The blue lights dance.

I expected this to feel peaceful. But I still have so much to do.

"Get up," I hear someone say. "Stop messing about."

I blink, surprised to find I still can. I'm impressed by Lulabelle's capacity for rudeness, even to the recently dead.

"Come on," the voice says again. "Hurry up and untie me."

I sit up and Lulabelle's body slumps to the ground. I look down and my new button-up shirt is damp. I touch a hand to it and realise that the fabric isn't torn. Neither is my skin below it.

"I'm alive," I say with mild surprise.

"For Christ's sake – are you just going to sit around all day?" Lulabelle grouches.

I pick myself up and look down at the corpse in her tacky tracksuit. She looks as surprised as I feel.

I untie the other Lulabelle. When the last knot is unpicked, she stretches like a cat in her pyjamas. When she stands up she goes over to prod the dead Portrait with her toe.

"She shouldn't have tried to kill me. Not like that anyway. We were just having a drink together. You know, I almost thought we were friends."

I stay quiet, watching the fluid running into little channels between the tiles in an expanding grid. It'll ruin the grouting, I think sadly. In the dark it almost looks like blood.

"Deliberate cruelty is unforgivable, and the one thing of which I have never been guilty," Lulabelle recites in a strange attempt at a southern-belle drawl. Seeing my face, she winces. "I know. She was always better at the accents."

"What do you mean you were having a drink? I thought she broke in."

Lulabelle doesn't seem to hear me. She's still looking at the Portrait.

"You made the right choice you know."

I watch her for some kind of hint. I think she might be

smiling, or at least, trying not to smile, but it might just be the play of flickering light across her face.

"I don't think I made a choice," I say, but she's already walking away, towards the sliding glass doors of the ugly house. I can see her reflection and my own held there, white ghosts in the dark garden.

She pauses and glances over her shoulder. "Well? Are you coming?"

I am. I trail obediently behind her, leaving behind the palm tree fronds and the sound of the artificial waterfall.

Inside, the lights come on automatically. The sudden flood of light illuminates an immaculate white and cream living room. There's a submerged firepit in the middle of the room. The flames are lit but there's something warmth-less and synthetic about the flicker of them. One wall is completely made of glass; through it I can see the distant ordered lights of suburbia on the other side of the valley.

"Don't sit down," Lulabelle warns me. "The dirt will never come out of the velour."

I look down and see I have already tracked a series of grimy footprints across the carpet. Lulabelle doesn't seem to have noticed, and I hover where I am, afraid to cause any more damage. Lulabelle stalks over to a cabinet and pours herself a very generous glass of something amber brown. She plunks in some ice from a tiny silver bucket and stands there in her pyjamas gulping it down. When it's drained, she pants and pours out another.

"I have something for you," I say and reach into my pocket for the letter. I hold it out to her but she stays where she is, glass in hand.

"You can just tell me whatever it is."

"It's not from me. It's from the last one who died."

"The last one you disposed of," she corrects.

I keep my hand outstretched and the letter trembles a little between us. "She ran your social media accounts."

"Oh," she says, frowning faintly. "Her. Just put it on the coffee table."

"Will you read it?"

"For God's sake, yes, just put it down."

I place the letter carefully on the glass table and smooth it out as best I can. Lulabelle glares at me over the rim of her glass.

She must be the real Lulabelle. I wouldn't hate her so much otherwise.

"Why do you really want them dead?" I ask. She goes still, but all I can see is the back of her platinum head.

"I told you," she says. "Didn't I tell you?"

She sounds as if she's genuinely asking.

"It was about your movie," I prompt. "But someone else said it was about exclusivity."

"Oh yes," she says distantly. "It was that."

"Which?"

"One of those," she says dismissively. I can see the gleam of the amber light in her glass as she turns it in her hand.

I should stop now, but I try one more time anyway.

"Don't you think…" I have to clear my throat. "Don't you think you'll be lonely when it's over? When you're the only one left?"

It's very quiet in here. I wish a radio were playing. I can still hear the waterfall.

"It's always been just me," she says at last. She sets down her glass in a way that signifies the end of the conversation and presses an unobtrusive chrome button. I half expect a trapdoor to open underneath me.

"You're taking too long," she tells me brusquely.

"I know."

"What did you think of Prudence?"

"Who?" I ask stupidly. "Oh. The Portrait in the suburbs. You already asked me that. She was fine, I guess. She fought me a little at the end."

"What did you think of her hair?" Lulabelle asks me. "Did she tell you it was natural? She's a big fake."

"Hmm," I say noncommittally. I don't know why we're talking about this Portrait out of all the others. My eyes slide to the windows and for the first time I notice the telescope set up in the corner. Did Prudence have one too? Is this how they spend their days? Watching each other over the abyss? I guess no one will be looking back now anyway.

"Did you see John–" Lulabelle begins, but she's interrupted when the Viking walks in from a doorway leading deeper into the house. Her mouth shuts with an audible snap.

"Is it done?" he asks. I study his face but I don't see any sign that he wasn't expecting to see this Lulabelle.

"Yes," Lulabelle says and then shoots me a warning glance. When the Viking looks over at me, I nod slowly. I'm not sure what I'm confirming. Am I complicit if I barely understand what's happening?

"Do you have it?" Lulabelle says abruptly.

The Viking nods and holds up a file. My file. For a moment I am struck by the urge to run over and snatch it out of his hand.

Lulabelle takes it from him and starts to rifle through it. Not looking up, she stalks over to the firepit; for a moment I think she's going to trip and fall down the step. I have a vision of her with her hair on fire but she just throws herself down onto the couch, glaring at the file as she flips through the pages.

"Where is it?"

"Where's what?"

When she looks up her face is a white mask. She looked less frightened by the pool with a gun pointed at her. "Don't be stupid. Did you give it to Spencer?"

"I didn't give him anything. What are you talking about?"

I look over at the Viking but his eyes are fixed on Lulabelle. A muscle in his jaw is making his beard twitch.

"There's a page missing," Lulabelle says, more to herself than me. "We need to move quickly now."

For a moment I wonder if she's talking to me or the Viking, until she turns and points an accusing finger in my direction. "You're taking too long."

"Yes. You said."

"You should have finished in forty-eight hours tops," she goes on, waggling the finger now. "Find them, shoot them, move onto the next. Simple. But instead you're wasting my time, playing dress-up and getting in fights and crashing very expensive cars."

"Just one car," I say, stung by the reminder. "Singular."

Across the room, Lulabelle slugs back the last of her drink and narrows her eyes.

"I'm told you're getting on well with the painter," she says. "I'm not surprised. She's my favourite too."

I feel the hairs on the back of my neck bristle. I want to ask for my file back but she's clutching it very tightly in her blue tipped hands. There's a page missing – what does that mean? When did I lose it?

"Can I ask you something?" I'm trying to choose my words carefully, edging a little closer.

She shrugs as if to say, if you must.

"I've been trying to work something out," I say. "About the order."

"Order?"

"Of my binder. The order of the list. At first I thought you were assigning me the easy ones first, the ones who wouldn't put up a fight. But that doesn't make sense, and then I thought you might want your favourites to go first. But you put Prudence in the middle. And it's not age."

I can tell from her face that she has no idea what I'm talking about.

"Does it – so it doesn't... What does it mean?" I finish, feeling strangely raw.

"Nothing," she says, and I can tell she isn't lying by the confusion in her voice. "I didn't make up the binder. I just gave notes."

"Oh," I say, looking down at the ruined carpet. I shift my feet and feel the carpet fibres peel from the soles of my boots. "Okay."

"It's obvious I can't trust you not to drag your feet about this," Lulabelle says. "I'm giving you a chaperone."

She waves her glass at the Viking who stands in the doorway, as scraggly and stone faced as ever.

"I don't need a chaperone," I interrupt. "I'll get it done. I just need another car. And another gun."

"You need a chaperone," Lulabelle says firmly.

"You already lost my gun?" The Viking raises an eyebrow.

I flush. "I don't want your gun."

Lulabelle rolls her eyes. All at once, she looks incredibly tired. Her posture doesn't change but I can practically see the strings being cut. Her arm moves, adder-quick and before I can move, the binder is tossed into the flames. I let out a strangled noise as the pages curl and smoulder.

She doesn't look up but when she speaks, there is no doubt that her words are for me alone. They come out in a flat, emotionless drawl that roots me to the spot.

"I'll give you a new gun," she says. "And a new car and a chaperone and on top of all this I will give you another chance to prove yourself useful. I will give you all these things even though I've given you so much already. I gave you my name and my memories and my face. I gave you everything you needed. I'll give you more than that if you want it. You want money? You want new clothes? Take them. Take the shirt from my back. All I ask is that you might, just once, consider what I am owed. What could you give me in return?"

The binder is letting out a noxious plastic smell that can't be healthy. The flames are a strange, unnatural colour.

I try to say three more. Three more deaths to go and all the others that came before. That's what I'm giving her. The weight of all those bodies is making my shoulders ache. Something of this must show in my face because her expression softens and she stands up and comes over, pressing her drink into my hands.

"Try it," she says, and it sounds pleading. "I hate to drink alone."

This close I can smell her perfume, overpowering and sickly sweet. I take a sip and the ice clinks against my teeth.

"I want you to know" she says, soft enough that I can tell it's for my ears only. "You weren't the first. I tried this before. With the one I made before you."

"You made her to eat brunch."

She just shakes her head. "I sat down across from her on that balcony just like you. I had the script all ready. I made notes on what to say. I had the binder ready and the car and the gun. But when it came to it, I couldn't do it. I couldn't think of a single thing to say."

I remember the glint of sun reflecting off the surface. The single blemish on her robe. I shake my head but she continues anyway.

"We sat there in silence for forty-five minutes just looking at each other. When the buzzer went off, I just sent her to brunch."

I think of the expression on the face of the Portrait on the bus stop. No reason at all programmed into her brain. Was that freedom? Is that what I should be jealous of?

"Why are you telling me this?"

"Because I want you to understand. That I know how it feels. I know how hard it is. Believe me, I wish there was another way."

"There could be–"

"Listen to me," she says and it's strange because even this close I can't smell the alcohol on her breath. "Listen, I want you to know. It's not your fault. It's mine. This isn't your decision. You never had a choice in the first place. I want you to remember that."

The relief comes from nowhere and is shocking in its

intensity. Suddenly all I can think is how easy it would be to let her take the guilt from me like this. I'm so tired of carrying it alone.

At this moment I could give her anything. I could serve up the Artist's head to her on a silver platter.

In the background, I see the Viking check his watch.

I wonder if this is what the Artist was talking about in her poem. It does feel like being a fish. It feels horrible. Maybe it is love after all.

CHAPTER ELEVEN

Justice

The face of justice is a blank mask. He sits upon a throne between two solid pillars and holds a set of scales in his left hand. His ruling will be impartial, apathetic and final. In his right hand he holds a sword, raised and ready to fall. He must consider carefully, however – the blade is double edged.

"Come along then," the Viking says and goes to the doorway. He looks at me and I look at Lulabelle. She looks at the ice in her glass.

"Will I see you after?" I ask.

She yawns widely. "Sure. Maybe. God, I'm tired."

I want to linger, to prod a little more, but the Viking is looking impatient. I follow him through the house and its cool, impeccable halls. Outside sits a car so white it glows in the dark.

"Get in," the Viking says. "I'll just be a moment."

It looks so much like the car I destroyed that for a moment I feel a lump rise in my throat. But when I climb inside, it's pristine. No scuff marks on the dashboard where the hitchhiker rested his feet. No peanut dust on the leather seats. No empty wrappers in the footwells.

The Viking climbs into the driver's seat and passes me a shiny silver box. I don't bother looking inside. The gun holds no nostalgia.

The valley side is full of sharp corners, but the car follows the road as smoothly as if we were on metal tracks. We sit in silence and watch the skyline unfold in a glittering web. From this vantage point, I can see the city in its entirety for the first time. When I arrived three days ago, the city was just a series of grey towers on the horizon. Now I can see that it isn't a city at all. It's a galaxy, spiky and bioluminescent like some deep-sea monstrosity. I look for the suburbs, the skyscrapers and small neighbourhoods and can't find them at all. They're part of the organism, impossible to define on their own.

I could live another eighty years and still not see it all.

I could live forever, maybe, if what Belle said was true. I don't know what I would do with all that time. Four more to go and what then? What will I be left with when it's all over?

Despite everything, there's a horrible sense of relief at sitting in this car with the Viking at my side. I'm back on the pre-ordained track again and Lulabelle has absolved me of my sins. It would be easy to see this as a second chance; a way to return to simplicity and order. Forget the Artist and the others. Forget Marie and the hitchhiker and all the things I've seen so far. It could be easy. Maybe I just need it to be easy again.

We glide through the city down streets which seemed darker from the valley. It seems the whole world is out and jostling the sidewalks. It's brighter than I've ever seen it in the daytime but, then again, I've only seen three daytimes. We pass a golden restaurant spilling over with people; a man in a red suit is busking outside. His electric guitar is covered in pink plastic roses.

We pass a multiplex cinema, lit up in blue and gold lights, with people pouring in and out of revolving doors. The building is plastered with posters and I recognise the man from the suburbs, his blue suit traded for a white snowsuit. There's a gun in his hand instead of a cigarette. Lulabelle is less obtrusive. Her poster is nestled between a preview for a musical biopic of Mother Teresa and an animated film about office supplies. Lulabelle stares blankly into space, a limp teddy bear cradled in her arms. I'm trying to read the tagline when the lights change and we move off again.

"Do you ever wish," I ask the Viking, forgetting my resolution to be silent, "That you could drive the car yourself?"

He shakes his head. "No. I like it this way. It gives me more time to think."

"Think?" I echo, genuinely baffled by this answer. "Think about what?"

I wait, and for a while it seems like he might answer. I wonder if maybe I misjudged him. If perhaps he's a secret poet or philosopher. A poet-warrior. Maybe he sat in the back of the longboat singing to entertain the rowers. Or maybe his job was to observe the battles and report back in verse.

He opens his bristling mouth; I lean in eagerly.

"We're here," he says. "Get ready."

The car stops and when I exit I'm looking up at another cold pillar of a building. I follow him inside, through another gilded lobby, into another elevator. My stomach jolts as we ascend. Is this where the next Portrait lives?

The last few have made it easy for me. The racer crashed before I could kill her; Belle sacrificed herself so that I could go on. What happened by the pool and with Prudence could be argued away as self-defence. Not since the secretary have I put a gun to anyone's head and pulled the trigger.

There's a choice waiting for me at the top of this tower. Maybe the first proper choice I'll ever make.

"I've spent my whole life going up and down in these things," I announce and watch the Viking carefully out of the corner of my eye. I wonder if maybe he will try and turn it into a metaphor or say something wise.

"Hmm," he says. I look away, scowling. Maybe not a poet at all.

"Are you claustrophobic?" I ask, somewhere around the hundredth floor.

"No," he says shortly. I give up on small talk.

The elevator doors open onto a draughty, unfurnished floor. I can't help but feel that this would be a good place for a murder. Buckets of paint and dust sheets hang around us like dirty ghosts. Construction equipment is heaped in one corner.

"I don't understand," I say. "Where is she?"

"Over here," the Viking says, and I follow him to where one pane of glass is missing in the panoramic wrap-around, floor to ceiling windows. The view through the gap is identical to the view I can see through the glass, but I root my feet to the ground, instinctively terrified. I can feel the cold air even from here. I have a sudden vision of a gust of wind swooping in through the hole and around the room, picking me up and tossing me out like a ragdoll. Like a shooting star in a cocktail dress, hurtling to the ground.

"Over here," the Viking says again, a bite to it now. I force my jelly legs to take tiny mincing steps over to his side.

"What is it?" I ask, very warily. I accidently look over at the edge again and I wobble, feeling a flower of nausea expand in my stomach.

"A gun," the Viking says. "All you have to do is pull the trigger."

I try to focus. I blink at what he's pointing at and then I see it. The thing he's standing beside isn't construction equipment at all.

"Oh," I say, surprised. "It's a gun."

I hear him sigh but I'm already dropping to one knee to take a closer look. If anything, the weapon looks more like the telescope in Lulabelle's sitting room, balanced on spindly tripod legs and pointed towards the gap in the glass. It still doesn't really look like a gun to me; it looks like a piece of complicated and expensive technology.

"There." The Viking guides my hand to a small raised button, like the one that had summoned him in Lulabelle's ranch. "Press down on that."

"What?" I yank my hand away. "That's not a trigger. Where is this thing aimed? Where's the Portrait?"

The Viking looks at me with a weary kind of patience. I wonder if he's ever looked at the real Lulabelle like this. "She's three buildings away in bed. Everything's in position. All you have to do is pull the trigger."

"You mean the button."

He takes my hand again and very gently guides it back to the weapon, as if he's teaching a child to hold a pencil. "She's asleep," he reassures me. "She won't feel a thing."

My breathing is coming faster now, in short sharp gasps.

"No," I say. "No, it's wrong to do it like this. I can't even see her. Which one is she? Why was she made?"

"Press the button. It's very easy."

I shake my head and stagger back. I'm afraid again of the gap and I reach out to grasp onto something. The only thing to grab is the weapon and I recoil back from it. The timing of this, the planning, the cost. All of it done so I could come along and press the button.

On that sunny balcony, Lulabelle had made it seem like a moment's decision. A whim. But I should have known better, even from the binder. This was all planned very carefully.

I had felt like a rogue agent out there on the streets, marking my own bloody path across the city. Now, seeing this, I realise I was never really alone at all. That tracking device in my fingernail – had Mitosis kept that for their own use or had Lulabelle been sitting hunched over her phone somewhere watching my little red dot?

"No," I tell the Viking. "No. I don't even know who she is. I don't know anything about her."

"Do you need to?"

"Yes. Yes, I…"

"You think that's kinder? To look her in the eye when you do it?"

"I should talk to her first. At least I can explain–"

"You sound like a serial killer," the Viking snaps, voice hard and angry. "You think it makes them any happier to know they're going to die?"

I flinch. Of all the names I've been given, serial killer seems cruellest. I take no pleasure in killing. I could have been an artist in another life. Or a housewife, or a socialite, or a hermit, or a winged tiger in a dream. I could have been anything, or nothing, but Lulabelle created me to kill.

His voice gentles, but his eyes remain flinty. "This is the kindest way," he says. "You won't do anyone any favours by dragging it out. Least of all Lulabelle. Just do it quickly. Do it quickly and then you can forget."

I look out towards the dark skyline, as if I could see the Portrait sleeping in the city beneath. But all I can see is my own pale face in the glass. I think of the Artist, even further away, and the unmade bed where I slept. He said Portraits didn't need to sleep, and I suppose I was never meant to. I was only ever wasting time.

"Look," the Viking says. "Killing isn't a game. Or a ritual. It's just a task. An unpleasant one. If you must do it, then it must be for rational reasons and with a rational mind. Remove all emotion from it."

"That feels wrong," I mumble.

"What?"

"It feels wrong. Worse, to do it like that. It shouldn't be easy."

He sighs and rubs a rough hand over his face. When he speaks, it's in the tone typically reserved for explaining difficult concepts to children.

"You think your emotions will help her? You think she'll care if you agonise over doing this? Forming attachments like that – it helps no one. Don't be so selfish. You can't ask them to absolve you."

When I don't move, he says, "You want to know why the binder was in that order?"

I give him a wary nod.

"Economy," he says. "I worked out the locations on the map

and found the most efficient route for you to take. That's all it was."

I look at him for a long moment, and then out of the glass towards the city and the window beyond that and the sleeping Portrait I'll never have to meet. I press the button.

Afterwards, riding down in the elevator, the Viking turns to me and says, quite conversationally, "Did you know they had these in the Colosseum?"

"Had what?" I hear myself ask. I bleakly watch the numbers on the display scroll past. 99. 98. 97.

"Elevators," the Viking says. "Lifts. They had twenty-eight of them. All powered by slaves of course."

"Of course," I echo. 79. 78.

"They were used to get wild animals onto the floor of the arena. It was really very sophisticated. They had whole labyrinths under there. Sometimes they would flood the whole amphitheatre, just to recreate battles at sea."

"Okay," I say. "Pretty cool I guess. Sophisticated."

"I'm not from here, you know," he says, just before the doors open. "When I first came to this city, that's what it looked like to me from the plane. A colosseum."

If this is an admission of some kind or even an apology, the message is lost on me.

When we step out onto the pavement the Mitosis van is waiting for us at the curb.

"Oh fu–" I say but before I can bolt, the Viking snags my arm.

"Listen," he says urgently. "It doesn't matter what you pick, just do it fast. Don't hesitate."

"What?"

"They track your eye movements," he hisses as the van door slides open. "They're looking for indecision."

The lawyer comes out first, her heels clicking onto the pavement. It must have been a long day; there are dark circles under her eyes and what looks like a mustard stain on the lapel of her suit jacket.

"Are you responsible for her?" she asks, waving her tablet at the Viking. "Can I see some form of ID, sir?"

The Viking sighs and pulls out a card from his wallet. Narrowing her eyes at it she begins to type rapid fire into her machine.

"Are you aware, sir, that Ms Rock's estate is required to inform us of any damage sustained to her Portraits? Harbouring and continuing to work with a defective Portrait is actually a serious breach of contract. If–"

"She's not defective," the Viking interrupts. "It's just her hand–"

I'm hardly listening. My whole attention is focused on the engineer as he emerges from the van.

We're beginning to make a scene as the late-night bar flies and club kids turn to look at us from the taxi ranks. A group of middle-aged women smoking outside the cocktail bar across the street are shouting something that gets lost in the traffic sounds.

"Hold out your hand," the engineer says to me brusquely.

The Viking stiffens beside me, his eyes narrowing but already that calm is slipping over me. I hold it out, palm up. The Engineer shines a light over it, clicking his tongue.

"Yeah, it's what we thought. Nothing's dislodged, it's been crushed."

"Is it fixable?" the lawyer asks, peering over nervously. I want to ask what happened to Belle.

"Maybe," the engineer says. "We'll have to take her in anyway. I'm willing to bet this isn't the only issue. If she's beyond repair you'll hear from our team about the warranty terms within the next three working days."

This last he says to the Viking, who shakes his head.

"I'm afraid that won't work for us. We can't afford to lose her right now."

"We can't let a broken Portrait just wander around wherever she wants," the engineer says. He's still holding my wrist and

I ground myself in the touch. It would be fine, I think, to go with him. If that's what he thinks is best. At least the Artist would be safe.

"She won't be wandering around, I'll be with her. Look, I've been with her ever since she sustained the damage and she's been operating perfectly normally. Just test her and see for yourself."

The engineer is silent for a moment, eyes flicking between me and Viking. Finally, he shrugs and, pulling out his tablet from the holster slung over his shoulder, he holds out the screen to me.

"Choose one."

"Red," I say, trying not to blurt it out. It's hard to keep my eyes from moving, from flicking to the mossy greens and sunset purples.

"Hmm," the engineer says, watching me carefully. "Well we'll still have to fix the hand."

"I'll drop her off myself with you this morning," the Viking says. "Or you can pick her up. Whatever is easiest."

At first I think the engineer won't budge. Then, the lawyer clears her throat.

"We can do that."

When the engineer looks at her, she shrugs. "It's been a long night. We still have to deal with that mess out at the runway afterparty."

I look at the Viking and he nods his head at the car. I take the hint.

"You should have let them take me," I say as soon as we're on the road with the van safely behind us. I should have failed it on purpose.

He just shrugs and looks out of the window. If I didn't know better I would say he looks unhappy. It's hard to tell with the beard.

As we drive I think about the Viking telling me I didn't need to eat. He said he was trying to make it uncomplicated. He gave me the car and the binder, arranged along an economic route. He must have known I was created for this. He must have known I wouldn't like doing it. From what I've seen, I don't think he likes his job very much either.

Was he fond of the first Portrait he chaperoned? It might have been just a job to him but something tells me different.

Maybe he was trying to be kind.

"Was the ice cream a test?" I ask him. Outside I can hear music and traffic but in here, in the muffled interior of the car, the words come out very small.

"You know the next address," he says, as if he didn't hear me. "Are you ready?"

I clear my throat. "Do we have to do it right now?" I ask, hyper aware of the childish break in my voice. "Couldn't we get to her last?"

"Only two left now," he says softly. "You'll feel better once we get it over with."

I know all at once that there is another weapon waiting in position, its sights trained on the Artist's bed. I wonder if she's sleeping, or if she's waiting for me.

"Can't I do it in person?" I ask and then I swallow hard. "Please? Even if it's just for me."

He turns away from the streetlights and towards me. He looks for a long time and then he sighs. "I suppose with her the damage is already done."

"Yes," I say. "It is."

It takes us nineteen minutes and thirty-seven seconds to reach the Artist's neighbourhood. I know this because I spend the journey with my eyes glued to the navigation screen, watching the distance counter tick down. She'll be gone, I think, with each stroke of the odometer. She'll have run.

By the time we pull up outside, I have almost convinced myself it's true.

"You have the gun?" the Viking asks.

"Yes." I don't want it. I want my grey A4 ring binder.

As we approach the building, a sudden burst of inspiration strikes me. I rush forward, nearly tripping over my own feet. When I reach the buzzer, I slam my finger down on the button.

"Run," the words trip out of me. "You need to run, we–"

The Viking is there in a second, pulling me back from the door with an arm of steel. I yelp and struggle and, in the end, he has to shake me like an aerosol can before I shut up.

"Are you finished?" he snaps. "Are you done?"

I go limp.

"Yes," I say, and then, because I mean it: "Sorry."

He lets me go and I step back meekly. With his back turned, I crumple the smug smiley face note in my hand.

He presses the buzzer and then, when there is no answer, presses it again.

"I guess she's not home," I say, frowning. "Let's come back later."

I turn around but his hand whips out and closes around my wrist, fixing me in place.

"Give me the gun," he says.

When I do, he fires a clean shot through the padlock. The noise ricochets through me.

"Give it back now." I say, panicking, and when he does I wrap my hands tightly around it.

"You don't have to worry. I can't kill her," he says. "It has to be you."

"I know that," I snap and push past him into the building's narrow staircase.

She's gone, I think with every step. She's long gone. I'm holding the gun so tightly it feels like an extension of my own arm.

"She won't be there." I look back over my shoulder. A pink flush has risen just above the edges of the Viking's rusty beard, but he isn't out of breath.

"What's that then?" He taps one finger to his earlobe. "Hmm?"

I take in a shuddering breath. So he's heard it too. The sound of a piano, inexpertly played, is drifting down the stairwell.

The music grows louder and louder as we climb, until my whole body seems to shake with the impact. By the time we are standing in front of the Artist's door, I want to clasp my hands over my ears. It feels as if my bones might vibrate right out of my skin. I raise my hand in a fist.

"Don't knock," the Viking warns.

I unclench my fist and the door swings open at my touch. She must have been waiting for me, just like she said she would.

She's sitting at the piano, wearing her paint-stained man's shirt and running shorts. Her hair is tied back with what might be one of my lost socks. When she sees me, her blue-brown eyes widen. I hold up my hand and give her a little wave.

"Hi," I say weakly.

"Hi," she says and then: "This is the bit with the words."

Before I can make sense of this she has begun to sing. The tune is disconcertingly jaunty.

"Growing old gracefully
Was never in the cards for me
From day one you seemed to be
The one inevitability."

"What is this?" The Viking says by my shoulder. I shush him. The Artist continues, unfazed.

"I dreaded you and dreamt of you
But never ever doubted you–"

"Stop now," the Viking says and then he turns to me. "Tell her to be quiet."

I shush him again, annoyed at the interruption. I'm hanging on every word.

"Rider on a pale horse," the Artist sings. "I met you in the mirror."

"Did you write this song?" I ask, unable to hold back.

"Yes," she shakes her head without lifting her gaze from the keys. "Do you like it?"

"I think you're in the wrong key," the Viking tells her.

"Am I?" she says airily. "Oh well. Too late to change it now I suppose. And till my final breath, I'll flirt with death."

"Better do it now," the Viking mutters and his hand falls heavily on my shoulder.

"I'm sorry," I tell her. "But it won't hurt. I think."

"It's alright," she says. "You already know I'll forgive you. Do you mind if I keep playing?"

"No, please," I manage to say. "Go ahead."

The Viking sighs.

"You're just making this harder on yourself," he tells me. "You're humanising her."

The Artist frowns and stops singing, her fingers banging out a clumsy improvisation.

"I've forgotten the next part," she says. "You know practically nothing rhymes with death."

"Macbeth?" I suggest.

"I couldn't think of how to work it in."

"I hate that play anyway."

"Oh?" she says with a sad smile. "Well, I love it."

We look at each other helplessly. Her fingers keep running into each other as they move up the keyboard in a series of fleshy, discordant traffic accidents. My lovely Hierophant. Gorgeously, impossibly untalented. My time is up.

"Your time is up," the Viking says. "End this."

There's a moment where her fingers falter on the keys.

I close my eyes and put the gun up to my temple.

"Wait!" The Viking barks and lunges forward. He pulls my arm up just as my finger tightens around the trigger. The Artist yelps and there's a shower of broken glass around us from the skylight.

The Viking curses and when he prises the gun out of my hands, I see he's bleeding.

"Sorry," I say stupidly. My ears are still ringing from the shot.

Holding one hand to the fresh cut on his head, the Viking takes a step back, bringing up the gun.

"Don't hurt her!" The Artist calls out from where she's frozen on the piano seat. For a moment the gun swings between us. I hold my breath and get ready to jump for it.

"Is that clock right?" the Viking asks. He gestures at the cat with the moving eyes and tail. Blood is trickling down the side of his face, matting in his sideburns.

I shoot a wild look at the Artist who looks back at me, equally confused. Her fingers play the same notes over and over like a needle skipping over a record.

"Is that clock right?" the Viking repeats. He's pointing at the cat with the moving eyes and tail. It reads ten o'clock on the dot.

"Yes," the Artist says.

"That's my shift over," he says.

"What?" I ask stupidly. "What are you doing?"

"I'm making a decision. I'm keeping a healthy work-life balance," he says and lets out a strange laugh. Then inexplicably and still holding his bleeding head, he wanders over to look at the paintings on the wall. "You painted these, right?"

"Yes," the Artist says, looking at me.

The Viking laughs again. I wonder if he has a concussion.

"Yeah," he says. "Yeah, I thought so. Well... I'm off."

We watch him as he walks out the door without a backward glance. The Artist and I stare idiotically at each other and then I rush after him. I catch him on the landing below.

"Wait," I say. "What happens now?"

He spares me a brief glance, one hand working at the top button of his shirt, his phone in his hand. Already he's unravelling before my eyes, dishevelling. "I start back at midday tomorrow. I would leave the city before then if I were you."

"What about you?" I ask, my hands clenching and unclenching at my sides. "Will you be alright?"

He looks surprised for a moment and then he laughs. "Me? Yeah, I'll be fine. I mean Lulabelle will be pissed."

"What if she kills you?"

For the first time he smiles. His teeth are a little crooked. "Kill me? I'm not a Portrait. I'm a human. That would be murder."

"Oh," I say. "Oh, of course. So, I guess you'll be getting on your boat then."

"A boat?" he says and scrunches up his face. "I can't even swim. You're a weird kid, you know that?"

"Not a kid," I tell him.

"No," he says, looking at me seriously. "I guess not."

I watch him leave, taking the stairs two at a time. As he's about to turn the corner, he looks back at me.

"It wasn't a test," he says. "The ice cream."

"What was it then?"

He shakes his head. "I don't know. A nudge. I wanted... I hoped maybe it would give you a chance."

"You did it for the others too." It's not a question. I think about what he said about killing and kindness. "You said it was selfish to get emotionally involved. You're a hypocrite."

He thinks about it and nods. "Yeah. I suppose I am."

Back inside her flat, the Artist is still sitting at the piano, but the lid is closed now. Her fingers are tapping out a nervous rhythm on its glossy surface.

We look at each other; I see my own exhaustion and fear and desire reflected back at me. The Artist was right: love is nothing like being a fish. It's taking a long time to say goodbye and it's watching cartoons but not really watching them at all. It's someone asking if you're okay and really wanting to know the answer. It's waiting longer than you should.

I don't know how this happened exactly. Maybe I only fell in love with her because she was kind to me. I don't know why she loved me back. Maybe because when I met her, I was a blank canvas. Or maybe because, out of all of us, the Artist is the only one who has put real effort into loving herself. I wonder if this is all just narcissism; I don't know if I care.

"I would have done it," I say. I feel like I'm standing on the precipice of a skyscraper with the drop looming in front of me. If she exhales too forcefully, I might topple over.

"I know."

"I wouldn't have killed you. I couldn't have."

"I know," she says and stands up, the stool scraping backwards. She holds out her arms.

Gratefully, I fall forward.

CHAPTER TWELVE

The Hanged Man

The hanged man is strung up by his ankle with a halo around his upside-down head. Not dead but still martyred, he surrenders totally to the world and in doing so, gains a new perspective. While his hands are tied behind his back, one leg swings free.

When we finally pull apart, she keeps her hand on the side of my face.

"She burned my files," I say. "I don't know what to do."

"You don't need them anymore."

I'm not sure that's true but I nod anyway.

We pack as quickly and as lightly as possible. For me this is easy; I tuck my tarot cards into an inner pocket and change into a clean shirt. With my files and car destroyed, I have no other possessions besides the cards in my pocket. While the Artist gathers her things I slip away to the bathroom.

The Viking's blood is drying on my hands. As I wash them with a bar of the Artist's lumpy homemade soap I look at myself in the mirror. With my bleached eye and soiled shirt I don't look much like Lulabelle anymore.

I can't help but miss her a little. Whoever she is.

When I come out, the Artist is waiting by the door with only a backpack.

"Is that all?" I ask. "What about the paintings? The ceramics? What about your embroidery? Don't you want any of them?"

She shakes her head and shrugs. "There's too much – I can't choose."

"You should take something," I press. How many paintings could I carry with me? The thought of leaving all of this behind is bizarrely upsetting to me.

"It's fine, really," she says and then, "It's not very good anyway."

I inhale sharply. Until this point, I wasn't sure if she knew that.

"It is good," I say stubbornly and then to my surprise I find I'm not lying. "All of it is good."

"I'm not talented," she tells me gently. "It's okay. I never thought I was an artist."

It almost feels like a personal rebuke. I feel the heat rising up in my face.

"Who cares about talent?" I say. "What about your poetry? You can carry a notebook."

Her jaw twitches and I know she is gearing up for an argument.

I brace myself but instead she says: "This is our first fight. You know that?"

I think about it and then I smile, feeling giddy. "Yeah. I guess it is."

In the end, she lets me take the knitted blanket I slept under the first night. I fold it very carefully before putting it in my bag.

Outside, it's very dark. For the first time, the birds are silent in the tree-lined street. I follow her down the alleyway, past the rusted fire escape and over to a graffiti covered parking lot that smells like urine and weed. Tucked into one corner is a defeated little three door car. Someone has written wash me on the passenger window but underneath the grime I think the paint job is white.

"Is it yours?" I ask and the Artist beams with pride.

"My Nissan Sentra coupe. 1985."

"It's manual?"

"When it works."

What a hunk of junk, I think, but I'm very happy to climb in and pull the door closed behind me. Inside, there are throw pillows on the back seat and a pair of fluffy dice hanging from the rear-view mirror. This car doesn't have a display screen so I don't know what the weather's doing but writing on the wing mirror tells me that 'objects in the mirror may be closer than they appear' so I try to take some inspiration from that. While the Artist tries to start up the engine, I count the dots on the dice. All together they add up to twenty-one.

"Right," the Artist says in satisfaction when the sputtering becomes a low growl. "Where to?"

I can't answer. I'm looking at the dice. I wonder if the Artist has them there for luck. The luckiest roll is two sixes and that adds up to twelve.

"Well?" the Artist says, eyes wide and mismatched. "Where do you want to go?"

The dice are getting blurry in my vision.

"I'm sorry," I find myself saying. "I'm sorry, I can't go. Not yet. I'm not finished."

There is a horrible silence that goes on for so long I have to shut my eyes.

Eventually, the Artist clears her throat. "I know."

"You do?" I ask, my eyes still shut tight.

"I do," she says softly.

"It's why I was made."

"You were made to be loved," she tells me, which is very romantic, but not particularly helpful.

"There's one Portrait left," I say. "But I don't – I can't. I–"

"What?"

"I don't have my binder," I manage, feeling devastated all over again by the loss of it. "I don't know where she is. I don't know who she is."

She thinks about it and then asks me about the last Portrait I killed, about the button and the expensive piece of technology. I tell her everything. When I'm done, she makes a hum in the back of her throat.

"That must have been Amelia."

"Who?"

"She called herself that. After Amelia Earhart. It was a joke at first but then it stuck. She spent her whole life on planes, practically. Lulabelle has a lot of overseas commitments. You must have shot at her hotel. I didn't even know she was in town."

I think of the postcards on the Hermit's fridge, the sun faded beaches and monuments torn a little at the edges. Not for the first time, I feel a sort of loneliness. I arrived too late to the party.

"Did you keep in touch with all of them?" I ask, and then I blurt out. "I read your poem. About the spider. You told her about the cards."

She hesitates, chewing at her lip. "Not all of them. Those of us who were older–"

"Let me guess," I say, narrowing my eyes. "The Secretary. The Hermit. The Tax Evader. Who else?"

"The others were younger. And they were made to be shown off, displayed. They were busier than us, they didn't spend any time alone. It made it harder for them. Everywhere they went people called them Lulabelle."

"What about Prudence? She told me she was one of the first."

"She didn't like us. Listen, I think I know who's left," the Artist says and then hesitates. "What will you do when you find her?"

"I don't know." I can't explain why I need to do this. It just feels right somehow. Like I would be completing something. If I don't see her then I know I'll always be looking back over my shoulder.

The Artist nods and reaches past me to the glove box and pulls out a folded piece of paper. I look at her and take it dumbly. When I unfold it I see two lines on a blank page.

Registration Code: PROCKL78900913
LOCATION: Saint of Immaculate Blood Hospital,
Seventh Floor, Room 14

"When you fell asleep that first night, I took it from your car."

"How did you get in?" I ask and then the pieces click. "Oh. Facial recognition."

"I couldn't let you hurt her," she says, hands twisting in her lap. "I couldn't."

"You could have destroyed the whole file. Why just her? What's so special about this one?"

She says nothing, chewing on her lip. I reach out and put my hand over hers, stilling them.

"Why don't you show me?" I say gently.

She nods and then, taking a breath, she turns the key to start the car. The sound of the engine startles me; this is no smooth and silent electric car. Easing the car forward she navigates out of the parking lot, through the narrow alley and into the dark street.

We drive for a long time, listening to the radio. I can feel every jolt in the road, and I flinch every time she hits the accelerator. She's not a very good driver, or at least she's not as good as Marie. I felt safer on the back of Velazquez's motorbike. We're lower to the ground and the windows aren't tinted. I am aware of the city streets in a way I never was before. It should be a good feeling, but I don't have time to think too much about it. I am too busy wishing that the Artist would indicate.

It's scary but I trust her, despite everything.

It's scary to trust her so much.

We rattle and bump and swerve our way through Bubble City

and then finally, at the centre of a tangled mass of motorways, we come to a building where all the lights are blazing, and people are gathered in the entrance. I check the time; it's 3AM.

"Busy," I say.

"It's a hospital," she says, pulling into a parking lot and narrowly avoiding running over a group of frat boys with what looks like beer cans stuck to their heads. "It's always busy."

"I guess people die all the time."

"And get sick all the time and get born all the time. And fall off ladders."

"And jump off buildings."

She gives me a long side glance. "It always comes back to death with you."

I shrug. Of course, it does. I'm number thirteen. It's my card.

She kills the engine and the sudden silence is rattling. "Should I wait here?"

"Do you want to?"

"No."

"Then come with me," I say, "If you want. I'd like you to."

The parking lot feels noisy, like emergency lights without the siren, like lightning with no thunder to follow. We pass a chaotic family trying unsuccessfully to manoeuvre a young girl out of a camper van. In the centre of the frantic movement, she stands, face tight, hunched protectively over one twisted arm. We pass an old man on a bench, staring at the ground and clutching at his walking stick. We pass a young drunken couple sitting on the hood of a car laughing at each other. One of them is missing his two front teeth.

I fit in here, I realise, with all my broken parts. No one looks twice at us when we enter the emergency room, which is all madness and hurry. We have to force our way through the crowd and the noise and the smell, and bright lights make me feel like I'm shrinking up inside my jacket. The Artist leads me easily through it all and down a series of wide wipe-clean linoleum corridors. We step into an elevator that isn't sanitised enough to cover the underlying smell. I want to tell her about the Colosseum and the staged sea battles but I can't speak.

We stop three times on the way up. People crowd in and out. Two nurses in blue scrubs sleep-walk their way through a conversation about television.

The episode with... one says and the other nods. Yes, yes I remember.

I listen in for a while and soon realise they're talking about different shows. Neither of them seems to notice. We all shuffle backwards for a woman in red lipstick on crutches. My chest tightens in slow degrees with every level we rise.

We exit on the twelfth floor in a gaggle of people. In the corridor there's a momentary confusion and then we all disperse to follow our different paths. I follow the bright glow of light around the back of the Artist's head.

We enter a ward with murals on the walls. A field of bubble-gum pink flowers. A pod of bulbous air balloons. A pair of jaybirds side by side on a wire. I slow down to look at it, dragging my feet.

They look just like I thought they would. Dusty pink and beady eyed, with a little flash of blue on the wing. I wonder briefly if I could paint something like that.

In another lifetime maybe.

We turn down another corridor and I realise that for the first time since entering the hospital, we are alone. I can hear our footsteps slapping across the linoleum. The Artist pauses at a door next to a large shuttered observation window. A clipboard on the door has a name scrawled in green marker. P. Craggs.

I know suddenly what this feeling is, the feeling that's been building in me ever since I entered the building. It feels like being sick. Portraits can't get sick, though, so I suppose it must be fear that I am feeling. I'm afraid of what lies beyond the door.

Perhaps she scares Lulabelle too. That was fear on her face

when she asked me if I had given the missing page to Spencer.

What was it he said on the phone to me? Have you found her yet?

"Just this way," the Artist says, holding out her hand.

There's nothing to do but keep going. Whatever I find here, I know it will be an ending of sorts. Maybe it's normal to be frightened of that. Maybe this is how all the other Portraits felt when they knew I was coming.

There's death on the other side of the door. In my short life I've never been surer of anything. The end of the list. The end of the line.

And I don't want it to end. Maybe that's selfish after all the deaths I've dealt out, but still I want to live very badly. I want the Artist to live. I want to walk out of the city.

"You want me to wait outside?" the Artist asks, her hand on the door.

I shake my head and the corner of her mouth twitches upwards. She opens the door and holds it for me. I step past her into the dark portal.

The light in here is green. It ebbs and flows in time with the beeps and slow wheezy rattle that comes from the machines. There are so many machines. They hulk like silent robotic mourners around the hospital bed. I can't tell their purpose but each of them look terrifyingly essential. Clear plastic tubes and thin black rubber wires ooze from various ports, stretching from one machine to another, like a complicated cat's cradle or tentacled prayer circle.

In the centre of the web, the final Portrait is strung up on a white hospital bed. She's so small and withered, so covered in blankets and equipment, that I almost miss her.

Her eyes are closed. There is only the dry rattle of the machine that breathes for her.

I feel the Artist step up close by my shoulder. "She hasn't got long left, I think."

"What happened to her?" I whisper.

"She's sick."

"Portraits don't get sick," I say. When I look at the Artist, her eyes are brimming with tears.

"No," she says. "No, they don't."

I look back at the tiny figure in the bed. I've seen so many Portraits by now. Every single one of them has resembled Lulabelle Rock more than this little raisin of a person. I see her hand, curled around a plastic button. It looks like a claw. The lines cut very deep. That's no tattoo. Now that I'm seeing the real thing, it's hard to believe I could ever have fallen for the fakes. She doesn't look glossy or efficient at all. She looks human.

"I don't understand," I say, but I do. I just don't want to believe it can be real.

"I'm sorry," she says. "I thought you knew. I thought you must have known."

"I can't kill her. Not if she's real."

"Would you have killed her anyway?"

"I don't know," I say. My headache is back. It's a sharp splinter in my right temple. "I don't know. No."

If I killed her, the blood wouldn't be fake. This is the moment Spencer was telling me about. If I do this then there's no amount of handwashing I could do to take away the stain.

I want to sink into one of the chairs but they look fragile and unsuitable for sinking into. I perch gingerly on it instead and let my head hang between my knees.

"So, if this is the real Lulabelle then who made me?" I ask my knees. "Who's the person in the villa? Who spilled the smoothie?"

"What? I can't really understand you–" the Artist says gently, and I cut her off with a groan.

"I don't understand at all. I don't understand anything."

She crouches down in front of me. Her hand comes to rest on my head, very lightly, as if I'm a wild animal she's afraid of scaring away.

"Lulabelle went to Mitosis ten years ago," she says, very patiently. "That's when they took the samples. When she was healthy."

"That's why Spencer can't just make more," I mumble and then my mind latches onto this with a horrible creeping suspicion. "Did he do this? Did he plan it?"

The Artist shakes her head. "No one did this to her. She just got sick. It happens. He knew about it, but don't blame Spencer – he needed Lulabelle to exist. We all do. She's an industry."

"She's a person," I say and then I wonder why I'm being so defensive. I don't know her. I've never known her it seems.

"Sometimes a restaurant becomes a hit," the Artist says. "And because it's so popular, it can open up more restaurants. Sometimes the original location has to be shut down. But the chain keeps going. You see?"

I clench my jaw so hard my molars squeak. "You don't believe that."

She pauses and then sighs. "No. But it sounds good, doesn't it? That's the way Spencer put it."

"Did he offer you a deal too?"

She nods.

"Why didn't you take it?" I ask, wondering if it's too late.

"I don't see myself as a redhead."

She offers me a shy smile, but I can't bring myself to return it. In every sense, I'm lost. This changes everything and at the same time, nothing at all.

We both startle at the knock on the door. A nurse in blue scrubs enters and nods at us politely. She begins to move around the room, checking the mysterious machines and fluffing the pillow behind the real Lulabelle's head. The Artist stands up and turns her back to me, wiping discreetly at her eyes.

"What will you do?" she asks me quietly.

I don't answer her. After a long moment she leaves.

I let her go. I feel somehow that she has betrayed me. Because I trust her so much, this hurts me very deeply. It hurts even more because now I know I still trust her anyway, that I will continue to trust her even if she keeps on betraying me for the rest of our lives.

In an effort to look somewhere, anywhere but the closing door, I look over at the painting hung opposite the bed.

I know it well, even though I've only seen it once. The white dome rising up in front of a blue sky. The straggly brown foliage I recognise now as hair. It looks a little bit like the hill of Rocher du Saint.

"Is this a reproduction or the original?" I ask the nurse, without looking away from it. "I know a painting just like this."

"They're from the same series," the nurse says. I know that voice too. When I look over, her back is turned to me as she pulls down blankets from a high shelf. As she rises up on tiptoes in her white orthopaedic shoes, I see the scars on her ankles.

"Marie," I say weakly. I try to get up, but my limbs feel weak and I only succeed in clattering the chair. "What are you doing here?"

"I work here," she says, adjusting a tube. "It's nice of you two to visit. She doesn't have too much time left."

"You keep turning up. Everywhere I go."

"I could say the same thing to you."

"It should be impossible," I say. "It's such a big city."

At last she turns and smiles at me. It's a sad, tired kind of smile. "Not really. It can be very small sometimes."

"Marie…" I say. For the first time I see the cruelty of making something that can't cry. "It's all gone wrong. I don't know what to do. I've made so many mistakes. I've only been alive for three days and I've already fucked it all up. It just keeps on getting more complicated and I can't fix any of the mistakes, I just keep making more. I don't have my files anymore. I left her on the roof alone. I should have stayed. I shouldn't have pressed the button. I shouldn't have left her there."

Marie looks at me patiently, though I'm sure that was mostly unintelligible. Without tears, the emotion is in my whole body, shaking my shoulders and ribs and wringing out my lungs. My stomach hurts. I want my grey A4 ring binder.

"Sorry," I say at last. "But I don't know what to do."

"That's alright," Marie says, tucking in the corners of Lulabelle's bedsheets. "Hardly anybody does."

I wait for her to go on but she says nothing. I watch her adjust the pillows and think of what the hitchhiker told me by the artificial lake. Fools, he had said. Saint of stitches, fools and travellers. Bubble City has a different name on some maps.

After a moment, I take a breath and try again, my voice steadier now.

"So, do you have any advice?"

She sighs and puts the sheet down on the bed. She looks at me, point blank and for the first time I notice her eyes aren't a shifting, ambiguous myriad of shades. They're just eyes, eyes with deep blue shadows underneath them. Her shoulders are a little slumped. There is a stain on the front of her scrubs.

"You can lead them to water," she says slowly. "But you can't make them drink."

I frown. This doesn't seem very applicable to the situation. "What does that mean?"

"It means," she says gently. "That you need to work some things out yourself."

I stare blankly at her for a moment and then I nod slowly. "Yeah. Yeah, okay."

She nods and then with a final adjustment, steps back from the bed. "She should probably get some rest now. You too."

"Yes," I say and stand up. "Yes, I think I will. Thank you. For everything."

I know suddenly this will be the last time I see Marie. I think about hugging her or maybe shaking her hand, but in the end I settle for a stiff nod.

"Goodbye," I say and then I hesitate. "I hope... I hope you get some rest too."

"I will," she says. "But it's a long shift."

"Good night, then."

"Good night."

I turn and start to go, but as my hand touches the door, the rasp of the machines call me back. I look at Marie again. "May I touch her?"

Marie nods. "Of course."

I reach for Lulabelle's skeletal, tube-encrusted hand. There's something under the edge of one of her nails. A faint smudgy blue shadow. It could be just a bruise but I know better. When I lean closer to look, her eyes don't flicker over the oxygen mask.

This is who I was made from. The blueprint. The original. She's looking in the mirror and I'm just the reflection. But she's still so small. I wonder what she thinks of us. Her Portraits. I don't think she hates us. I don't hate us. Or at least not consciously. I think maybe the hate came later for the others, the ones who had to live in a world crowded with other Lulabelles. I'm still young; maybe I'll grow to hate the others too. Perhaps I'll even hate the Artist one day.

Maybe. It could happen.

But I don't think it will.

"Well…" But I can't think of a single thing to say to her. I squeeze her hand gently. "It was nice to meet you. Sleep well."

As I let go of her hand, her eyes shoot open and fix on mine. I fight the urge to recoil. Her mouth moves beneath the plastic.

"What's she saying?" I look to Marie anxiously.

"Water," she says. "She wants water."

Marie goes to a small plastic jug and pours out a cup. Then to my horror, she passes it to me.

"Are you sure?" I ask.

Marie nods. "She prefers to do this herself anyway. She likes to be self-sufficient."

Marie removes the mask and I hold the cup to Lulabelle's lips. My hands are shaking. Lulabelle drinks with surprising strength; gulping greedily as if she has been dying of thirst, as if she was walking in a desert and only just reached the edges of the rainforest. When the cup is drained, she falls back wearily and Marie pulls the mask over her slack mouth.

I think this might be the first time I have helped Lulabelle in any real way. Looking at the empty cup, a plan comes to me, all at once and perfectly formed. I turn it over in my head and examine it from a few different angles. I'm not used to making plans and there's a good chance this one might be terrible. But it might work. It might.

Maybe you don't need to know judo if you have a gun.

I'm still thinking about it when I feel a hand on mine, the skin paper thin and very soft. When I look down, Lulabelle is looking back at me.

"What is it?" I ask her, leaning in close. She gestures at the mask and I pull it down for her, bending my head so she can whisper into my ear.

"Is there a problem?" Marie asks, with the faintest edge of impatience.

"No," I say. "She just wanted to say thank you."

When Marie turns to adjust a monitor, I take the cigarette packet from my jacket and slip it under Lulabelle's pillow. She needs the luck more than me. And I don't feel much like a girl anymore.

"Those things will kill you," I tell her, speaking quietly so Marie doesn't hear. One brown eye closes slowly. A wink.

I swallow around the lump in my throat and give her a final wobbly smile.

Then I ask Marie if she has a pen I could borrow.

Outside, under the fluorescents, the Artist is slumped against a mural of yellow ducks on a dark pond. When I come out, she straightens up.

"Listen," she says quickly, with big anxious eyes. "I want you to know that–"

"Give me your hand," I say and then, softening my tone, "Please."

She does, without hesitation. I turn it palm up and then I uncap the pen with my teeth.

"Hold still," I warn. "It's hard to do this one-handed."

She stays as still as possible but her hand trembles as I draw a new line across her palm. When I'm finished, I give it a critical onceover. Wobbly and blue, but not so bad if I squint.

"What does this mean?" the Artist says, eyes flicking up at me and then down again, like it will disappear if she looks away.

"It means you're going to live a long and happy life," I say. "Now let's go murder Lulabelle."

CHAPTER THIRTEEN

Death

Death rides into town on a white horse. A skeleton in a dark suit of armour, a twisted reflection of life, a shadow, a mockery. He cuts down kings and children alike and grins at the holy man who pleads with him. Behind him, a boat floats down a dark river. In the distance, the sun is setting behind vast and ancient towers.

"Is that really necessary?" the Artist asks dubiously. "She's halfway dead already."

"Not the real Lulabelle. The one who made me. The one who tried to kill you. The one on the hill."

The Artist pulls back and frowns. "I don't understand."

"We'll talk in the car," I say and start walking.

This time, I drive. I do it fast and I use the turn signals. It's harder driving with a manual gearbox with all the noise and dirt of a petrol engine but Lulabelle remembers this too. Buried under the convertible and the coastline are less glossy memories. Of stalling at red lights and standing in the sticky heat filling up her car and hating the smell, hating the cost, hating that she wasn't where she wanted to be. Now I've met the real deal these memories feel more precious to me, more finite.

"The one on the hill is the first, isn't she? The one who made me. The firstborn," I say, taking a corner at 75 miles per hour. "And I'll bet they hadn't got to grips with imprinting yet. What instructions did they give her? Did they give her any at all?"

The Artist's knuckles are white around the seatbelt. "I don't know. We don't talk."

"But you knew she had replaced the real Lulabelle."

"Spencer's Secretary was reading all his emails. Spencer, he... well, he helped her at first."

"They made a deal."

The Artist nods. "When the real Lulabelle got sick, the Firstborn took her place. She got to be Lulabelle and Spencer got someone who would follow orders. The real Lulabelle didn't trust him, they were always fighting. She was turning down parts, she was talking about retirement..."

"What happened then? Why is he so pissed?"

"Well the Firstborn didn't trust him either. He got greedy. He wanted more samples, more Lulabelles..."

"You said they only took thirteen samples."

"Thirteen healthy samples. Spencer is desperate – he's sloppy, he doesn't care if the new ones are bad quality or if Lulabelle is... if it... The process of extraction isn't easy."

I think of the machines around Lulabelle's bed. "It would kill her."

The Artist takes a shaky breath. "They've been hiding her from him. From everyone. They made a new crop of Portraits, spread them through the city to confuse him. Even I didn't know where the real Lulabelle was until I saw that file – none of us did. We thought they had her locked up in that villa in the countryside."

"Wait, who's they? Who knew about this?" I ask and then smack my forehead with my palm. "The Viking. He was her handler, wasn't he? He got attached."

"Viking? What are you–" the Artist asks and then yelps when I cut through an intersection. "Jesus, slow down!"

I don't, and for a moment our headlights splash across a

tall gangly figure dressed in black leather by the side of the highway. One hand is held up to the road, one thumb jutting out. The other clutches a sign that reads, Anywhere But Here. On both, the nails have been painted a deep occult black and for a moment I swear I see the eyes of the Hitchhiker flash green in the dark like a cat. But we are going too fast to stop now and so I just press my foot down on the accelerator.

"It's all too complicated," I say absently, watching the white lines flash by. "It's too tangled up, don't you see?"

"Watch the road!"

"There should only be one of us. The moment we started multiplying, that was where the problem started. I understand her now."

"Well I don't."

"Look… when the original dies we would all be turned off automatically, right? Mitosis would have tracked us down, one by one and decommissioned us personally. Unless…unless we were already dead. Thirteen deaths, thirteen, very public deaths in the week leading up to her premiere. Medea was never the point, it was just a cover. She was never trying to distract people from bad press – she wanted it, you see? Medea was the distraction!"

"And the real Lulabelle is quietly taken out in all the chaos," the Artist says and then frowns. "But wait… Mitosis collects the bodies. They would know that Lulabelle… the real Lulabelle wasn't a Portrait."

I open my mouth and close it again. "…Okay, I'm not sure about that part. I think the Firstborn might have switched their trackers but beyond that… Look, I'm sure she would have found a way. The point is, with thirteen bodies and no original to make copies from, the firstborn would have been free."

"One Lulabelle standing."

"But who says it has to be her?" I say and smile as I swerve in and out of traffic, followed by a series of horn blasts. I am starting to feel like myself again. Everything seems so clear now. I had forgotten this joy, the joy of simplicity, of being fixed on a single point.

"What?" the Artist echoes, gripping her seatbelt with white knuckles. "What do you mean?"

"She won't stop chasing us if we leave. She'll send more men like the Viking or she'll send Mitosis after us. It has to be you, don't you see?"

"No. No–"

"It has to be you," I go on, narrowing my eyes against the red glare of the taillights. "It has to be you that's left. You're the best of us."

The Artist splutters while I take the exit ramp for the hillside. It feels very different from the last time I drove up the side of this dark valley. Back then, I felt like I was drifting. I was on a conveyor belt. I have been on a conveyer belt my whole life. All three long days of it. Now the car rumbles and roars and whines under my control. I press down on the accelerator and catch a glimpse of my own white teeth in the rear-view mirror. I smile like a wolf and change gears.

"So what?" the Artist asks. "What's the plan?"

"You'll like the view from the hilltop," I say. "You can get all your stuff and bring it up. The house is ugly but it'll look better once you have your paintings up. You can sweet talk Spencer into staying quiet. Tell him you'll do all the sequels he wants. He can help you get surgery for your hands."

"You want me to take her place?" the Artist asks and then, sadly: "I don't want to have surgery on my hands."

"It won't hurt," I reassure her. "You'll be playing the piano again in no time."

"But Lulabelle doesn't play the piano," the Artist says quietly. "And what about you? What happens to you?"

"You won't need me. My job will be done." I throttle our way around another switchback. We are climbing higher and higher now; there's a horrible feeling building in my guts. It could be relief. It could be.

"What does that mean?"

I'm silent. We both know what this means. It means nothing has changed. I've always known that I would be the last one to die. I knew it from the moment I saw that first Portrait waiting at the bus stop. I had never wondered why she never ran away. I knew the answer. We are what we do, and when we have nothing to do, we are nothing. When my job was finished, I would have been just like her. Defunct. Pointless. I always knew that the last life I took would be my own.

Maybe it had bothered me before – when it could never be my choice. But it can be now.

"It's okay," I tell her. "I want to do this for you. That's all I want."

"But why? We could run or fake your death or something, there's no reason why–"

"It's okay," I tell her and smile over at her. I reach out my hand.

She looks down white-faced at it hanging in the air between us. She doesn't take it. She mumbles something.

"What?" I ask.

"Watch the road!" she snaps, and I jerk my head up just in time to see the white headlights erupt in my vision. I swear and yank the steering wheel to one side. The truck barrels past, inches from my window, horn blaring.

"Oh fuck, fuck, sorry," I say, glancing over. "Are you okay?"

"Pull over," the Artist says tightly.

"Right now?"

"Right now."

I ease my foot off the accelerator and pull in at the next turn-off I see. My headlights splash over a sign that reads Bubble City Scenic Vista in a curlicue font. I park and turn off the engine. A ramshackle wooden fence is the only thing separating us from the sudden drop of the valley's edge.

In front of us in glorious spreading technicolour lies Bubble City. I avert my eyes from the glimmer of it; I look at the Artist

instead, the soft outline of her in the shadows. She's easier
to make sense of. I don't know everything about her yet, but
I'm learning every day. I know what she looks like when she's
naked and happy. I know what she looks like when she's fully
clothed and angry; she looks like that right now.

"You want to die so badly?" she asks me, hushed and raw.
"You think that's what you deserve? Here. I'll kill you myself if
you're that desperate."

I think for a moment that she's going to ask me for the gun.
Maybe this was her plan after all. I would give it to her.

But instead, she holds up her hand and points it like a weapon
with the thumb cocked back and two fingers extended. Very
gently, she touches the tips of those two fingers to my forehead.

"Bang," she says. "There. Now you're dead."

"I am?"

"Yes," she says and then I feel it.

Bang.

The button under my finger. The blue light of the swimming
pool. The crowd gathering around the car as it burns. Blood
seeping into the pale sofa.

Bang.

Follicles of hair fading from red to white. A gold comet
plummeting through the dark.

Bang.

Polka dots. Bagels spilling into the gutter.

Bang.

And it's a good death. Maybe this is what I deserve after all.
I have to make it all count for something.

"Now do the same to me," she says.

I blink. Very hesitantly I hold up my two fingers to her
forehead. She closes her eyes. Nothing happens.

"Why isn't it working?" I ask.

"You didn't say bang."

"Bang." As I say the word, I feel an electric pulse travel
down my shoulder, along the length of my arm and jump up

into my fingertips. I almost hear the sizzle of it as it passes into the Artist's brain. She opens her eyes.

"There," she says. "Now we're both dead. Your job is done. Who are you going to reincarnate as? I'm toying with the idea of being a Cindy."

"Who's Cindy?" I ask, feeling a little jealous.

"Cindy or Artemisia," she says. "Or maybe Vincent. I'm torn. Who are you?"

I think about Simon the hitchhiker and the Viking whose name I never asked. I think about Marie and Velazquez who gave me a ride on his bike.

"I think…" This is an important decision. "I don't know."

"That's okay," the Artist says, smiling. "You don't have to know right now."

"I have time for that," I say hesitantly. I'm not sure if I'm asking a question.

"You do," she says. "I think we should leave the city."

"Is it that easy?" I wonder. "Can it really be that easy? Can we just leave? Without making any more of a mess?"

She nods. "Yeah. I think it can be easy. If you let it be."

"And will we be happy?"

"I don't know. Maybe."

"And will we be together forever?"

"I don't know," she says again and this time she laughs.

"But will we be safe?" I press. "And will we live for a long time?"

"It might just be for a few days. Or it might be a long time. Whatever's left we'll make the most of it."

"It won't be long," I warn her. "Not if they catch us. Even if we disable your tracker, we can't run forever."

"It always comes back to death with you."

"Of course, it comes back to death," I wail. "That's who I am. I'm the thirteenth card."

I pull out the cards from my pocket and in my haste, I spill them out over the car's interior. I scrabble for them on the floor and as I do, I hold whatever card I find up to the Artist and try to explain.

"This one is you, you see, the Hierophant and here are the lovers, that's six and the hermit and the high priestess... thirteen of them and thirteen of us, don't you see?"

"But there's more than thirteen cards," the Artist frowns. She picks them up blindly and shows me. "Look, there's the tower and the devil and the sun... How do they fit?"

I stare at them for a moment and then I scrub a hand over my face. "I don't know. Oh fuck, I didn't even think about that. Do you think there's more to come?"

She laughs softly, fondly. "No. I think that it just doesn't fit your pattern. I think it's all a lot more complicated than that. A lot simpler, too."

I try to process this. I look out at the city in front of us. The sun will be rising soon and then it won't be a dark field studded with pretty lights. It'll be a thousand different buildings that don't match up, it'll be heat and skyscrapers and slums and suburbs all crowded in on each other and mixed up and jostling for space.

"I need it to fit," I say and there's more, but I don't have the words to explain. I don't know how to tell her that I need the cards like I needed the grey A4 ring binder. That I need them just like she needs her art and the others needed their poems and minimalist cream and white living rooms and their yellow polka dots and knowledge of Excel spreadsheets and martial arts and their fast cars and their cats. That I don't know if I can understand without my cards. That the world won't make sense. That I don't know what comes after without the next card in the deck.

In the end I just gesture helplessly at the city. "It's too big. All of it. It's too much."

"Oh," she says and for a moment we watch it together, side by side. Then she holds up her hands again and makes a square with her index fingers and thumbs. She closes her brown eye and leans back to look through the frame they make.

"It's not so big," she tells me. "Look."

I lean over and look. It takes me a moment to understand.

"Oh yeah," I say.

Like this, Bubble City looks just like a postcard. It looks just like a painting.

"You see it now?" She asks.

"I see it."

And I do.

EPILOGUE

Temperance

The angel stands upon the rocks, carefully dividing water between two cups. Behind them a path stretches away through the mountains. Their wings are the colour of dawn.

And I do, but something still bothers me.

"Hold on," I say. "I'll be back in a moment."

I get out of the car and walk to the edge of the scenic view. The tarot cards are in my hand. I think about saying goodbye to Lulabelle. Lulabelle dying in a hospital bed, Lulabelle dead on a boat, on a couch, on a pavement. Lulabelle still living, up there in her high tower, jumping at shadows and afraid of her own reflection. Out of all of them I think most about the Lulabelle at the bus stop with her dirty feet and crumpled white paper bag.

When I get back in the car, the Artist is talking to someone on a pink flip mobile. When she sees me, she smiles and gives me an A-OK sign.

"Uh-huh," she says into the phone. "Uh-huh. Under the nail? How deep? Okay, I can do that."

Who is it? I mouth. I'm angry at myself for not thinking of the tracking device myself. Everything had happened so fast but this could have cost us our lives.

She puts a hand over the phone and whisper, "Craig."

I make a face. "Who?"

"Hold on," she says and then after a moment she holds out the phone. "He wants to speak to you."

I take it gingerly, frowning at her. "Hi?"

"I've bought you some time with Mitosis." It's the Viking's voice. He sounds tired. Craig? Hmm.

"I thought your shift was over."

"It is. I guess you could say this is pro-bono."

Next to me, the Artist has pulled out what looks like a small fabric sewing kit from her backpack. Unrolling it she selects a small pair of gold scissors. They look wickedly sharp. My stomach roils and I look away quickly.

"What about Lulabelle?"

There's a pause from the other end and then the Viking clears his throat. "Actually. She wants to talk to you."

"She's there?" I make the mistake of looking over at the Artist in my shock and catch a glimpse of her wiggling the scissor edge under her nail.

"Can I put her on?"

"Um."

Before I can say no, there's a click from the other end of the line. It's faint but I recognise it. The sound of a lighter.

"So, I hear you're dead," Lulabelle says, just as the silence is becoming unbearable.

"Yes."

"And I guess you know everything now."

"Most of it. I still don't understand what you planned to do with the real Lulabelle."

"The plan was… well I'll be honest I was making up some of it as I went along. It could have gone more smoothly, I'll admit."

"A total flop," I say. "A disaster."

There's a strange noise down the line. It takes me a moment to place it as laughter. "Yeah, I guess you could say that."

"What happens now?"

"Well…" she pauses. "I guess this is the part where the two of you ride off into the sunset."

"Sunrise."

"Whatever." Even without seeing her I can tell she's rolling her eyes.

"Are you really going to let us?"

There's an even longer pause, so long my palms begin to itch.

Then, finally, in a tone that sounds almost surprised. "Looks that way doesn't it. I suppose I can dredge up a few dead Portraits to take your place. Maybe you had a car crash. But you have to change your hair."

"Okay."

"And go very far away. Maybe to some cabin somewhere."

"Done."

"And maybe plastic surgery."

"Hmm. Maybe. I'll think about it. Can I ask you something?" I say, leaning back in my seat. From here I can see my reflection in the wing mirror and beyond that, the coloured lights in the dark.

"Shoot kid."

"Why are you okay with this?"

"Well, that's the point of you, isn't it? That's why you were made," she says. "To do all the things I don't have time for... I just don't think I can fit a happy ending into my schedule."

I think about this for a moment and then I try my luck. "Can I ask something else?"

"Ok. But make it quick. I have to paint my nails."

"What did she tell you when you first woke up?"

"Oh. That's all?" she says and laughs. "That's easy. She told me to be Lulabelle Rock."

I nod to myself and then hang up. When I look down at my lap I realise I'm still clutching the cards. My hands are getting sweaty. I realise now she never answered me about the real Lulabelle. I think about the way she had looked for the missing page. Maybe she hadn't been sure either, right up until the end. I think about her putting Lulabelle in the file and then trying to take her out. The frantic way she had looked for the missing page. I hope she'll go to visit her in the hospital again.

I think they might need each other.

"You're holding onto them?" the Artist asks. She's cleaning off the scissors on her sleeve.

"Yeah." I rub a thumb over the cardboard packet and it feels a little warm. They don't have to be the whole world. Just a little part of it.

"I thought you were going to throw them over the edge," she says and then she gives me a lopsided kind of smile. "I would have."

"I don't know what to do next," I admit and then I don't know how to say it.

I look over at her but she's silent, waiting for me to go on.

"It's not that I want any more death," I say. "But it's what I was made for. I guess I don't know... I mean I'm not sure what's left."

I expect her to have an answer ready. Something easy, like everything or even nothing.

But instead she just shrugs. "I don't know. I guess we'll find out at some point."

"And until then?"

"We'll just have to make it up as we go along."

I nod slowly and as I start the car, I ask her, "Do you think it matters? That you and I started out the same?"

"I don't see why it should," she says. "Pretty much everyone does."

ACKNOWLEDGMENTS

This book simply would not exist without the help of so many people but let me try and highlight a few.

My agent Lina, who took a chance on me and did so with incredible enthusiasm and tireless attention to detail. My beautiful and clever friends, whose creativity and drive inspire me every day. My exceedingly lovely girlfriend for staying up till 4am to talk me through crises of confidence. My family with all their fierce devotion and unquestioning support. The amazing team at Angry Robot who've guided me through everything with such generosity and patience.

Above all I need to acknowledge and thank my first readers. Not only did they stop me from tearing the whole book up after writing it but they helped shape it in countless ways with their practicality and wisdom. This includes all the friends and relatives who read over all my countless drafts but especially the handful of you who I gave the book to the minute after writing 'The End'. I'm forever grateful.

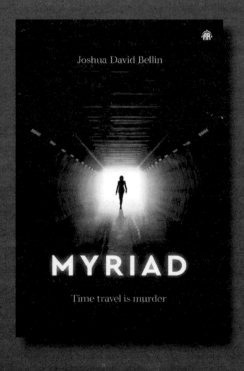

CHAPTER 1

I step through the doorway five minutes before the man kills his wife.

The penumbra crackles like a thunderstorm played in reverse. Nausea folds me in two. I fang my lip to make the pain my own. There's a taste of blood on my tongue, but the world grows sharp, reality replacing the memory I relive every time I travel.

I'm standing in a guest room in the Sleep Rite Motor Lodge, just off the interstate in Monroeville. Low cost and proximity to the highway make it a favorite spot for a midday frolic. It's the tail end of another sweltering Pittsburgh summer, the blinds closed against a hot, bright sky. The room has that baked-in smoky smell universal to such places, adding insult to injury since I haven't had a cigarette all day – no stimulants allowed on the job.

In the dimness, I scan the unexceptional décor. Ersatz wood paneling, faux-bronze floor lamp, rustic paint-by-number scene above a nickel-plated headboard. The rattletrap air conditioner competes with a daytime soap, *Days of Our Lives* or something, while the shower hisses and spits behind the door to my left. More like the Last Rites Motor Lodge if you ask me, but the clientele this place caters to aren't choosy.

A specimen of that clientele stands by the rumpled bed, waiting for the other occupants of the room to emerge.

He's in his forties, badly overweight, sweaty in his brown business suit. Graying, unshaved. Whiskey on his breath. So nervous his hands shake. I know what he's going through, and I feel for him. He doesn't want to be here any more than I do. But the gun he's holding doesn't leave either of us an option.

I train my eyepiece on his trembling hand until the AI returns a match.

Smith & Wesson M&P 380.

An older model, the kind the trade shows used to pitch as a safe bet for newbies. Even if I didn't know that, even if I didn't know every salient detail of this man's recent history, the tentative way he handles the weapon would tell me he's never fired a handgun before, possibly never touched one until today.

He looks amazed to see me. They always do.

His story's the oldest one in the book. Businessman gets a funny feeling, decides to turn detective. Tracks receipts and bank transactions, pockets the pistol his wife bought for home protection when the kids were babies and follows her to the Sleep Rite, where she's been humping his business partner on her lunch break. This shouldn't come as a surprise, since the husband's a neglectful lover at best and the twentysomething year-old partner has the time – and stamina – to give the wife what he can't.

But the hubby's not thinking clearly, what with the booze and betrayal. He confronts them in the act, shouts, threatens legal action. Only means to scare them, but gets so worked up when his wife taunts him, he squeezes the trigger like he's letting out an accidental fart. After a single, stunned moment to eyeball what he's done, he turns the gun on himself in a spasm of guilt and despair.

The result: two dead bodies, lots of brains and blood, a pair of orphans. A tragedy any way you look at it.

That's where we come in.

The blinds rustle as Vax arrives a second later. Thunderclap played backwards, face fighting the urge to vomit. He holds his trusty Glock out straight, left hand cupping the grip to steady it over the nausea.

The husband's eyes flick from me to my partner. Obviously terrified. Absolutely no idea what's going on.

Vax briefly takes his left hand from the gun to flash his badge. "LifeTime Law Enforcement. Place your weapon on the floor and raise your hands above your head."

The man stares, chews the end of his mustache as he nervously processes what must look like two glowing aliens who've unaccountably crash-landed in the motel room. Will he feign bravado, misunderstanding, innocence? Or will he be a good boy and do as my partner says?

None of the above. He blinks, stares, but holds on.

"Sir," I say, trying for a steady, soothing tone. "We're going to have to ask you again to place your weapon on the floor and raise your hands above your head. You're under arrest."

"What for?" A primal wail.

"Attempted murder."

"I didn't kill anybody."

"Not yet."

He sucks in a breath, looks us over again. His eyes are teary from the strain or the hooch or both.

I've often thought we could save ourselves a lot of trouble if, instead of confronting imminent murderers at emotionally fragile moments like this, we nabbed them well before the act. But the law's the law. You can't arrest someone for a crime they haven't committed, even if they've already committed it, until you have what the government calls "reasonable inference" that they're about to commit it again. Booking the husband in the motel room passes the test as, say, collaring him while he's downing his last shot of Jack Daniel's at the neighborhood pub doesn't. We've debated among ourselves whether anyone could actually make a violation of the timecode stick, but in the end, we've opted for playing it safe.

"Sir," I say. "Make this easy on yourself."

He wavers. I see it in his eyes. Like most people, he's naturally timid, doesn't want to hurt anyone. If we can get the gun off him, set him up with a cup of black coffee and a long talk with the court-appointed shrink, he'll be all right. At least he won't have to carry around the burden of knowing that, the first time around, he did exactly what he never dreamed he was capable of doing.

He's edging toward me, the gun held gingerly like a bag of dog doo he's about to drop in someone else's trash can, when the bathroom door bursts open.

All eyes shift as the two emerge from the steam. They're naked, beaded with water, the wife's legs wrapped around her lover's waist, his face buried in her long black hair. Both of them so focused on the moment they seem unaware that their exclusive party has become something of a social hour. She moans as he carries her to the bed, arranging her in what must be one of their tried-and-true positions.

The husband takes a step back, his fleshy face turned scarlet. I see the change come over him, and I know what he's about to do.

"Now, sir!" I say. "Drop your weapon!"

The wife screams. Untangles herself from the business partner, who drops to the floor, shouting something incoherent. The husband bellows right back as he stumbles toward the bed. I've got him lined up for a shot that should hobble him, not kill him, when he slips in the pool his wife and former partner left. His hands flail to catch himself against the headboard.

Deafening explosion. Blood smears the sheets. After a moment of silence, the word "Babe!" comes from his mouth.

Vax leaps for him.

You'd think the newly minted murderer would be too paralyzed by the sight of his wife's head pumping blood to react, but no. He dodges, shrugs off my partner's charge. Vax goes for him again, but now that the man knows what he's capable of, he eludes his much fitter adversary and wields the gun with newfound purpose. Vax should be over the wobbles by now, but he seems more sluggish than usual, and the husband has weight and desolation on his side. He throws Vax against the lamp. The bulb shatters, plunging the room into deeper dark.

"Vax!" I cry.

He's rising woozily. I can't see if he has his Glock. The husband is a lot closer than I am, and he takes aim like a sharpshooter. He even smiles, his teeth gleaming in the TV's ghostly glow.

I fire two rounds from my Beretta. The first hits the husband in the chest, spinning him against the wall. The second reddens the paneling behind his head, and he slumps to the floor.

Blood. Brains. Bodies. The only one left alive of the original three is the cowering, whimpering business partner, who's curled into the fetal position beside the puddle his bladder left on the shag rug.

Vax stands, feels the couple for a pulse. A mere formality. He shakes his head.

"You OK?" he asks.

I nod.

"I had to do it," I say.

He looks me in the eye. "I know."

My hands fumble as I holster my gun. My partner peels the sole survivor off the floor while I make the call.